If You Were Mine

CARRIE ANN RYAN

NEW YORK TIMES BESTSELLING AUTHOR

If You Were Mine

A ONE ROOM ONE BED EDITION

THE CAGE FAMILY
BOOK THREE

CARRIE ANN RYAN

If You Were Mine

If You Were Mine
A Cage Family Romance
By: Carrie Ann Ryan
© 2025 Carrie Ann Ryan

Couple Cover Art by Sweet N Spicy Designs
Special Edition Cover Art by Wildfire Designs
Couple Image by Wander Aguiar

All content warnings are listed on the book page for this book on my website.

Praise for Carrie Ann Ryan

"Count on Carrie Ann Ryan for emotional, sexy, character driven stories that capture your heart!" – Carly Phillips, NY Times bestselling author

"Carrie Ann Ryan's romances are my newest addiction! The emotion in her books captures me from the very beginning. The hope and healing hold me close until the end. These love stories will simply sweep you away." ~ NYT Bestselling Author Deveny Perry

"Carrie Ann Ryan writes the perfect balance of sweet and heat ensuring every story feeds the soul." - Audrey Carlan, #1 New York Times Bestselling Author

"Carrie Ann Ryan never fails to draw readers in with passion, raw sensuality, and characters that pop off the page. Any book by Carrie Ann is an absolute treat." – New York Times Bestselling Author J. Kenner

"Carrie Ann Ryan knows how to pull your heartstrings and make your pulse pound! Her wonderful Redwood Pack series will draw you in and keep you reading long into the night. I can't wait to see what comes next with the new generation, the Talons. Keep them coming, Carrie Ann!" –Lara Adrian, New York Times bestselling author of CRAVE THE NIGHT

For Echo.
As I type this, we're headed for a new journey to a new country.
And I know I couldn't have pushed through this book without
you and our plans.
Harper is for you.
But Dorian is mine.
Just saying.
And don't forget The Box.

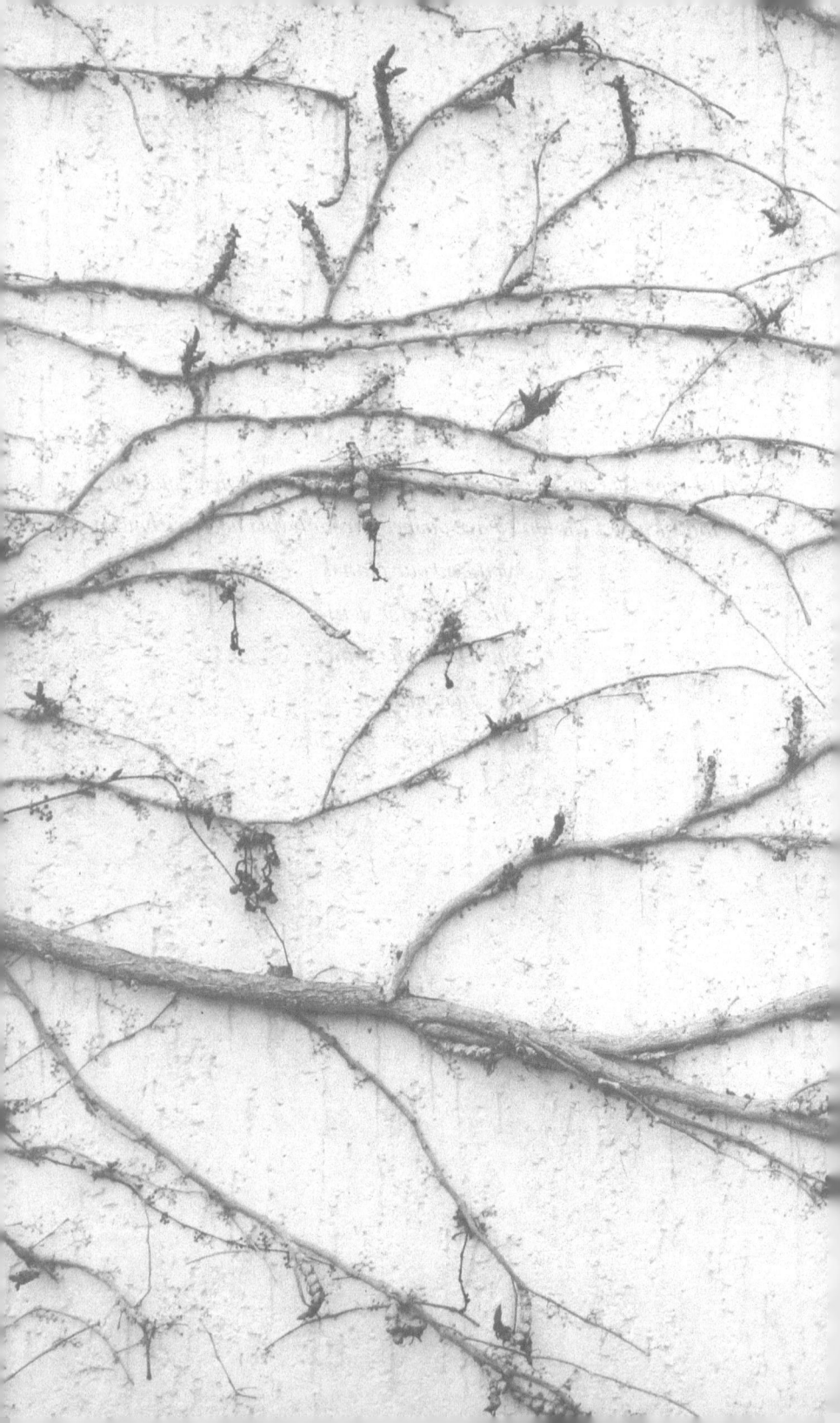

Prologue

DORIAN

"It kind of worries me that I'm so easily persuaded to get in this thing."

My best friend just beamed at me as we looked over at the Cessna Skyhawk. "Isn't she gorgeous? I realize she's not mine, however, my boss lets me borrow her."

"When you say borrow, do you mean *borrow*, or are you stealing this from your boss?" With Joshua, one never knew. It wasn't that Joshua was reckless, far from it. But we had been in our fair share of scrapes throughout the years.

I had many friends throughout my life. Some that I worked with now, some that I had gone to school with. Joshua was the only one I had met on a summer vacation that had turned into a full semester vacation when my father hadn't wanted me to come back to town.

That wasn't a time in my life that I liked to think of, but throughout all the pain and rejection, including neglect, I found my best friend.

Joshua worked with me sometimes at the various clubs and businesses that I owned, but he also worked with a billionaire who liked to have his hands in every single pot he could find.

When I had been shipped off to Cage Lake to stay with my mother in one of the various houses that the family owned, dear old mother had been too busy to pay attention to me for many hours of the day, so I had strolled the small-town streets and found my best friend. Seriously, we had clicked just like that and got in enough scrapes together that the local sheriff and deputy probably still had our pictures as teenagers up somewhere.

We'd grown up, of course, and quit doing stupid things that could get us sent to jail, however, I needed to be a little clear on this.

"Who do you take me for? Of course I'm not stealing a damn plane. Adam wants me to fly it, because he just got his new baby, and he wasn't sure if he wanted to sell this or not. So I get to take it out after they work on maintenance, just to make sure she's doing good."

"That still doesn't fill me with confidence," I said dryly.

IF YOU WERE MINE

"I've had enough flying hours solo that I could be a pilot if I wanted to. You know this is what I've always wanted to do."

"Why weren't you a pilot?" I asked, interested. He met my gaze, and I got it. "Harper."

"Yes and no. When Mom and Dad died, flying didn't feel like an option. We were spiraling trying to deal with custody and what I'd do for school. Then when the grandparents died and Harper was getting out of school, I didn't want to leave my baby sister alone all the time flying back and forth. You know that pilots don't get to spend as much time with their families as they'd like. And I couldn't do that to Harper. Plus, I liked working with you and Adam. And a business degree isn't anything to laugh at. Hell, I'm making more money now than I would have as a pilot. Which means I can have a hobby now, instead of having to fly from one place to another."

"I guess the glass is half full in your case."

"Damn straight."

"So where are we going in this thing? Vegas?" I teased.

"No, I'm not taking you to Vegas in a piston single engine aircraft. This baby has six hundred nautical miles of range, can seat up to four, has over an eight-hundred-pound useful load, and needs a little over fifteen hundred feet of takeoff distance. It's the best training plane out there."

"Did you read that in the manual?" I asked dryly.

"You know I did. I know every inch of this baby. It's going to suck when he sells her."

"You really think Adam's going to sell her?"

"Probably. He got a green Caravan, which seats up to fourteen, and I don't know if he wants this tiny plane."

"Maybe he doesn't want to waste that much fuel, or deal with that many people. He won't give up your baby easily."

"I hope not because I love her. So get in, and I'm going to do my normal preflight checks. You just sit there and look pretty."

I batted my eyelashes. "It doesn't take much."

I got into the co-pilot seat and did what I did best. Nothing. At least that's what my father had said.

I frowned, pushing those thoughts from my head. Why the hell was I thinking of my dead father today? He truly didn't matter. He was gone, and while his sharp talons of control were still dug in deep in some of us, I didn't really care about him. He had never liked me, pretty sure he had never loved me, and so I wasn't going to give him the time of day.

My phone buzzed and I looked down at the readout as Joshua did his preflight checks.

Flynn:

Are you heading to town this weekend? Hudson isn't answering my calls.

I rolled my eyes because those two might be twins, but they sure didn't have that twin-speak like others did.

Me:

Probably. We were just there, but Amy liked the place. Plus, it's always good to check on Harper.

Harper was Joshua's little sister. Eight years younger than us, barely out of college, and owned her own business that was doing damn well in town. Yes, she rented from us and had taken a loan from the Cages, but it was better us than the bank. At least, that's what my father had said.

I frowned, annoyed he was in my head once again.

Flynn:

Get him to call me. I have paperwork to go over, and I don't have time to head out to the lake this weekend.

Me:

I thought you had to work on whatever the mayor had asked of you?

While our family owned and operated much of the town, Flynn was the one who took care of many of the businesses in Cage Lake. With Hudson being his proxy, as our brother was the only one who lived there full-time. Of course, that would change in the future since Isabella was moving there for most of the year to be with Weston. And wasn't that a change? I had known Weston for as long as I had known Joshua, though he had been a couple of years older than us. It was a damn small world it seemed. But that was small towns for you. Even though I didn't live there, I stayed there enough that I got the idea of it.

Flynn:

I have a meeting that I can't get out of. And I need Hudson's help.

Me:

I'll take care of it if he can't. Maybe he's working.

Considering Hudson got lost in his work when he was painting, it made sense.

But I knew we were both worried about the unsaid things. That maybe Hudson was in another spiral. Neither of us wanted that to happen.

Me:

I'll check on him, and whatever business things you need me to do. I don't mind.

Flynn:

You're a lifesaver. And please check on my twin for real. He's scaring me.

Me:

I've got it.

I nearly put my phone away when it buzzed again,

and I smiled down at who was calling. I picked up and wiggled my brows over at Joshua.

"Hello Harper darling."

Joshua curled a lip at me, and I just laughed.

"Hey, is my lovely brother with you?" she asked, her voice all soft and happy. She also sounded a little tired, but considering what hours she worked at the bakery, that made sense.

"He's right next to me. We're about to take off, though."

"Hand me your phone," Joshua grumbled, and I did as he ordered, grinning.

When their parents had died, Joshua hadn't been able to get full custody of Harper. She had been shipped off to her grandparents, since she had been a minor and Joshua had just turned eighteen. It had been a huge fight for custody with only partial visitations. My best friend had done his best by Harper, but I knew he didn't feel like it was enough. Then their grandparents had passed right when Harper had graduated high school, so she had come back to Cage Lake, at least for the summers while she finished school. I didn't know exactly what it had done to Joshua to lose out on being with his baby sister for so long. But they made it work. They were all each other had now.

"Yes yes. I'll bring home milk too, how's that?"

I rolled my eyes at the two, though I didn't know

what they were talking about, and held out my hand when he hung up.

"We ready to go?"

"Almost. Your girlfriend texted when I was on the phone. Sorry."

I frowned and looked down at the readout.

Amy:

I miss you. Are you coming over tonight?

Me:

Yes. As soon as I'm done with Joshua. Need me to bring something for dinner?

Amy:

I think I can be dinner. What do you think?

Then she sent a photo that made my eyebrows raise, and Joshua whistled through his teeth. "Well then. That's an invitation."

"Hey, eyes on the runway and not on my girlfriend."

"I didn't see much. Although you should probably put a screen on your phone or something if she's going to send so many of those."

I made a note to do just that and was grateful I didn't have to adjust myself. Flying with a hard on didn't sound like a picnic. "My girlfriend likes me. And she's hot."

"Well that is true," Joshua said dryly. I said my goodbyes to Amy, as Joshua did the rest of his checks, and soon we were going down the runway, and in the air.

Despite my joke to my best friend earlier, I loved flying. It didn't matter what kind of plane. I loved being in it. I also liked bungee jumping, skydiving, and just anything that gave that little burst of adrenaline. And Joshua always did it right with me. My best friend had had his license forever, and I was thinking maybe it was time to get mine. Everything just felt right. After so many years of bullshit and stress, things were finally coming together.

"I'm thinking of asking Amy to move in with me," I blurted.

We spoke through our headsets, the sounds of the engine loud within the small compartment. But even with sunglasses on, and that huge headset, I saw the way Joshua's eyes widened with his eyebrows lifting. "Really? I didn't think she was really your type."

I frowned. "What the hell do you mean by that?"

My best friend winced. "Sorry. I just, well, I thought you guys were just having fun? I didn't know it was serious."

"I think it is."

"Do you love her?" Joshua asked.

Surprised, I just blinked at my friend. "I don't even know what love is really. But I like being with her. And she makes me happy."

"Okay, so that's a no."

"Why are you acting like this? I figured moving in with each other was just the next thing to do, right? I suck at dating. We both know this."

"Considering Amy's your fourth girlfriend in how many years?"

"In a year." I swallowed hard, ignoring that familiar sliver of doubt that always threatened when it came to settling down. "Which seems like a lot in retrospect, but Amy's great."

"I'm sure she is."

I glared at my best friend. "I'm not a player like some people think. I just can't find the right person."

"And Amy's that right person?"

Unsettled, I shrugged. "Maybe."

Joshua fiddled with a few things on the dash. "Okay, if that's what you think."

"That doesn't sound very helpful."

The other man let out a breath. "I'm not trying to be helpful. I'm trying to be your friend. I mean, you were there for me when Harper needed me. When my parents died and the grandparents were hell-bent on trying to split us apart. *You* were there for her to open up her shop. To make sure I knew what I was doing in each of our businesses. You're the *best*, man. Fuck whatever your daddy thought. And fuck the fact that your mom thought that she was going to mold you into a perfect pawn."

I swallowed hard at that diatribe, wondering exactly how long Joshua had been holding on to this particular rant. "Why does that make me sound weak?"

"No, it makes you sound like you had family issues. Believe me. I know what you mean."

"This is about me and Amy. Not my past."

"Okay then. Ask her to move in. If she says yes, I'll be right there with boxes and tape to help. I promise. But Amy—"

"But Amy *what*?" I bit out, annoyed now. I thought Joshua would be happy for me finally trying to settle down. Joshua didn't have a serious girlfriend, but he had one at one time. And he was still looking for that perfect person. They didn't have to be perfect, just perfect for him. That's what I thought I was doing with Amy.

Once again, Joshua was quiet. "I love you, Dorian. You're my best friend. And I'm sorry if I'm off base. If I'm wrong, then you can punch me in the face later. But I don't know if you're truly seeing what we see."

"Who is we?"

"I misspoke," he said quickly, and I didn't believe him. "But Dorian? Amy likes Fun Dorian. Club Owner Dorian. Cage Money Dorian."

"That's a fucking lie." I practically spat the words into the headset.

"If that's what you think. But I think it's the truth."

"Just because you can't get a woman to actually love you doesn't mean you have to shit on my relationship."

I didn't even realize the words were out of my mouth until they filled the small cabin. And they were such a goddamn lie, that I hated myself.

"Well, good to know how you really feel, Dorian."

"Joshua. I'm sorry. I didn't mean that. Seriously. I don't think that. At all. I love you, damn it. Just like one of my brothers. I didn't mean it."

"Whatever. Shit." There was an odd sound, and I swallowed hard, realizing we were descending faster than we had been before. Joshua had started the descent for our landing earlier, but now, everything got oddly quiet.

"What's going on?"

"The engine stalled." Joshua cursed again. "Mayday, mayday, mayday. November-niner-seven-eight-Charlie-Papa. We have engine failure upon descent and request immediate landing. Mayday, mayday, mayday."

He continued to say a few other words, and I barely swallowed, panic rising. I knew Joshua trained for something like this, but the ground was coming up really fucking fast.

"What can I do?" I asked, bile coating my tongue.

"Just breathe. Tighten your seatbelt. And hold on." He let out a slow breath, his entire body focused as he worked. "We've got this, Dorian. I've got you."

He met my gaze for a bare instant before turning to once again to speak to the control tower, his gaze on the runway. The engine sputtered once and started again, and my heart leapt out of my chest.

"I trust you," I repeated.

"I know, buddy. I know."

And then there was nothing.

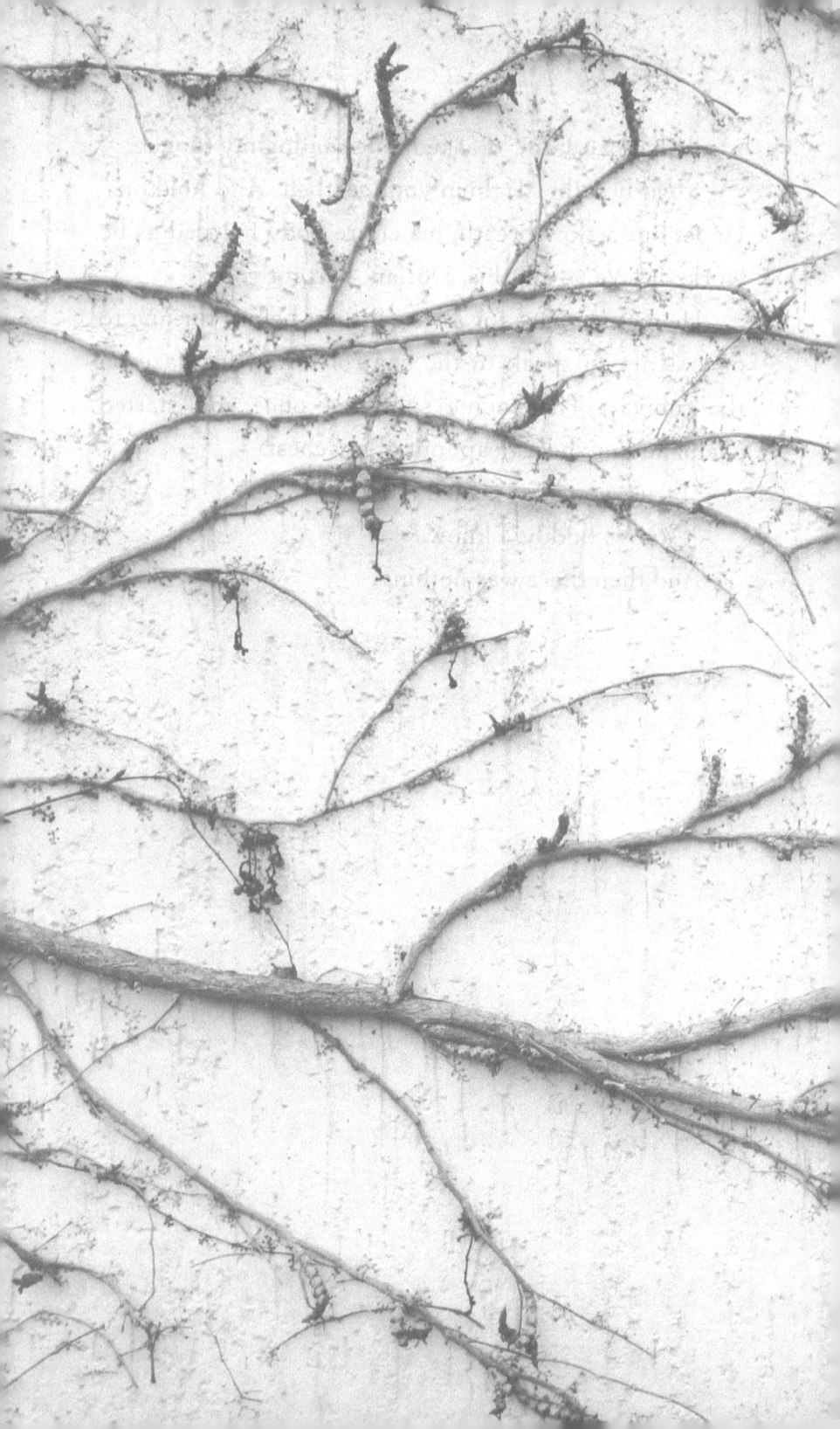

Chapter One

HARPER

LIFE ROCKED.

Seriously.

Sure, life had its hardships and was never truly easy, but sometimes I knew if I just let my face tilt up to the sun, even in a Colorado winter, I'd be able to let life touch me once again.

Because it *rocked*.

I looked down at one of my best friends and couldn't help but smile. "You are living up to your name today, because look at that sky." My loving and adorable golden retriever tilted his head up to follow my gaze, and I knew I had the smartest, sweetest boy there ever was.

Yes, even at four years old, his face had already gone a little white, but he was still my puppy. And I always loved the fact that golden retrievers looked as if they were smiling sometimes or had the saddest expression with those big eyes. I blamed their eyebrows. They were just so expressive.

Lucky shook his head at me, a very human expression on his face, and then rotated his hips back to stretch.

"Oh, big stretch." I paused, wondering when exactly I was going to stop saying that phrase. However, my cutest boy did just stretch, and he deserved to know I had noticed.

Lucky had been my graduation and birthday present from my big brother, and I had a feeling Joshua had known exactly the perfect puppy for me. Because Lucky was just as exasperated as my big brother when I didn't do exactly as I was told.

"Okay grumpy Gus, it's time to head to doggie daycare."

At the sound of my voice, he wiggled his butt, went to go get his favorite stuffie, which today happened to be a stuffed rabbit from two years ago. He'd been a little spoiled during our Christmas celebrations, but then again, he was my child. He deserved the best.

"No stuffies today. You're allowed to bring your ball though."

His ears perked, and he did a little circle dance,

before dropping his stuffie and picking up his orange and blue ball.

I rolled my eyes, because I should have said toy. Now that I had said the word ball I was going to have to play outside of the building for a couple of minutes before walking him to doggie daycare.

I was grateful that the Cages had not only rented me the building with my bakery inside, but also the apartment above. Yes, my home constantly smelled like baked goods, but considering I was the owner and head baker, I always smelled like sugar, flour, and yeast.

One day I would have enough saved to get a little home around Cage Lake and be able to let Lucky roam around in a large yard to his heart's content with ball time and outdoor time.

Until then however, the bakery did host a small outdoor eatery area where pets were allowed to hang out, and I was right across the street from a large park. That meant he could get his ball time off leash, at least during certain times of the morning, and then we'd head out to doggie daycare.

I grabbed my purse, and flashlight, because while the sun was out, there were enough trees that if the ball went where it shouldn't, it was going to be annoying to find later.

Lucky, still attached to his leash, bounded beside

me down the back stairs, thankfully not knocking me off.

As soon as we hit the park, I let him off his leash, and without looking back, he darted towards the corner of the flat area of the park. I rolled my eyes, because he didn't even have to look at me. No, Lucky he knew I would throw the ball. Because if I didn't, I would get those huge puppy eyes. And even after four years, I couldn't say no.

I tossed the ball, and of course it hit a tree, then a limb of another tree, before hopping down right next to Lucky. He looked at me, those eyebrows so expressive I saw the disappointment in them, but picked up the ball anyway. Then he ran full speed towards me before daintily dropping it at my foot.

This went on for another six throws or so—thankfully I hadn't hit another tree—and after he took care of his business, and I cleaned it up, it was time to go to doggie daycare.

The owners had decided to call it Dog Gone It. I still had no idea why they had gone with that, but if it made them happy, and it made Lucky happy, that was all that mattered.

At least it didn't have the name Cage in it.

My lips twitched, because my bakery was called Rising Cage.

The Cage family pretty much owned Cage Lake.

They had founded it generations ago, and before it had become a tourist destination, thanks to the resort, also owned by the Cages, it had been a mining town. And when the mines had closed, the Cages had turned it into this.

Or at least the past two generations had. They had plastered their name on everything they could, gobbled up any land they hadn't already owned, and hadn't quite turned into robber barons.

Thankfully this new generation, the ones that included my friends, were the good sort. They were kind, even while grumpy, and cared about the people in town. They also didn't want to own everything.

Aston Cage, the eldest Cage, had helped me open up the bakery of my dreams less than a year ago. The town's original bakery had burned down in a fire and the three built since either shut down or went out of business. The final one had closed while I was in high school, and the town was sorely lacking.

Not everybody would have taken a chance on a twenty-year-old with an associate's degree. But Aston had. So when I had worked on finishing up business classes to make sure I knew what I was doing, I had begun working on the bakery.

Now I had employees, ledgers, overhead, and I was in the black.

The Cages had taken a chance on me, and I knew it

was because I was a family friend. And I wasn't going to look a gift horse in the mouth. Or whatever that expression was.

I dropped off Lucky, and thankfully he was on his ball-high so he wasn't sad that I had abandoned him.

I winced at that. I always hated leaving my baby boy at doggie daycare, but he was a large golden retriever, at least seventy pounds, but we weren't going to talk to him about that, and I owned a bakery. The health code violations alone would be too much. And I wasn't going to have him locked up in my small apartment all day.

For now he got to play with his friends, and I knew he would be taken care of.

Maybe having a large dog at this point in my life wasn't the smartest idea, but I wouldn't change Lucky for the world.

After all, Joshua was rarely in town, and that meant Lucky was my only family sometimes.

Though if I said things like that to Joshua, using my big eyes just like Lucky did, my brother would be at my side in an instant.

Overprotective, slightly overbearing, and growly.

But then sometimes he would bring a certain Cage with him, and all would be right in the world.

I rolled my eyes as I began my morning prep. My employee, Melody, whistled under her breath as she worked on the sourdough that we were setting up for the afternoon.

Thankfully she couldn't read my mind, but as soon as *that* Cage walked in, she'd be able to read my face. She had always been able to.

Thankfully she didn't tease me. And thankfully my brother had no idea that I was totally crushing on his best friend.

His much older best friend.

Well, Joshua and Dorian were the same age, but I was not.

No, I was eight years younger, and even though I was an adult, out of college, and a business owner, I was still the baby sister.

But first crushes never went away.

As I set the frosted cookies aside and rubbed my lower back, I caught a glimpse of myself in the mirror. Flour coated one cheek, and I was pretty sure there was some form of frosting in my dark red hair. I dyed it different colors constantly, because it was fun. The only color I never truly went was an orange, mostly because the one time I had it had been a total accident, and it was *not* my color.

"You look a fright," Melanie teased.

I rolled my eyes. "That's what happens when I get to work, and I'm thinking about too many things at once."

"Joshua should be back in town today, right?

"Yep. He's in Denver right now but plans on being here for dinner."

"I'm glad that he has an apartment here, and he doesn't have to sleep on your tiny couch."

"If Joshua had his way, I would be living in that apartment with him. Or he would in fact be living on my couch. I don't think he likes the fact that we live separately. It's not like he actually lives in Cage Lake year-round."

Cage Lake was a beautiful town with memories and a thriving historical community. It had been growing over time, but the Cages made sure it didn't explode.

There were laws in place by the town governance to make sure that things didn't hurt the environment and grow exponentially. Even the resort on the east side of town had strict limits on how many people were allowed to be there at a time.

It brought in the income our town needed in order to take care of itself, but as of yet, it hadn't overflowed into making Cage Lake inhospitable or unlivable.

It was home. Unlike some who were transplants, I had been born and raised here—except for a few years after my parents died.

I ran my hand over my chest. No, I didn't like to think about those years.

"What are you planning on making him?" Melody

asked as she flipped the sign to open. People walked in with coffee in their hands and smiled. Our regulars.

"Stew, I think. It's already made."

"Good. He can cook for you from now on." She rolled her eyes.

I understood. I did tend to mother my brother sometimes just how he liked to be overprotective.

But it was what we did.

We were each other's family, along with Lucky.

We went through our busy rush, selling out of bagels and muffins far quicker than I was planning. However we had backups of other things, and Melody was fantastic at selling what we had on hand.

The Caged Bean was close by and was the town's gourmet coffee shop. While we sold drip coffee, and any type of sugar or creamer that you wanted, the Caged Bean was where people got their cappuccinos, Americanos, specialty coffees, and even a coffee flight featuring sweet and elaborate lattes.

We worked together, rather than as adversaries. They sold my baked goods, and I made sure that my customers knew exactly where they could easily get coffee, and at a discount if they found my card.

It worked well for me, and for them, and I was just happy that things were working out.

Even if, once again, the Cages were involved.

As Melody worked the front, I went back to decorating a few cakes that we had as orders, as well as a few that I wanted to set out front. Sometimes people bought cakes on the fly, and that was always a sight to see.

By the time lunch rolled over, I remembered I hadn't eaten, but I knew I would get to it eventually. I had a few big orders to get through, thanks to a family reunion taking place up at the lake, and I didn't want to get behind.

However, as I turned the corner, my chest seized, and I had to stop and slowly let out a breath. Thankfully Melody didn't see and wouldn't ask questions.

She didn't know after all.

No, the only one who did was Joshua, and I was glad that my brother wasn't here yet.

I told myself to breathe, going through the exercises I had learned as a child. When I caught my breath, I looked down at my phone, and realized it was later than I thought.

Joshua should have been here by now.

Well, I'm sure he would text soon. Maybe there was traffic getting up the mountain.

I went back up front to work with Melody, when a familiar face walked into the shop.

I smiled at Hudson Cage, one of Dorian's numerous brothers. The fact that Dorian had not only one family, but two thanks to his dad's philandering ways, still surprised me. He had *eleven* siblings.

I wasn't sure how that had happened, but then again, remembering Dorian and Hudson's dad, I guess I knew exactly how it happened.

The man had always been a jerk to me, but then again, he had been rude to anyone he thought beneath him.

Hudson however was not like his father. In fact, other than the growliness, he was the exact opposite. He was a loner and liked being the cabin man. You know, the type of guy who lived and worked in the woods, and you never knew exactly what he did. Some of the women in town couldn't help but fall for him, you know because he was the broody, bearded type, the one with secrets and stories to tell even though he would never tell them.

I just thought he was Dorian's brother.

There was probably something wrong with me. Okay, there was *seriously* something wrong with me and I knew what it was.

A crush that wouldn't quit.

I opened my mouth to tease Hudson since he rarely showed his face these days. He liked staying out of the spotlight now that one of their many sisters had moved to town and had taken up some of the Cage responsibilities that Hudson had been forced into.

But then I saw the paleness of his features underneath his beard, and my throat went dry.

"What's wrong?" I asked, my voice soft.

"Oh my God, there's been a plane crash out on the private airfield!" Ms. Patty screamed before Hudson could say a thing. She was the mayor's wife, a busybody with a heart of gold, and bile crept up my throat.

Because I knew exactly what airfield she was talking about. Because if it had made the news here so quickly, there only had to be one.

The one where my brother worked occasionally.

"Hudson?" I asked, my voice shaky.

A beat of silence. A growl of a voice. "You need to come with me."

Everyone stopped moving as they stared between us.

"Oh my God, is it Joshua?" someone asked even though I couldn't pay attention well enough to figure out who it was.

Hudson didn't answer, instead just stared at me in that stone way that he always did. I immediately undid my apron and grabbed my bag from under the counter.

"Melody." My voice cracked and I cleared my throat. No. I would not react. Not now. Not when others could see and gossip. All was well. I had to show that. I couldn't break on the outside when it was as if I were ready to shatter on the inside.

Melody, my full-time employee and friend gave me a sad look, her eyes filling. "I got it. And I'll make sure that Scarlett or I can take care of Lucky too. Just keep us updated."

"Okay," I said, my voice low.

Melody looked over my shoulder. "Take care of her, Hudson."

"Don't worry, she'll be safe with me."

I wanted to believe that, but I wasn't sure I was going to be safe ever again with the way he just stared at me. The way he wasn't giving me a single update as to what he was thinking.

"Hudson?" I asked after we got into his truck, and I pulled out my phone. "What am I going to see when I look up the news?"

He tapped his fingers on the steering wheel and took a moment to respond. I hated how careful he was being. "Small plane crash. They don't know what happened, though I'm sure they're just saying that. There were two people on board."

My hand squeezed my phone so tightly that my knuckles whitened. "Who was it? I mean, if you're here, it's got to be Joshua. Right? Is my brother okay?"

"Joshua and Dorian were in the plane."

Silence.

A void of emotion.

A crack in the world that began to erode beneath my feet.

My throat tightened, and I just stared at him, wondering if the ringing in my ears would go away soon. "Do you know anything else? Hudson. What happened?"

"I don't know, Harper. All I know is that there was an accident."

I studied the line of his jaw as he wove down the mountain with such ease and practice like he had been doing it all his life. But then again, other than the time when he had been overseas, he had been.

And so I knew he was lying to me.

"Hudson? What else do you know?"

He let out a breath, and it took me a moment to catch the stress and cracking beneath it. "Harper."

"Just tell me. If it's both of them, I need to know. Because it's them."

My family. Two men that I loved. Not that I could tell Hudson that.

Not that Hudson didn't already know or could guess.

Hudson's growl of a voice filled the cab of the truck. "One is alive. In surgery. The other didn't make it."

And with that, a screaming void wrapped its skeleton-like hand around my neck and squeezed. I didn't say a word, I couldn't. Instead I turned to face the front and tried not to focus on the trees passing by, or the others going about their life as if the world hadn't ended.

"I'm sorry, Harper. I wish I knew more."

I reached out and grabbed his hand, and he squeezed it back. The man who didn't like touch, who didn't like most people, gave me comfort when he didn't know if his younger brother was dead or not.

We made it to the hospital in a little over an hour, with our service spotty at best. Nobody had texted me or reached out. I had a feeling that Ms. Patty and Melody had ensured that none of the town would bother me. And that the Cages were all talking with Hudson.

But when we walked through the emergency room doors, and I saw so many of the Cages there, so many of Dorian's family members, I'd never felt more alone.

I didn't know who was dead—Joshua or Dorian.

I didn't want to think about what would happen when I knew the answer.

I didn't want to choose who I needed, who I wanted to be alive.

Amy, Dorian's girlfriend, came forward and wrapped her arms around Hudson tightly before giving me a nod and going back to the group. Dorian's mother was there as well, speaking in hushed tones to one of his brothers. I knew she had a complicated relationship with the rest of them, but right then and there, I couldn't focus on anything but needing answers.

And then Aston Cage, the eldest of them all walked forward, and I knew. In that moment of peace before a shattered soul, the guilt, the worry, and the absolute pity on his face.

I knew.

My knees gave out, and Hudson was there, trying to keep me steady, and I screamed.

Because Dorian's family was there. Nearly all of them, filling the waiting room to the brim. Because he had family. A big one. One that loved him with every single complicated and tangled relationship they had.

And I had lost the only family I had left.

And I ignored the part of me that screamed in relief that it hadn't been Dorian.

Because my brother was dead.

And I let the darkness take me.

Chapter Two

DORIAN

~ *One Year Later*

"All I'm saying is that you have a wonderful house outside the city. And a perfectly reasonable apartment in the city. With a doorman and an elevator so you don't even have to take the stairs. Not to mention *my* home has a space for you. I do not know why you need to stay and involve yourself with your brother and that woman."

I leaned against the back of the armchair, rubbing my temples. Aston had decorated my guest room to be soothing while I recovered. Dark blues and grays, memory foam pillows and fluffy duvets. A walker in the corner. A medical tray to the side so my former nurse could change my bandages. The bandages and nurse were long gone, but the tray remained. Aston had tried to take it away multiple times, but I'd refused. I needed the reminder. The symbol. The dreams ensured I'd always remember. The fact that I would never be getting on a fucking plane again deserved something more than a forgotten time of healing.

Or hiding.

Yet I hadn't hidden deep enough in the cave if the woman in front of me could so easily find and annoy me.

I loved my mother. I didn't like her, but I loved her.

Perhaps it was only out of necessity some days, but sometimes my mother was a good person. Sometimes she cared for others. I would like to think that her incessant need to put me where she wanted me, and to control the situation, was because she loved me too. And wanted what was best for me—and wanted me to keep her secrets.

Only I had a feeling it was partly because she wanted to be a raging bitch and stick it to my brother Aston and his amazing and take-charge wife, Blakely.

My mother had it in for Blakely, and I still didn't know why. Of course, a reason could be because one of my favorite people in the world, my sister-in-law, didn't take my mother's shit.

And yet here my mother was. In my room. And I

had no idea why I even bothered anymore. I'd kept her secrets for years. I'd let the burden wear on me, stripping me of who I was until I was just the playboy the world thought I was. That went up in flames the same day the plane did.

"Mom. Leave off, will you?"

Melanie Cage blinked at me and took a step back as if surprised I would dare speak out loud to her in any way. She shouldn't be too surprised considering this wasn't the first time I did so. It was just that I was usually the person she listened to.

I had an idea why, hell, anybody who knew the truth knew why she called me her favorite, and why she actually paid attention when I spoke usually, but in this moment, it had nothing to do with that.

She let out a long breath and rolled her shoulders back. "Dorian. Don't talk to me in that way."

"In what way? Mother. Seriously, breathe. You're talking so quickly without inhaling, you're going to pass out at some point. There's only so long you can stand there with that stick up your ass and pretend like you care about me in this moment."

Okay, that was probably a little too on the nose.

Her eyes narrowed, the pink stains on her cheeks darkening.

Thanks to a wonderful surgeon, and Dysport versus Botox, my mother did not look her age. I was all for doing whatever you wanted to your own body. As long as you had the money, and were doing it safely, go for it. Hell, I might even try it one day if I ever ended up with crow's feet. Why not? It didn't hurt anyone but myself if I chose to do it. My mother's attitude on the other hand, that hurt.

But in this moment, she didn't look like a woman in her fifties, let alone a woman who had birthed seven kids.

She looked like a terror. "Dorian Cage. What the hell is wrong with you?"

"I guess answering with the whole 'Daddy had a secret family and then I almost died in a plane crash' is a little too on the nose?"

Even as I said the words, I knew I had gone too far. Not with mentioning the plane crash, because I was too numb to even think about that.

No, it was Daddy's secret family.

A secret family my mother had known about.

Because of course the Cages could never be simple.

My father apparently had quite the stamina. Not only had he decided to have seven children with my mother—he had a whole other family. One that my mother had known about and had colluded with the other woman in order to make the timing work out.

Considering my father had been a CEO of a billion-dollar company, one that not only worked in real estate and property development, but countless other assets that were all tangled up in his will, he had somehow made it so that he could have two sets of families.

The main one, as my mother called it, had lived in decent wealth. I hadn't quite been born with a silver spoon in my mouth, but adjacent. And now the silver spoon was right next to me, and I wasn't hurting for money anytime soon. Especially with the settlement that was coming out of the plane crash.

No, I didn't want to think about that. I wouldn't think about that.

The other woman, my dad's mistress, was a pretty decent person. Once she had begun to shave off some of the bitterness of her own situation, Constance Cage Dixon was a pretty cool person. She'd been able to come back into her children's lives and they'd all found a way to make it work.

All five of her children from what I could tell.

Yes, dear old dad had twelve kids. *Twelve.*

I would wonder how he could do it all. But it wasn't as if he had ever come to any of our games, or cared about our school beyond making sure that we didn't disgrace him. He hadn't been in our lives enough to care. Of course, maybe he had been in Aston's life a bit more considering Aston was the prodigal eldest. And he had been in and out of the other Cages' lives enough that they barely knew him.

But the asshole had made it work for him.

Not us. But it wasn't like we could ever make it work for us.

Not that I was bitter or anything.

Okay that was a lie.

"Why do you have to bring up your father?"

"You're the one that married him, Mom. And stayed married to him." I gave her a look that spoke volumes, but she just rolled her eyes. Because we weren't going to talk about that, or the other thing. Or the other secret thing that we never talked about.

Secrets tended to add up, and my mother was the queen of them.

She was also the Queen Bitch, and I hated even using that word. I didn't use that word for women. My new sisters and sisters-in-law were the prime examples of what goodness could be. Even if Isabella had a bit of an attitude, I loved her. And I would never call another woman a bitch and degrade women in any way. But my mother personified the word most days.

"I don't understand why you're here though. Dorian, it's been a year. I know that you're still hurt, and being crippled —"

"Fuck off. Don't use that word. Don't even go down a path where you're going to say something so ignorant that I'm going to have to scream."

"That's not what I mean. But you don't even go to physical therapy, Dorian."

"I do. I just don't let you take me. Because I'm not a toddler."

"A toddler wouldn't have gone up in that plane with that man to begin with. What were you thinking even getting in that small plane with a pilot who wasn't even a pilot, just your friend?"

"Don't talk about Joshua. Don't even mention him."

"I know. I know he's gone. But his lack of skill almost killed you. And now you have all those scars, and you're never going to be able to walk again."

I had to count to ten, slowly, breathing in and out so I didn't get up and beat my mother with my cane.

She had never understood my friendship with Joshua. Because every time I went to Cage Lake, the small town that my family literally owned because we were ridiculous, she had always thought any relationship with the townies—in her words—would be slumming. Also in her words because my mother could never look for the good in people. Only who could do good for her.

Because Joshua hadn't been the rich boy in town. But there weren't many rich boys in Cage Lake other than the Cages themselves. So I hadn't known what my mother was thinking to begin with.

Joshua and I clicked from the moment we had seen each other and had been friends through everything. Some of the last things I had said to him were so cruel that I could barely breathe. I pushed those thoughts from my mind, because dwelling on them didn't help anything.

And the more I dwelled, the more I thought about her.

No, I wouldn't think about her. I couldn't.

"Mom. I use a cane occasionally. Because sometimes my leg fucking hurts. But I'm fine. Sure, I'm going to be able to tell when the air pressure changes and a storm's coming when my knee aches, so that just means I've reached a version of old age a bit earlier than some. But I'm fine."

"Then why are you here and not at home? Why aren't you working on any of your businesses? You're just letting it go to waste. That is not what your father taught you."

"We both know my father didn't teach me anything. And I can handle my businesses. I have managers for a reason."

"And they're going to manage them into the ground without you there overseeing things personally. They need a Cage."

"Contrary to popular belief, not everybody needs a damn Cage."

"Is everything okay up here?"

I sat up straighter and turned towards the doorway as Blakely stood there, her dark blonde hair pulled back from her face. She glared at my mother for an instant, before her expression softened as she looked over at me.

I loved my sister-in-law, but I hated that look.

It wasn't quite pity. Because she knew I hated a pitying look. But it was care. And I wasn't sure what the hell I was supposed to do with that.

"It's none of your concern. But why don't you go get my son something to drink. Do something for him for once."

"Your son can walk to the kitchen and get it himself. As he told me this morning." She winked at me as she said it, helping my shoulders drop.

My lips quirked into a smile. "I was a bit of a bastard this morning, wasn't I?" My mother was lucky Blakely had spoken first or I'd have kicked the woman out myself for daring to speak to Blakely like that.

"You had just done your PT, so you were in a mood. It's okay." She gave a pointed look to my mother that told me our argument had carried throughout the house.

"Dorian—" my mother began.

"Just go home. I'm not staying with you. God, I'm never staying with you."

"And so you're just going to live on your brother's charity."

"Yup. That sounds pretty good." I turned to Blakely, grinning. "What do you say? Do you mind if I live here forever? Oh, maybe you can marry me as well, and we can get a whole poly going on. But not the way that Ford is with his husband. You know, as Aston's my brother."

"Why did you have to make it weird?" Blakely said as she walked into the room. She ran her hand through my hair and rolled her eyes. "But I'm not going to marry you. Aston's possessive."

I could practically feel the heated rage radiating off my mother as she moved forward. "I don't understand you. Either of you. And then you just bring up Ford and his lifestyle."

"Get out," Blakely said, her voice sickly sweet. "Get out of my home. You're not welcome here. Not if you're going to talk about our family that way."

My hands fisted at my sides. As much as I wanted to handle this myself, if I stepped in front of Blakely like I wanted to, my sister-in-law would kick my ass. I'd throw my mom out if my body had the energy, but I wasn't about to step on Blakely's toes.

"This is my son's home. You just latch onto him."

"You're right. I think I really latched onto him when I learned how to give that perfect blowjob. It's all about learning how to swallow and hollow your cheeks."

I threw my head back and laughed, ignoring the pain in my side. The scars of the burns on my side ached, but after a year now, they were healing up well enough.

My mother looked as if she was ready to strangle Blakely, but I knew for a fact that Blakely could take her. Instead my mom picked up her purse and stomped out of the room.

"I cannot believe I just said that to your mother," she said as she put her face in her hands. "I don't think I've ever said anything like that in my life."

"I love you more than you know. And I realize that a triad relationship really isn't what you're looking for, but if you ever leave Aston, I'm all yours."

She shoved gently at my shoulder, and then took a step back, eyes wide. "Did I hurt you?"

I sighed, shaking my head. And just like that, reality was back. "No. You didn't. Promise. I didn't feel a twinge that time."

"I just want you to be okay, Dorian." Her eyes began to fill, and I cursed. I gripped the edge of the chair and forced myself to stand, ignoring the twinge. When I wrapped my arms around Blakely, she settled into me, but didn't hug me back.

"The burns won't get any worse if you hug me you know."

"You just have to tell me if it's too much," she whispered. And then she wrapped her arms around my waist, settling her cheek on my chest.

I sighed. "Thanks for standing up for me."

"I was mostly standing up for Ford," she mumbled.

I chuckled, resting my cheek on the top of her head. "I don't know why my mother's getting worse day by day, but I'm sorry she was here at all."

"She's your mother. She should have a right to see you."

"No. She shouldn't."

"Is there something I should know?" Aston asked dryly.

I looked over at my suave older brother as he strolled into the upstairs parlor where we all stood. His hair was a bit longer than usual, and it looked like he had finger combed it back numerous times during the day. He had undone his tie, his suit jacket long gone, and while he raised a brow at me, he truly only had eyes for his wife.

Fricking newlyweds.

Right after I had gotten out of the hospital, I could have stayed with any one of my family members. Even Hudson offered to take me in. My brother was enough of a recluse that he didn't like anybody near him, but his words hadn't been a surprise. He was a good man who'd seen shit no one wanted to deal with. Even Kyler, the brother I barely knew and was currently out on a world tour since he was a damn rockstar, had offered to stay home and help me.

The siblings I hadn't grown up with had each opened their homes for me, and I hadn't been able to say yes.

Instead, I had stayed with my older brother, because sometimes you just needed the one you knew who could take your attitude. Or maybe I was just the little boy again, looking up to the one person who had been able to see through my lies to myself.

"I'm trying to steal her away, but she won't have me."

Aston shook his head and tugged Blakely to him. She freely went, and I didn't try to hold her back. Mostly because I'd hurt myself if I did. From the way Aston was looking at me, I had a feeling he knew exactly what I was thinking.

"Mine," Aston bit out slowly.

"I do love being fought over like a dog toy," Blakely added dryly.

"But like one of those homemade dog toys, not the mass-produced kind," I put in.

"You are so weird. But I love you, Dorian. Do you

want me to go get your pain pills? I know it's almost time."

Resentment split through me, but I put on a bright smile, trying my best to ignore it. "I've got it. Don't worry."

"No, let me help. You don't have to go all the way downstairs."

"I've got it, Blakely," I snapped, and immediately regretted it.

It wasn't Blakely's fault I was in a pissed off mood.

"Dorian," Aston's voice cooled. I wanted to slither up and hide under that stare.

Blakely patted her husband's chest. "It's fine. I'm going to go start dinner. Come with me. I want to tell you the whole blowjob thing I talked about with your mother."

Aston blinked slowly, and I pressed my lips together so I wouldn't smile. "Well, that's one way to distract me. I'm very confused and I'm afraid I don't want to know."

"You actually want to know this one." I winked and Aston's shoulders relaxed.

"You're getting dinner with us, right? You're not going to hide up here?"

"Aston," Blakely whispered.

"Yeah. Don't worry. I won't become the crazy recluse in the attic. At least not yet."

My brother shook his head. "Dorian. We only want what's best for you."

"That's what everybody keeps saying." And with that, I turned to go back to my room on the other side of the hall. Of all the homes that we Cages owned, this one was the largest. But considering we Cages needed to meet up *en masse* often, it was good that at least one of us had the space.

I closed the door behind me, ignoring the worrying whispers between the married couple.

I was exhausted, and it had nothing to do with PT that morning. No, I didn't want to think about exactly what it had to do with.

I sank down into the comfortable chair in the corner that I knew Blakely had put up here so I would be able to sleep at some point. I hadn't been able to sleep on my back at first, so the armchair La-Z-Boy had been my saving grace. But even having my feet up didn't help keep away the nightmares.

My phone buzzed, as the family group chat went on about something or the other. I stopped paying attention. I used to be the one to instigate shit, but I wasn't in the mood. I was tired, and I had no idea what the hell I was doing.

I hadn't been lying when I told my mom that my managers were handling my four high-end bars.

The Golden Cage was the highest-end bar that I

owned, and the clientele tended to be the wheelers and dealers of politics for the area. Some came from Old Money; the others made a name for themselves. Either way, the drinks were top notch and we'd spared no expense at making the place comfortable yet ornate.

I had three other places that varied in degrees, but they were still doing well. And though I had told my mother my managers were handling everything, I still looked in on them, at least through emails and spreadsheets. I wasn't in the mood to be gawked at, so I didn't go to each of them. My managers could handle them without me. Hell, I should have been letting that happen anyway. I was the CEO. I didn't need to show my face.

I ran a hand over the scar on my jawline, the one that would one day be covered with a beard. Most of my scars were underneath my clothes, so they wouldn't be gawking for long. I didn't want them to see. Didn't want the questions. Those pitying looks.

And that meant I needed to get out of here.

Not just from work, but from the others.

Because the Cage family dinner would be happening at Aston's soon, and I didn't want to deal with that. When dear old daddy had died, the true nastiness of his secrets had been revealed. Meaning each of the Cages had found out they weren't the only

Cages in town. I didn't only have six siblings, I had eleven.

But of course dead old dad couldn't just stick with a secret family. No he had to screw us in the end. In order for the family company to stay as is and not be divided into so many parts that thousands of people would lose their jobs and ways of life, we had to have family dinners once a month.

With three people from one side of the family and two from the other. We had to document it and send it to our handy-dandy lawyer. And once that was done in a couple of years, there would be more hoops to go through. It was one of the worst wills ever in the history of time, and we still couldn't get out of it.

My father was a mastermind and hypocritical asshole, and he didn't stop there. Each one of us got a letter from our father. I knew some of us had opened ours, and others hadn't received theirs from the lawyer yet.

I knew what was in Aston's because he had showed us, but I didn't know anyone else's.

With a sigh I opened the hardback book I had been trying to read through the headaches and pulled out the letter that I barely cared about.

Dorian,

It's time for you to realize who you really are. For you to stand up against the blood in your veins and the history of where you came from. It's time for you to do something with your life for once. To stop being the playboy who fucks around and never amounts to anything.

Take this. Take what I wouldn't bother giving the others. Do whatever you want with it. But you know what you need to do.

For once in your weak life, make me proud.

Loren Cage.

My lip lifted in a snarl, and I resisted the urge to crumple the paper.

I had never liked my father. And truly I never loved him. And what kind of thing was that to think of the dead? I didn't really care about what my dad thought. But he had given me a way out.

Because in addition to the main will, there had been a side benefit just for me.

I took the keys from the night table and looked down at them in my hand. The weight of them far heavier than it should be.

With a sigh I stood up again, but too quickly. My knee gave out, and I cursed, falling forward. I tried to catch myself at the edge of the bed but missed and ended up on my side.

Pain spliced up my side, and I cursed through gritted teeth, trying to breathe through the acidic taste on my tongue. The sound of running on stairs echoed through the area, and I cursed, trying to sit up before Aston barged his way in the room. But I was too late.

"I'm fine."

"You're on the fucking floor, Dorian. Let me help."

"I've got it! You don't need to help the invalid. I'm fucking fine!" I shoved Aston away and forced myself to stand, straining my side in the process.

"Dorian. I love you. You're hurting. Just let us help."

I whirled on my brother, one of the people I loved most in the world, and tried not to throw a punch. Because maybe hitting someone I knew loved me back would make things better.

"I'm fine. Okay? You don't need to worry about me. I've got this."

"You always do. But you can lean on someone."

"So says Aston Cage. *The* Cage."

I could have cursed myself at that, from the way that Aston staggered back.

Our father had been *The* Cage. The asshole name that came with the responsibility of an empire. And all the weight of the disappointment and cruelty of our father.

"I'm going to go help Blakely with dinner. I'll see you in a bit."

I should have opened my mouth to say I was sorry, to do anything. But instead I watched him walk away and then looked down at the keys in my hand that I hadn't dropped.

It was time to go because I couldn't be here. Maybe I could be near her. After all, I had promised Joshua. I didn't want to see that look on my brother's face again. So maybe it was time to open up the closets and search for all of those skeletons.

Because I wasn't going to do that here.

I just didn't know if I was going to be able to figure out what the hell I was doing in Cage Lake either.

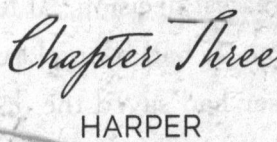

Chapter Three

HARPER

"OKAY, LUCKY. TODAY IS GOING TO BE A GOOD DAY. The bakery is doing well. I have three cake orders coming in. The sun is shining. The tank is clean." I paused and looked down at my amazing dog and realized he did not get my humor. "*The tank is clean?* You know, from one of the best movies of all time. *Finding Nemo?* We just watched it like last week."

Lucky yawned, showing all of his teeth, before he padded to the front door.

With a sigh, I stuffed my feet into my running shoes and tossed my hair up into a bun. I caught a glimpse of my face in the mirror and held back a wince.

I dyed it dark a few months before on a whim and didn't quite regret it, but I still wasn't sure what I thought of it. I missed my red hair, just like I missed being blonde, or having pink hair that one time. But going at my hair with boxed dye during a night where I hadn't been able to breathe out of loneliness and fear, hadn't been the greatest decision. At least I hadn't been drinking at the time. It had been close, but no. Thankfully my hairdresser had saved the day and made sure that I hadn't completely destroyed my hair. But I was stuck with this color for a while. Because if I went and tried to bleach it, it would probably fall out.

Of course, the dark hair just made my face look paler than usual, and I couldn't help but notice the dark circles under my eyes.

"It'll get better. They say it gets better."

If I kept telling myself that, maybe I would believe it. Not yet, but maybe one day.

Lucky barked, something he really did well inside, and I cringed. "I'm sorry, baby boy. Let me get your things. And we'll go on your W-A-L-K."

His entire body wiggled, starting from his tail all the way to his nose, and I couldn't help but laugh. I loved my baby boy. Yes, we were both getting older, and the white around his face was growing over time. But we were okay. We had to be. After all, it was just the two of us.

I swallowed hard, ignoring the familiar sharp stab

of pain that came whenever I thought about that. It didn't help anybody if I dwelled on what I didn't have. I could barely dwell on what I *did* have.

I hooked Lucky into his harness, and we headed down the stairs to the small walking path.

I wasn't opening today, and for that, I could only thank the gods. I needed some time to just breathe. To get ready for the day.

My team could handle the bakery, and then I would work on the baked goods in the back. I had a whole list of cakes and cookies that I needed to make, and others that I wanted to. The others could deal with customers and put on the smiling faces they didn't have to lie about. And hopefully nobody would notice I spent less and less time up front.

And if the others never noticed that I'd stopped going out on dates or letting them set me up, the better. I hadn't meant to be a twenty-something virgin, but the idea of dating or dealing with people made my entire body stiffen.

I was just fine as I was, thank you very much.

Again, the lies seemed to be coming easier.

I began my jog, Lucky prancing beside me. I was barely above five feet, so my version of a jog for anyone else would be a fast walk. But Lucky didn't mind my pace.

A few people nodded at me as they walked past, and I was grateful that the first set had been tourists who didn't recognize me. It was still cold enough outside since it was late January that, though the sun was beginning to shine brightly, there was still snow on the ground and an icy chill in the air. But I had warm enough clothes on, and Lucky was in his element. My dog loved snow.

Thankfully we lived in a mountain town in Colorado, so he got his fill of it. I probably wasn't going to get tired of it anytime soon, but if I did, I would head to the resort and go annoy Scarlett. She was the manager, and I'd be able to sit in front of the large fireplace with a book and pretend that I was happy.

I nearly tripped over my own feet.

Pretending. Well, that wasn't the greatest thing to come to mind. I didn't want to pretend I was happy. I wanted to *be* happy.

It had been a year now since Joshua had died, a year since my life had changed radically.

How was I supposed to go back to normal?

"Harper. Oh Harper."

I held back a cringe as Ms. Patty came forward. She was bundled up and looked adorable in her white puffy jacket and cashmere scarf. Her hat was perfectly knitted, and I knew she had done that herself. The mayor's wife was the Jill of all trades as she called herself. Everything she touched was perfect.

I tried not to think about the stains that were probably on my leggings, or the hole in my glove.

The idea of using Joshua's life insurance had nearly broken me. I'd done the only thing I could with it, however—other than leaving it in the bank—and put it toward the bakery. He hadn't had too much equity in his home, so all that money had just gone into overhead with the increasing cost of being a business owner.

And it wasn't like I had the energy to go out and shop and buy pretty things. Who would see them anyway?"

"Hi Ms. Patty. Good morning."

"Good morning. I went over to the bakery to get a Danish and didn't you see there. But I see you're here with this lovely boy. Hello, Lucky."

Lucky sat, wiggling, and held up a paw.

"Good morning, dear boy." She shook his paw, despite wearing cream-colored gloves, and I warmed towards the older woman.

She loved gossip. She didn't thrive on it like some people, but she always wanted to know what was going on. The mayor's wife was also kind enough to back away if someone truly didn't want to talk about it. She didn't dig deep. Didn't play with lives in a callous way. She was the queen of all things Cage Lake news and knew everything that went on in Cage Lake. Including as much as she could about the Cages themselves.

That hollow feeling echoed inside, but I ignored it. I didn't see much of the Cages these days. It wasn't that I was actively avoiding them, it was just easier if I did. Now that Isabella had moved to town, I saw her often enough, but she and Weston had spent most of the winter down in Denver with the other Cages, so I hadn't seen her too much recently.

And Hudson liked hiding in his cabin. He still came into the bakery every once in a while to check on me. I wanted to think it was because he liked me, but with the scowl on his face, I had a feeling he was doing it because of Joshua.

Because somebody had to do it. It wasn't as if Dorian was doing it anymore. He hadn't been back to town since the accident. I hadn't seen him since the funeral. Just a few texts here and there to make sure I was where I was supposed to be, and then the person who had mattered more to me in my life than anyone other than my brother had ghosted me.

But that was fine. I needed to learn how to be alone. I was getting better at it.

"How are you feeling, Harper?"

Ms. Patty reached out and gripped my forearm gently before patting it, bringing me out of my reverie.

I hated that question. What kind of answer were

they looking for? If I wasn't doing okay and I told them, they wouldn't know what to say. Nobody wanted true honesty when they asked you how you were doing. You were just supposed to say you were doing fine so they could cither believe you or see through your lies and pity you. Nobody had any answers.

What were you supposed to say when your brother died in a fucking plane crash?

My brother had only reached thirty a couple of months before he died and hadn't even settled in on who he wanted to be in his life. And now he was gone, and I was just supposed to move on and pretend like I knew what the hell I was doing.

"It's a lovely day, isn't it? As long as I have the sun on my face, and this guy right here, it's going to be a good day."

Not quite a lie, and not quite an answer. And Ms. Patty saw through it all. But thankfully she let me off with just a smile.

"It's good to see you. I'll stop by later. I want to get Mr. Mayor something special for his birthday. And you know how he loves that fudge cake of yours."

I held back a smile at that, because I loved how she called him Mr. Mayor. I had a feeling that when the man finally stepped down from his position and somebody else took his place, he would always be Mr. Mayor to her.

The two loved each other more than anything, and though sometimes the cloying and closed-in feeling of living in a small town was almost too much for me, I did love Ms. Patty.

"Well, you know me and fudge. I can't say no."

"Same here, but I try not to overindulge."

"There's no such thing as overindulging. Not when it comes to fudge cake. You can have as much as you want and never feel guilty."

"I like that. What a great concept."

"Food is food. Not bad, only food. Don't worry, I'll keep you both happy with fudge."

"Now, that's what I like to hear. I'll let you finish your run. I know we're going to get a couple flurries later, so I will see you soon."

"Sounds good."

"And take care of yourself, Harper. We're all here for you. You are not alone. Not in Cage Lake. We're always here for each other."

I hadn't been prepared for the blow. I should have been, because Ms. Patty was truly trying. She wasn't being cruel, just being herself. A caring person who wanted me to know I wasn't alone.

Only I was.

When death broke through the darkness and stole life from the young, people crowded in, ensuring that you were never truly alone for the first moments. They had phone trees and casseroles. There was always a covered dish ready for me to dive into so I wouldn't have to cook. Only cooking and baking was how I focused, how I was able to push through my own thoughts.

Eventually the visits ended and they went back to their own business. Their own lives. People moved on, because life continued. Even when death lied.

Part of me wanted to scream at the world and ask why it kept moving on. Why it kept trudging through as if my world hadn't ended.

But that would just be selfish.

So I smiled at Ms. Patty, squeezed her hand like she needed me too, and continued my jog with Lucky.

We trekked up a hill to the edge of the forest where the trail continued on. We would have to turn around soon because Lucky would get cold, but he was still having fun, and I just needed to focus on trying to breathe. Of course, the pace was a little more than I bargained for, and at this high elevation, my lungs seized.

I was an idiot. I hadn't brought my meds, hadn't even thought about them. So when the first sting sliced into my lungs, I tried to suck in a breath. Only shards of glass replaced my air, and I gasped.

I ran my hand over my chest, forcing myself to stop

as I bent over, trying to catch my breath. Lucky nuzzled my face, and I ran my hands through his fur.

"I'm okay. We just should head back."

He gave me a look as if he were judging me, or maybe he was just worried. Or maybe I was losing my damn mind.

I knew better than to jog in the cold at this altitude without taking care of myself. After everything my body had gone through, I knew I should take it slower. Who was I trying to impress? Why was I even bothering?

No, I wasn't going to think about that. That was a very bad road that I was not going to go down.

Instead, I turned back down the path and went over the hill so I could go back to the center of town and get through my day.

One step at a time, and then maybe it would stop hurting. Maybe the numbness that they kept telling me would sweep over, would finally settle in.

Lucky barked and sped up. I groaned and tried to keep up, but the leash slipped from my grasp.

"Lucky! Stop. Heel. Lucky!"

He sped up, leaving me behind, and I ran, ignoring the sharp pains in my lungs as panic seized me.

"Lucky!"

As I turned the corner, I slid on an ice patch, and my feet went out from beneath me. My hips slammed into the ground, an arc of pain radiating through me as I landed awkwardly on my shoulder.

Of course, that wasn't the only pain that decided to make itself known as I realized why my damn dog had run away from me.

"Harper. What the fuck?"

Dorian limped towards me, Lucky at his side, as he scowled down at me.

"What the hell were you thinking? Running out here alone? You've hurt yourself, dammit."

I hadn't seen the man in almost a year, and the first time I do I'm bruised and battered on the ground, and humiliated, and he was yelling at me.

Sounded about right.

I tried to shove off his arm as he reached for me, but the man was too big, even though he had lost weight since I had last seen him. Instead, he lifted me up, and I couldn't help but notice the pain in his eyes as he did so.

It seemed I wasn't the only one hurting. Not that he would ever admit it. But hell, I wasn't about to admit it either.

"Are you okay? Let's go to the hospital."

"I'm fine. My pride hurts more than anything." Though I did rub my hip.

I scowled down at Lucky. "Traitor."

He just did his little golden retriever smile before he looked longingly at Dorian.

"Seriously. Are you okay?" His hands went to my hips, and my cheeks burned before I batted at him.

"Stop it. I'm fine. I'm a klutz. We both know this. You're the one limping. Are you okay?"

I could have rightly bit off my tongue at that. Because we both knew he wasn't okay.

He had been badly burned on his side, and he'd broken his leg, twisting it in a way that I couldn't even bear to think about. According to Hudson, eventually Dorian would walk without a limp, and his scars would remain, but it could have been worse. That's what everyone kept saying. It could have been worse.

But it had been worse for Joshua. No, I wasn't going to think about that. I couldn't. Not if I wanted to stay sane.

"I'm fine," he bit out. "Let me walk you home."

"You're here. In Cage Lake. Why didn't you tell me you were coming?"

"We need to get you back to your place," he said in lieu of answer.

"That's where I was going until my dog deserted me. I need to go home and shower and then get to work. How long are you in town for?" I asked, trying to keep my voice level. I didn't want to sound accusatory, or like I was begging, because being in Dorian's presence was always a war of emotions.

Because I had loved him since I was eighteen, in the way that the younger sister loved the older brother's best friend.

But he had always been there, always sweet, always caring.

And always not for me.

"I don't know. I'm just here. So, let me take care of you."

Exasperated, I shook my head. "I'm an adult, a big girl. You don't have to take care of me, Dorian. But I'm glad you're here. You haven't been back in a while."

"I've been a little busy," he ground out.

"Doing what?" I asked before I held up a hand. "No, that's not my business. I'm sorry. Are you staying at your place? I know Hudson's been keeping it up."

"No. I got another place."

I frowned. "What? Where?"

"The old Ackerson place."

My brows winged up. "Really? That place has been abandoned forever. I didn't know it was habitable."

"It's fine. I'm working on it for a while."

"So you're here working on a house? In the dead of winter?" Confusion didn't begin to explain the emotions running through me.

"It doesn't matter. I'm here because I want to be.

And fuck, I told Joshua that I would take care of you. So I might as well live up to the deal."

It felt as if another slash to my heart would be one too many, but I was used to this. Because of course he was here to take care of Joshua's baby sister. That's how it had always been.

It didn't matter that I was in my twenties and a woman. I was the baby sister.

But from the strain in his eyes, and the dark circles that rivaled my own, Dorian needed to take care of himself.

"Is Amy with you?" I asked, and I was happy I kept the bite out of my tone.

Storm clouds covered his eyes, and he glared. "I have no idea where Amy is. Seems she didn't like staying with a cripple."

I fisted my hands on my sides. "Oh, I'm going to find that bitch. Did she say those words?"

He shrugged. "Water under the bridge. She's gone. Your brother was right, and I'm going to be here for a while. So stop running alone and hurting yourself, okay?"

"Are you serious right now? You haven't seen me in nearly a year. You don't answer my calls or texts. And suddenly you show up and try to order me around, while you're being all secretive with the Ackerson place. What the hell, Dorian?"

"Stop arguing and just get back to a safer place. And make sure that you don't have anything worse than bruises. You need to be more careful, Harper."

I stared at him, wondering who this Dorian was. Then again, I didn't think I was the Harper he had seen last.

Death was inevitable, and it didn't judge you. It sliced through you and left nothing but agony in its wake. There was no numbness, there couldn't be, not for the living.

"Whenever you decide to stop being the grumpy Cage, let me know. Because I'm pretty sure Hudson already has the mountain man, grumpy asshole Cage locked in. I don't think we need a second one."

"Watch your tone and watch your language, Harper. That's not like you."

"You don't know me, Dorian. You never did."

With that, Lucky and I moved past him, and ignoring the pain in my lungs, I jogged back to the bakery.

I ignored the worrying looks from others as they milled about Main Street, and as I bumbled up the stairs and back to my apartment, I locked the door behind me, only then realizing that I wasn't shaking from exertion, but from the sobs racking my body.

Dorian Cage was back.

The one man I had ever cared for.

But the Dorian Cage I had just seen wasn't the man that I knew.

But that only made sense. Because I couldn't recognize the Harper that I saw in the mirror as it was.

Two peas in a pod. Joshua would be so proud.

Lucky slid his body against mine as I sat on the floor, held my dog, and let the sobs come.

But no amount of crying would bring Joshua back. And no amount of crying would help me figure out what the hell to do about Dorian, let alone myself.

Chapter Four

DORIAN

THE THUD OF MY AXE HITTING WOOD ECHOED IN MY ears and felt good. Of course, I was going to regret this later. Hell, I was already regretting it. I was a damn idiot, but then again, this was something I knew. Me being an idiot wasn't anything outrageously new or fantastic.

After all, hello, I woke up being an idiot, went to sleep being an idiot, and would remain one until the end of my days.

Another whack, as I split a log and tried not to groan. I rolled my shoulders back, the axe nearly falling out of my hand. I set it so it rested against the larger base log, before I tossed the split logs of the wood onto the pile.

The old Ackerson place, as it had been named years before I was born, wasn't exactly falling down around itself, but close. It was larger than a cabin but not a huge estate like my father would have preferred when we'd been growing up. I didn't even know why we still called it the old Ackerson place considering a Cage had owned it for nearly two decades. Only he'd done it in secret.

It would take months of backbreaking labor for me to get it into shape to sell, but that's what happens when you neglected a place for so long.

It seemed only fitting that the place that my father used for whatever illicit practices he decided to under-take away from the prying eyes of town, and both Cage mothers, would be the one falling into pieces. Neglect had no better name than Loren Cage.

I set up another log, rolled my shoulders once again, and let out a grunt as I split it in two.

With each movement my burn scars twisted and stretched, and the bile rising in my throat told me I was probably going to end up in more pain than I should be —I deserved it.

Especially after what I had done with Harper.

Talk about fucking up a reunion. I had just been tongue-tied seeing her. I knew it. But what the hell had she been doing out alone?

Whack, another log, another wheeze from my throat because I was out of shape when it came to this type of movement.

My knee was already swelling, and I would have to limp back up the deck stairs that would probably crumble beneath me thanks to the rotted core of them. Yet part of me whispered I deserved it—just like my father.

I had a feeling I knew why dear old dad had left this place to me in the will outside of the other Cage's purview. Only the damn lawyer had known about it and hadn't had the grace to tell me until after the plane crash. It most likely had been stuck in probate and had been an addendum in some will that no one had seen.

I didn't know the timeline, and I frankly didn't care. Maybe he had just hidden it until the perfect time to annoy the fuck out of me. That seemed like something a lawyer my dad would employ would do.

I hated this place. Every time I walked through that door down the hall with the tattered wallpaper and partially rotted subfloor, I could scent Dad's cigar smoke. That tobacco wafting through the air and seeping into the walls themselves. The sound of ice clinking against glass as he sipped at his bourbon, talking in wild tones to whoever dared to listen.

This was the place he made his deals, the ones that

were above board, because Dad never broke the law. Not when it came to making money. Because those who had shady assets were prone to lose them. They soared far too high in the sky, daring the sun to shine upon them as if they were Icarus.

It only made sense that my father would go about making his millions the legal way. Everything else in his life he tended to go about ass backwards. Not only having a secret family, but a mistress or two along the way.

I swore I could hear the sound of that giggle, and then maybe that hearty laugh of another woman. Countless women who had strolled through this house because they had wanted a piece of a Cage and hadn't cared that they were the other woman. Or even the other woman's third-placed trophy.

I hated it here.

Yet I was going to fix it up. Sell it. And never look at the damn place again. Maybe I would get tired of it and burn it down to the ground so nobody could live underneath its roof. Honestly, that probably sounded like a better idea.

Ignoring my obvious thoughts that were going in a direction I did not want to think about, I went back to splitting wood so the house would be somewhat warm for the rest of the winter. It had a decent heating system, but for all I knew the wiring was going to catch the place on fire. Which again, wouldn't be a bad thing most likely.

After another twenty minutes, my knee finally decided to say enough was enough and nearly buckled.

Annoyed, I tossed the last log on the pile, then used my forearm to wipe the sweat from my brow.

"Wow, I didn't realize that you were going for the mountain man look. The Henley works, but I think you need to add the flannel like your dear old brother does."

Shoulders tensed, I carefully set the axe aside and turned to see Weston, my brother-in-law, a man that I had known for years and called a friend, as well as Hudson, my brother who happened to live in Cage Lake full-time.

When the Cages had built the town, they had decided to do it in sections. The main houses of the family were situated around the lake itself that was on the north end of town. Then the main street of town bisected where the residential and commercial areas would be.

Each of the residential areas tended to be off the side streets and blended into the river area on the west that butted up against the mountains, and the resort area passed the forest on the east side. And of course, because the Cages were Cages, they owned the resort as well.

When Dad had overseen everything, we hadn't had the ability to take care of the town as much as we wanted.

And when Hudson had finally gotten out of the service, and found himself in need of solitude for reasons that he wouldn't tell us to this day, he had ended up moving to Cage Lake full-time and taking care of all the minor business issues that came when you owned many of the buildings in the city.

Rent had to be dealt with, as did little things like repairs and upkeep. We also owned enough land in the area so people couldn't build on any more than they already had.

For all my dad's faults, he did care about preserving this town. It had never become too commercial, and if my generation had anything to say about that, it would continue not to be.

"What are you doing here?" I asked, trying not to let the bite in my tone sound too annoyed.

But when both men just gave me a look, I knew I hadn't succeeded.

"You don't call. You don't write. You just show up, pretend you're a mountain man." Weston drawled. "I thought the surly asshole Cage was the guy next to me. Not you."

"Fuck you," Hudson rumbled, before he moved forward and yanked the last piece of wood from my hand.

"You do realize you're doing all this all wrong, don't you?" he asked. For a moment I thought he knew exactly how I had fucked up seeing Harper again. But instead he gestured towards the log pile.

"You stacked it wrong."

"How the hell can I stack wood wrong?"

"Like how you did it. Because if you're not careful, it's going to all roll on top of you."

"It's fine."

Hudson mumbled something under his breath I didn't hear before he moved forward. "I'll fix it."

"You don't need to fix my mistakes," I grumbled.

Hudson didn't listen. Instead he picked up the axe and continued my job, rearranging things when I couldn't even say a damn word about it.

"I see he's still the grumpiest of us." Weston shook his head. "Come on, you can get me something to drink."

I pinched the bridge of my nose, my knee aching. "You invite yourself here and then you expect me to entertain you? That sounds brilliant."

Weston smiled though I wasn't sure it reached his eyes when he looked at me. Of course, that was probably a projection. "I *am* brilliant. Thank you. Your sister tells me that all the time."

That made me snort, the smile on my face feeling slightly disused. "I'm pretty sure Isabella has never said that."

Weston smiled like a man in love. A man who had his life before him and was damn happy with the outcome. "Your sister loves me. And one day she's going to marry me, and you're going to have to deal with me as your real brother-in-law, rather than just playacting as we're doing now."

That made me roll my eyes. "I call you my brother-in-law in my head, so whenever you get the balls to actually propose, it won't change much."

"You always say the kindest things." He shrugged as I followed him into the old house.

The place had already been furnished when I moved in, and though there had been a caretaker thanks to the lawyer, they hadn't done much. It left little to be desired. And from the look on Weston's face, he agreed.

"By the way, I'll propose eventually. When Isabella's least expecting it."

I snorted. "Seriously?"

Weston leaned against the counter, that knowing and secret smile once again on his face. "That woman is amazing at everything she does and likes things in a certain way. So I'm going to surprise her. Because you know how she loves surprises."

"I might not have grown up with my sister, but I know her well enough to know that you are delusional." Isabella was headstrong, brilliant, and always spoke her mind when it came to protecting those she loved. As the eldest of her branch of the family, she reminded me of Aston in a lot of ways. And oddly enough, a little bit of Theo in the way she pushed in a kind way.

"But she loves me." Weston just smiled. "And I was waiting for the twins to be settled in college and my brother to be set with his next phase in his career, that way I didn't have to play big brother."

Weston, much like Joshua, had lost his parents when he was younger. But unlike Joshua, Weston had been forced to raise his three younger siblings. From the time the twins were ten, Weston had been their guardian.

Joshua on the other hand, hadn't had the chance to be Harper's guardian.

My hands fisted at my sides for a moment as Weston opened my fridge to see what meager offerings I had. I'd picked up a few things from the main general store, but there wasn't much.

I had a feeling that's how everyone knew I was in town, because you couldn't walk through the small downtown of Cage Lake as a Cage without people noticing.

My business was always out there for everybody to see. I had grabbed a few things to get me through and really missed delivery already. I did not like the stares, because they weren't as kind as the ones from my family. No, my family had good intentions. I didn't know what the town wanted.

Because the town and Joshua hadn't been able to keep Harper safe. Not when she had been a kid. Joshua hadn't been able to keep custody of Harper, not until he had won a vicious battle with their grandparents.

My best friend had hidden most of it from me, at least the parts of why he was able to get his kid sister back. And I didn't dare to think about what Harper had gone through in the process.

But now I was back in town, and my best friend was gone, and that meant I was the only person left to make sure Harper was okay. That she had someone in her corner.

I was doing a piss poor job of it.

"Do you want a beer? Water? Because we don't have much else," Weston drawled.

"I'm fine."

Weston gave me a look that spoke volumes. "You're not in the city. There's no food delivery.

IF YOU WERE MINE

Though the pizza place does have a delivery boy. Just not when there's ice. Or heavy wind. Or a chill. And since you're in the middle of the forest in this shack, that makes the chance of him showing up around zero."

I laughed at that though it was a hollow one. The place was three stories with six bedrooms and four bathrooms, let alone countless other tiny rooms with different names. It wasn't a shack.

"It's fine. I have enough food to get me by."

"And I have a feeling you're not going to want to go into the restaurants to eat there, so we're going to need to make sure you get more."

"Do not text Isabella," I warned, but Weston just smiled at me.

"Too late. I snapped a few photos of your bare cupboards, so the love of my life will probably be over soon with a color-coded spreadsheet and a meal wheel for you."

"What the hell is a meal wheel?" Hudson asked as he stomped inside, kicking off snow as he did. "Wood's done. But fuck, Dorian. What the hell are you doing in this place? Do you even know how to fix the subflooring?"

There was probably a metaphor somewhere in that but I didn't have the energy to find one. "Contrary to popular belief, I did help build my clubs. I didn't just sign a check and call it a day. I know how to fix this place up."

At least I hoped I did.

Hudson tilted his head as he studied me. "You might have the skills, but I still want to know why."

"There's no reason. It's just what I'm doing right now." *Lies. Lies. Lies.*

"Well, doing something is good," Weston said as he met Hudson's gaze.

I ignored them both, gritting my teeth "Please don't send Isabella over here. I don't need a nanny."

"I'm pretty sure my Bella would hate even hearing that phrase."

"Well, I don't need her to take care of me. And technically, she's my younger sister." My shoulders sagged as I let out a breath.

"So?"

I shrugged. "She has the older sibling mentality. You're going to have to deal with it, middle child."

"Our family tree confuses me," Hudson said with a sigh. "I didn't used to be a middle child. Not really. Why aren't you staying at your house? I keep up with it for a reason."

"I have things to do here."

I didn't elaborate, and when I didn't lean into their conversation, they finally let me be. But not without a stern look, a glare, and a promise they would be back with tools and their sweat.

I didn't want their help. I just needed to get this done and out of my hair.

And I needed to fix what I had already broken.

With a sigh, I closed up the house and got into my truck.

I needed to fix the driveway, not only clear it, but repave some of it, but for that I would have to hire someone. While I knew how to fix the house, I had no idea what to do with that part. The trees needed to be trimmed, and there were probably a dozen other things that needed to be done with the land.

I knew I was in over my head, but it was better to deal with this than go back to one of my clubs and deal with the stares. Of course, as I drove through downtown and parked in front of Harper's bakery, the stares followed me there too.

I didn't look that much different. Yes, my beard was longer, so I could try to cover my scar, and they couldn't see the scars on my side. And as long as I practiced, I didn't limp.

They couldn't see the evidence of me surviving a plane crash.

But they also saw the lack. I did.

Joshua had died. And I had survived. Only I had no idea what to do with that.

With a sigh, I got out of my truck gingerly and made my way into the bakery. I did not understand why she had named the place Rising Cage, but it had made her laugh, and I had shaken my head when she signed the lease with Aston.

I had been so damn proud of her for going for her dreams. Not everybody at her age or position would have even thought to get where she was. The place was bustling. She was damn good at her job, and Joshua had always been so proud of her.

I was proud of her too.

She had grown into this person that surprised me every day. And I had ignored her for too long. I hadn't truly known her when she had been younger. She had always been in the periphery when I visited. It wasn't like I had grown up in Cage Lake. So it wasn't until she was out of high school and living with Joshua that I had fully gotten to know her.

Maybe that was why every time I saw her, I had to remind myself that she was Joshua's kid sister.

And not a full-fledged adult in her early twenties with a career, an apartment, and a dog she loved.

Sometimes I felt like I was failing in that though.

"Dorian, so good to see you." I looked up at the older woman behind the counter and frowned.

"Melody, right?"

"You remembered. It's good to see you. Harper is in

the back if you want to head over there. She's been decorating cakes all day."

I saw the frown on her face for a blink before she smiled, but I leaned forward anyway. "What's wrong?"

Melody blinked. "It's just good to see you."

The worry in her tone dripped like syrup, and I ignored it. "Is Harper okay?"

"She's just been baking. It's what she does these days."

That was weird because Harper usually worked up front. She loved talking with customers, figuring out their favorite desserts, and working them into her schedule. I suppose it made sense. As I could feel the stares on my back, people on pins and needles waiting to ask how I was, at least those who lived in town, it must be twice as bad for Harper.

She lived with it day in and day out. No wonder she wanted to stay in the back.

I cleared my throat—the stares on my body digging in. "I'll go visit."

"I think she needs that."

I moved past Melody, ignoring the slight wince in my step, and walked to the back of the kitchen. Harper stood there, hands on hips as she frowned at the book in front of her, and I couldn't help but smile at the studious look on her face.

"So...Wellesley. This is what you do all day? Frown at books and flour?"

Her gaze shot up, her eyes widening. "Oh. You're here. Are you okay?"

I ground my teeth and told myself she didn't mean anything by it. "Just here to say hi."

"You called me Wellesley." That little line between her eyebrows deepened, and I wanted to rub it away.

I hated when I got that urge, the same as that little squeezing thing that happened to my chest whenever I saw her. "What?" I asked, trying to remember what she said.

"You called me *Wellesley*," she repeated, her eyes wide and her voice curious.

"I always used to call you Wellesley. Or Wells. It's your name."

"You've been calling me Harper. I mean, it's my first name, but I always liked that you called me Wellesley." Her cheeks pinked as she lowered her head and shrugged, wiping her hands on her apron. "Anyway. Is there something you need?"

She'd always been my Wellesley. Sure, she was Harper in my head too, but she was Wellesley too. And I hadn't even realized I'd called her the wrong thing. I was a damn asshole and needed to get my head on straight. Her clipped tone could have been daggers for the way she looked, and I swallowed hard. "I'm sorry, I'm an ass. Yesterday, the past year. I'm sorry."

She looked over my shoulder, a frown on her face.

I followed her gaze with a frown. "What is it?"

"I was just wondering if someone was there pushing you to say that."

An odd feeling slammed into me. Was I that much of an asshole? Yes. Yes, I was. Joshua had asked me to do one thing in his life—to take care of his baby sister —and I'd been doing a shit job of it so far. "Nobody is pushing me to be here. I'm here because I want to be."

Her eyes widened for an instant, and she swallowed hard. "Oh. That's good. I'm glad you're here. I know I didn't sound it yesterday, but I am. And you're allowed to be an ass. Of course, that's not saying much, as am I."

My lips twitched. "Language, Wellesley."

"I'm an adult, Dorian. I probably curse more than you do."

"I'm not quite sure about that. But why are you allowed to be an ass too?" I asked, tilting my head as I studied her face.

The circles under her eyes had darkened, but then again so had mine. But she was still so damn beautiful. She'd colored her hair darker since I had last seen her, and I liked it on her. It made her cheekbones pop, not that I would tell her that. It seemed like a weird thing to say to your best friend's little sister.

But I had always liked Harper's smile, and the way that she leaned into everything she did.

"I'm allowed to be an ass because my brother is dead and he was all that I had left," she said point blank, pulling me out of my attentions.

Again. A kick to the chest. "Wellesley," I whispered. I had moved in front of her without thinking, and now we were less than a foot away.

Her lips quivered and it took all within me not to reach out and bring her close. I didn't think she'd let me, nor did I think Joshua would want *that*. And hell, my leg ached enough at the moment that I'd probably fall on my ass in my rush.

"Sorry. I didn't mean to blurt that out. But it's true. He's gone. So I guess we're both allowed to be asses."

"You still have me you know. I mean, it doesn't seem like it recently, but you do."

Her eyes filled, and I cursed.

"Dorian."

Panicked, I ignored my earlier control and reached out, not knowing what to do, but she wrapped her arms around my waist and hugged me tightly. Awkwardness settled in for just a moment, but then I realized this was Wellesley. *Harper.*

I swallowed hard and held her back, holding her

tightly. And when she nuzzled into my chest, I leaned down and rested my cheek on top of her head.

I didn't mean to, but I inhaled, that sweet vanilla scent of hers filling my nostrils.

"I miss him," she whispered.

I sighed, running my hand up and down her back.

"I miss him too."

And we stood there, ignoring her work, ignoring the world.

Because I knew I couldn't go anywhere. Not with Harper in my arms.

Where she should have always been.

Chapter Five

HARPER

THE DARK CIRCLES UNDER MY EYES NOW MATCHED the bags that would probably forever remain. I hadn't slept well since the plane crash, and honestly, I wasn't sure if I was ever going to. It ached just to think about, however, I was getting decently good at learning how to function while on little to no sleep. Having practiced when I was younger and living with my grandparents had been a saving grace I'd rather not think about.

Everything I'd gone through over the past weeks, however, was worth it. I was finding my place in town, my role in a way that had nothing to do with my life before. And the best part was reconnecting with the women in this town who I'd left behind when I'd been torn from Cage Lake's grasp. While I was alone, I wasn't truly alone. And in the darkest of days I needed to remember that.

Ivy and Scarlett were on their way over, and we were going to have a girls' afternoon, which wasn't exactly like a girls' night of lore, but as each of us had full-time jobs that tended to create chaos it made sense that we had to schedule out our get-togethers with a multicolored calendar. One that got a lot of use considering Scarlett worked more hours than I thought was physically possible. Though I was no slouch considering I owned the business, my friend took dedication to a whole new level. Ivy sometimes pretended that she had a decent work-life balance, but all three of us were terrible at it. Ivy traveled often, even though she was a Cage Lake resident like the rest of us, so her sleep schedule was probably just as bad as mine.

However, my lack of sleep last night had nothing to do with the usual. No, it had everything to do with him.

How he had held me. How I was Wellesley again. Wells.

It had almost felt as if we were back to what we had been. Only I knew that wasn't the case. There was no way we could have been when it felt as if that hug had been a dream.

Because he had walked away after that moment, that sense of a new reality shattering in a blink. He'd grunted something about needing to be somewhere for the house and then scurried away. If he was anyone else, I would've thought it had been because he couldn't stand me. But perhaps, I was closer to the truth of that than I cared to admit.

With a sigh, I finished putting my hair up into a ponytail that would fit at the back of my hat and went to find where the love of my life had scurried off to.

Lucky stood in front of the door, doing his big stretch, and I snorted. "The girls are almost here and then we will go on our you-know-what."

He gave me a look with those expressive golden retriever eyebrows that told me he knew exactly what I was talking about, and I should probably give up the whole not speaking out loud thing when it came to the W-A-L-K word.

But seriously, my dog was a menace, and I loved him more with each passing day. He would never run away from me as if I were the problem.

I tried not to think about what would happen though, when time moved far too quickly.

I set Lucky up in his harness, pushing my doom and gloom thoughts out of my mind. They weren't going to help anyone.

As soon as I opened the door, my two best friends glared up at me from the bottom of my staircase.

"Since when are you the late one?" Scarlett asked, a smile playing on her face.

Ivy threw her head back and laughed. "She's right about that. I'm the one who forgets what time it is unless I look at the sun while on a hike."

"It's because you always go off to places that don't have enough service, and you refuse to wear a regular watch because of that one time that you shattered it and somehow cut yourself." I jogged down the stairs, Lucky at my side, and rolled my eyes as both women pretty much gave up all sense of sensibility and treated Lucky like the king he was.

"Are you ready for your day?" Scarlett asked, and for some reason I knew she wasn't talking to me.

"Who's the best boy ever? The one man who won't ruin the day?" Ivy asked.

I met Scarlett's gaze again. "First, you guys are early, I'm not running late. Meaning I have a feeling you told Ivy a different time?"

"No, she told me the correct time. I'm not that late. I'm not rude," Ivy said primly, her eyes dancing.

I winced. "That is very true. I'm sorry."

Ivy waved it off before looking over at Scarlett once again. "And not all men are jerks. Remember, we actually like Ronan."

"Your boyfriend does seem like one of the good ones. I'm sorry," Ivy said, though the darkness in her gaze took more than a couple of blinks to finally go away.

"Plus, you have pretty much the last decent guy in Cage Lake," Ivy added.

"That is true. Considering I had yet another fight with you know who."

My lips twitched as we began our walk, the three of us letting Lucky decide where he wanted to go at first. "What did he do this time? I thought Isabella was the Cage in charge of the resort now."

Scarlett was the manager of the Cage Lake Resort. Yes, the Cages owned it, but Scarlett was the one who made sure it did exactly what it needed to. She excelled at her job, and that was why the Cages trusted her to handle it without their constant oversight. I also knew they had no idea how many hours she worked because Scarlett hid it. If they knew about it, the Cages would put a stop to it. The fact that she could hide it from Hudson, Flynn, and Isabella meant she was damn good at it. I just hoped she realized she could lean on them at some point.

"Isabella is amazing, but she also has a full-time job doing other things. So we're easing her in to doing the oversight of the resort."

"I totally agree on Isabella. Who, by the way, should be here any minute. But what did Hudson do you that angered or annoyed you?" I asked, imagining Dorian's grumpy, growly, and sometimes mean if you didn't look closely enough at his intentions brother.

"Well, he wasn't too much of an asshole. But it was a look. You know that look." Scarlett scowled, and her pace sped up.

I glanced over at Ivy who was holding back a laugh.

It wasn't that Hudson was generally mean—it was that I wasn't sure he liked people. Which made the fact that he was still the Cage in charge of going to a resort that had countless strangers as part of the clientele funny to me.

He hadn't always been in Cage Lake. Just like the rest of them he had spent his childhood down in Denver. But their summers had always been part of our small town. Considering the family owned the damn thing, it made sense to me.

That was how my brother and Dorian had become friends after all. Because he didn't need to live in the same town to be a best friend. We just had to make it work.

"I'll continue my story if you tell me why you're frowning," Scarlett said softly.

I blinked and shook my head. "It's nothing. I was just thinking about how Hudson didn't used to live here, and then it reminded me that the Cages didn't always use to live here at all, but two of them are here. Well, three."

I was rambling now and had to hold back my

wince. Because my crush on Dorian that had started as a little girl's crush but had nothing to do with real feelings and had morphed into something more, as I had become an adult, was something both of my best friends knew.

"Okay, we can come back to that in a second," Scarlett drawled. "As for Hudson, he stomps into the back offices as if he owns the place." She held up my hand. "I'm well aware the family owns the place, but that flannel wearing, growly asshat doesn't actually have his name on the deed." She winced. "His last name. Still."

"I'm pretty sure all of their last names and first names are on those deeds," Ivy sing-songed. "Especially since with the famous will, the other Cages were added. Why are you being so growly about that?" Ivy asked.

"You've all confused me, but it's just that he acts like he doesn't want to be there and then is there all the time."

"It's his job." Ivy added.

"Is it? Is it his job to follow me around and make sure that I know what I'm doing? I'm the manager. I know more about that business and how everything works than any other person in that building."

"That's true. Is he questioning you? Thinking that you can't do the job?" I asked, angry on her behalf.

Hudson did have an attitude problem, but I always thought it was for a reason. Not that I knew that reason. The Cages all had their own secrets.

"I don't know." She threw her hands up in the air. "It's not like he tells me what those grunts mean. He just shows up, asks to see what he always does. The stupid paperwork that he can send over to the others. And then he stares."

I met Ivy's gaze again, intrigued.

Scarlett raised her chin. "No. Don't give each other that look. It's not like that kind of staring. I know when a man is hitting on me. Or wants me. That's not it. I promise you. It's more that I confuse him."

"Probably because you don't swoon at the sight of a Cage," Ivy said, wiggling her eyebrows.

"That is true. There's only one of us that swoons at the sight of a Cage."

At her smirk, I scowled. "Hey. Don't bring me into this."

Ivy burst out laughing as we took a turn to go down Main Street. We were heading to the local restaurant, where we could eat outside, and Lucky would be welcome.

"You're the one who got all defensive. I didn't even say your name."

"What else did Hudson do?" I asked, not doing a great job at changing the subject.

Scarlett didn't even bat an eye, which surprised me. "He just...he always catches me at my worst. And I hate it. It makes me feel like I don't know what I'm doing even though I'm good at it. I'm not egotistical, I'm not an asshole. I know I have room for growth, but I'm damn good at my job, and he only sees the worst."

"What happened?" Ivy asked. We took a seat outside of Cage Free, the local diner, and I tied Lucky up where he would be comfortable. There was already a doggy bowl full of water, and I smiled at how happy my precious boy looked.

Scarlett glanced over her shoulder and leaned forward to whisper. "I just had to deal with this stupid thing with the resort guest, and I ended up with coffee all over my shirt. And then when I went to go change, I hadn't realized that Hudson was in the room."

My lips twitched. "So you flashed your boss?"

"No. Maybe. I don't know if he was looking. But as soon as I ran away, which I'm not proud of, he didn't even dare to follow. And then, I was trying to work on four projects at once, because two of my people had called in sick, and when I bent over to keep a small child from knocking over one of our precious vases, another kid ran me into a wall, meaning the vase fell anyway."

I cringed. "Oh no."

"Oh yes. Hudson, of course, caught it, and me." She

rolled her eyes. "Because of course Hudson Cage can do everything. The vase was fine, and I didn't hit the floor. And the parents were all apologetic. Not to me, mind you, but to the precious Cage."

"Did he say anything about it?"

"Of course not. He grunted, glared at me, and stomped away. I cannot wait for Isabella to take over."

"It sounds like I need to," a familiar voice said as she walked up.

"Oh. Hi. Pretend you didn't hear any of that. And I'm totally professional." Scarlett's face turned the color of her namesake.

Isabella just shook her head before taking her seat. "First, sorry I couldn't show up for the walk. I had three online meetings in a row, because for some reason the love of my life and I decided to live in two places, so traveling is trying to break me. However, I might've heard some of it. I'll take over for Hudson soon. I wasn't planning on doing it for a while because I thought you two had it covered, but I can. If there's a problem."

Scarlett shook her head and began to play with her napkin. "No, no, it's fine. I was overreacting. Plus, as soon as I stood up and tried to talk with the family, my boyfriend walked in and apparently had seen Hudson's hands on me, and well, it was another scene. I'm sorry. Your brother's great."

"Are you okay?" Isabella asked, voicing the same question Ivy and I clearly had.

"Oh, I'm fine." Scarlett smiled brightly. "Promise. Ronan has always growled about the Cages more than I do." She winced again. "Sorry."

"It's okay. I'm just now learning how to be a Cage, and I don't know Hudson that well. I'm still learning about these new brothers of mine. So I don't know why he growls like he does, or why it seems like the Cages that grew up here during the summers seem to know more than they're saying."

"Hudson was always pretty doom and gloom when we were younger," Ivy put in. "At least, in that broody sort of way." Her lips pressed into a line.

"And he was deployed a few times," I added. "Though I was really too young to know what that meant at the time."

Hudson was a full decade older than me, and Dorian was eight years older than me, so it wasn't as if I could throw stones at my own crushes. But it had never been Hudson for me. No it had been my brother's best friend instead.

"He changed when he got back, but it's not like we really knew him."

Ivy continued. "I think you're always going to be different when you come back. I hope he at least told some of you what happened over there," Ivy said on a whisper.

"And now I feel like an asshole for even complaining about him," Scarlett said with a sigh. "My twin would be so disappointed."

Isabella's eyes widened. "I forgot you have a twin."

"Luna lives down in Denver, so I only get to see her when we make plans. Though we talk every day on the phone. I miss her being here."

"You'll have to introduce me sometime. It's nice getting to know more people in Cage Lake."

"Honestly the two of you would get along so well. I'll make it happen." Scarlett immediately picked up her phone, and when Isabella's vibrated, I knew there was now a new group chat in effect.

"You are efficient. So if my brother has said anything different, I'll beat him up for you," Isabella said with a wink.

I grinned as our favorite waitress came and took our orders. It was a quick lunch, and a beautiful afternoon. Yes, it was cold, considering it was winter, but they had the heat lamps out, and everything oddly felt good.

And just like that, guilt settled in.

Because I wasn't supposed to feel good.

How could I?

After a few bites of my sandwich, I set it to the side

and listened to the others as they spoke about the ongo-ings and stressors of Cage Lake.

Isabella gave me a concerned look when I shook my head infinitesimally, hoping the others hadn't noticed. Lucky put his head on my thigh, and I rubbed his fur, trying to feel connected to the real world, rather than the dreams that kept trying to set me under.

"Wellesley, shouldn't you be at work?"

The hair on the back of my neck rose, as I swallowed hard and looked at the man who kept invading my dreams.

Dorian had a to-go cup of coffee in his hand, not one from the specialty coffee shop, but mine. Because apparently, he wanted plain coffee today. I didn't want to think about the fact that maybe he had gone to my own bakery to check on me. No, that wasn't it. He just liked coffee.

"I do take one day off a week. Apparently if I work seven days a week, people glare at me."

"As we should," Ivy put in. "Hello, Dorian."

At the dryness in her tone I blinked, focusing on Dorian's face. That's when I realized that he hadn't looked at anyone else. Not even his sister. What on earth was that about?

"Ivy. Scarlett. Isabella. So I guess we're all playing hooky today?"

"I should ask you the same thing, brother of mine,"

Isabella teased, though I saw the concern in her gaze as she studied her brother's face. They might not have grown up together, might not know each other, but they were blood, nonetheless. I didn't know how that family dynamic worked, how they were figuring out this new phase of their life. But I knew Isabella was trying. And Dorian had done his best before the flight...

Only I didn't know how he fit himself into the family now. He'd hidden himself away from Cage Lake for the past year and I'd heard he'd done the same within his family, but I didn't know the connections they'd made along the way. If any. How was one supposed to create familiar relationships in such a short time after finding out your father's life had been a lie, breaking the rest of the family along with him?

"Like you I'm taking a break from the house."

"That's not the work I meant," Isabella said softly.

"It's fine." He shrugged. "My managers know what they're doing."

"At least one Cage believes that their managers can handle things," Scarlett put in, and I knew she was trying to help Dorian, because the awkwardness had settled in. Of course, with the way that Dorian's brow rose, maybe it wasn't the greatest thing to say.

He cleared his throat and then looked straight at me once again. That feeling that I couldn't quite name settled over me, and I wasn't sure what I wanted him to say. What I needed him to say.

"I'm headed back to the house since the place won't fix itself sadly. But if you need anything, Wellesley, you let me know."

"Sure. Um. You too."

And with that, Dorian left, and I tried not to watch him and failed. The way that he filled those jeans nearly broke me, but not as much as the way that he tried to hide his limp.

"So..." Isabella drawled. "What was that?"

Sadly my two best friends didn't speak up for me, so I just cleared my throat.

"It's not like that. He's just trying to fill my brother's place. You know, in that overprotective stance. Seriously. Not like that."

Except the more I tried to deny it, the more I knew they didn't believe me.

Oh, how I wanted to believe them.

But Dorian was not for me. He never had been, and frankly, he never would be.

Chapter Six

DORIAN

"It could be worse. We could be having this at your ghost house."

I glared over at Hudson as we scrambled up the stone pathway to Aston's home on the edge of the lake.

Each of my siblings—at least the ones I had grown up with—had a place on the lake. I wasn't using mine currently, and Hudson's was farther back into the forest, but we each had a place that we used when we visited. For some it was an oasis. Some an escape. For me, it would be my reward if I ever actually finished this particular project.

Currently we were walking up to Aston's place since he and Blakely were in town for the lovely family dinner we were required to have every month.

Because when our dear old dad had died, he hadn't

just decided to throw a few skeletons out of his closet directly into our faces. No, he had decided to make it complicated for us.

While most people may have realized that their parents had secrets, I felt like ours were a little special.

Some cheating fathers had a single kid out there with a woman who had been forced into silence.

Not us.

We had an entire family out there who had thought their dad took far more work trips than was reasonable.

Then again, we had thought the same. Well, knowing what I knew at the time, it was more that my parents had probably hated each other in some way, so being apart would be easier than having to deal with one another face-to-face. But for some reason, both of the moms had been in on it. I didn't know their motivations; money, a twisted form of love, or exhaustion, but here we were. Dealing with the consequences.

Because if our family did not have dinner once a month, we would lose everything.

I wasn't sure exactly which crackpot lawyers had allowed this to happen, but because it was so tangled in red tape, we were leaning into it.

At least five of my Cage siblings had to be in residence for a dinner once a month. We had an actual spreadsheet and calendar to ensure this happened. Because it couldn't just be five from one side of the family and not any from the other. There had to be at least three from one side at a time. Usually that meant the siblings I grew up with because we were seven. And the ones who had grown up farther south, and in a different tax bracket thanks to Dad's cruelty, were only five.

The fact that I had eleven siblings truly made my stomach hurt.

Then again, for all I knew there were more siblings out there. I swallowed hard. Countless other siblings that we would never know about until a new skeleton popped up out of nowhere.

Hell, maybe one of Dad's special letters would show up and at the end of this torment and betrayal, we'd have a whole new surprise.

I shuddered to think there was a third family out there. Because no, there couldn't be. If there had been, Dad would've mentioned it at some point in the will.

It was how he fucked with us.

It wasn't that we would just lose everything. It would break the shaky foundation that Cage Enterprises and Cage Lake sat upon.

Cage Enterprises was a billion-dollar company that fed into real estate, development, environmental concerns, research and development, and countless other departments. My family that worked with the main part of Cage Enterprises were brilliant at what they did and wanted it to succeed. Thousands of jobs would be lost if the company was dissolved. Not only that, but real people would be hurt without some of our research.

Aston, Flynn, and James worked on Cage Enterprises, and they split it into three main sections. Blakely and Isabella now worked with them. Our family was a tangled mess, but it made sense.

With so many siblings there were bound to be knots and tangles.

We didn't always have family dinner up in Cage Lake, sometimes we had it in Denver. At some point if anybody decided to move outside of the state, maybe we would have it there.

That reminded me. "Is Kyler going to be here?" I asked as we walked into Aston's home without knocking.

Hudson shook his head. "He's still on tour."

"So now he's coming to fewer of these than you are," I said drily.

Hudson shrugged as he hooked his jacket on the rung and reached for mine.

I raised a brow. "I can take off my own jacket."

He glanced at my leg. "You've been limping. Didn't know if your ribs still hurt."

Glaring, I handed over my jacket before stalking away. Hudson rarely came down to Denver, so he didn't go to any of the family dinners in the city. And Kyler was a famous rockstar, which always made me laugh. Meaning he was out of town often. I didn't even know if he had a place in Denver. That was shitty of me. My own sibling and I didn't know where he lived. Then again, it wasn't as if Kyler spoke up in the group chat. Or even talked to us often. He talked to his sisters, I knew that much. But I didn't know him.

I didn't really know any of that side of the family.

"Well, that makes five," Aston said as he lifted up his lowball of whiskey in a toast.

"Let's get this damn photo over so we can actually have a dinner without losing everything and having it tainted." Isabella pulled out her phone, and before I could even get a drink, she snapped a photo of the five Cages as well as a couple of spouses.

I looked around the room and realized that yes, we were five. Now that Hudson and I were there, it added to Isabella and Aston, their significant others, and Sophia.

My lips curled into a smile as I looked over at my sister, and the fact that she couldn't help but glow. She'd not only married the love of her life who cherished her, making her the center of his world, she'd gotten pregnant soon after the wedding. Now a new mother, she'd settled into her role with such grace, it was as if she'd only been waiting for her person to come along. My brother-in-law, Cale—yes, the man was named after a vegetable but spelled with a C—was a nice guy. He was a little quiet compared to the rest of us, but you couldn't help but be quiet with so many Cages in the room. In fact, I knew the guy more than I even knew Kyler or Emily, my youngest sister. And how shitty was that?

But Emily rarely came to these dinners, since she lived the farthest away other than Kyler. And well, apparently, she had more of a life than the rest of us.

"Where are my favorite people?" I asked as I moved past the others without even bothering to say hello.

Sophia just smiled in answer. "They are sleeping upstairs in their cribs. Because why wouldn't my sister-in-law build a nursery for them?"

Blakely moved forward and wrapped her arm around my waist. I couldn't help but do the same over her shoulders. "Hi there, Dorian. Good to see you."

"Hi," I mumbled.

She just laughed. "I mean, of course I'm going to have space for them. My nieces need all the love and nurture. Plus, I'm sure that there will be more in the future considering how many Cages there are."

I looked down at Blakely with a raised brow. "Oh? Something we need to know?"

She choked on air, waving her hand in her face.

Aston was there in a second, glaring at me.

I blinked. "Seriously? I was only kidding. Well fuck."

My brother let out a dramatic sigh. "Of course we aren't. We'd announce it better than this. You know my wife. She knows how to plan things."

Blakely rolled her eyes. "And please, give me time before you start making me grow a football team."

That made everybody laugh, and I nodded in thanks as Hudson handed me a beer.

"Actually, Ford was supposed to be here too, and he wanted to announce something," Aston put in.

Ford was our younger brother and had married before all of us. In fact, the precocious asshole who I loved dearly had married not one but two people. His best friend and their favorite woman. Dad hadn't been happy with that but fuck it. Fuck *him*.

"Really? Greer is pregnant?" Sophia asked as she clapped her hands.

Aston nodded. "Yes and he was going to announce it tonight at family dinner, and maybe even do a group text or something, but something came up."

"Is Greer okay?" I asked, my heart racing.

"Greer is just fine," Blakely said with a bright smile. "There was a family emergency with Noah, everyone's okay, but they couldn't make it tonight. And they wanted to make sure that we knew about the pregnancy, because the Montgomerys just found out, as well as Greer's brothers."

"The Montgomerys keep beating us, and I don't think I like it," I said, trying to infuse the humor that I usually brought to an occasion. But from the worried looks on my siblings' faces it wasn't really getting there.

"I think I hear a baby's cry," Sophia said before she rushed off. I gave Cale a look.

"I don't know how she does it either. But now I hear it," Cale said as he followed her. I couldn't help but do the same as I gave my beer back to Hudson.

I hadn't been the greatest brother in the past year, and I knew it. Between pain, dealing with Mom, and just well, everything, I was an asshole. But Sophia's twins? I loved them more than anything.

And when Ford's kid came into the world? I couldn't help but be their favorite uncle. I might as well have one title like that.

I heard the others behind me cheering on Ford and his family, and I would text him later, but for now, I needed to check on the girls.

"They're just wanting to be picked up, everything's okay, Dorian," Sophia said softly as she held one of them close to her chest. Cale held the other, and I couldn't help but go over to the man and hold out my arms.

"You're lucky I like you," Cale mumbled as he put a small bundle into my hands.

"She's so tiny," I whispered. Her bright baby blue eyes stared up at me as she reached for my finger. "Strong grip."

"I swear you Cages melt so quickly as soon as you have one of the girls in your arms."

"I can't help it. She's beautiful. Are you sure they're okay coming up to this altitude?" I asked as I tore my gaze from the baby and to Sophia. Cale hugged her close from behind, so he was holding both Sophia and the baby. If I didn't have such precious cargo, I'd take a photo of the family. Hell, sometimes these kids were the only things that made me smile these days. That and Harper, but I wasn't going to think about that.

"Yes. We're doing well. And you have Violet by the way."

"Well say hello to Hazel for me and tell her I have dibs next."

"You may be getting favorite uncle status, but you might be going lower on the rungs of favorite brother status if you're not careful," Sophia said with a laugh.

"I'll fight my way through the family later. I can't help it. I love these kids."

"Oh, am I interrupting?" a familiar soft voice said, and I turned, forcing myself not to whirl since I had the baby in my arms, and blinked at Harper.

"What are you doing here?" I asked, my voice coming out far gruffer than I wanted it to.

"You invited me? Remember? I'm sorry I'm late, I had to drop Lucky off at Ivy's, so he wasn't alone tonight. And I wasn't sure if he could deal with so many strangers. I can go."

"Stay," Sophia said as she moved forward. Cale glared at me, and I pretty much earned it. "Harper, you are always welcome."

"Thank you," she said softly as Sophia gave me a look.

"Sorry, I forgot. I got distracted by this one." I lifted Violet up a bit, and Harper couldn't help but melt.

"They're adorable. Seriously. You guys did good."

Cale puffed up, and Sophia just smiled. "I think I'm going to feed them real quick right before we go eat our big person dinner. And thank you. I love them with all my heart."

"Seriously. I didn't know how I was going to be being a girl dad. But I can't wait to see them grow up. They're the best things to happen to me—other than Sophia of course." Cale leaned forward and kissed Sophia softly on the mouth, and I cleared my throat.

"There are virgin eyes in this room, be careful with all that kissing."

I had been talking about the babies, but with the

way Harper blushed, I couldn't help it when my mind wandered.

No, I was not going to think about that. Not at all.

"So proper," Sophia said with a laugh. "Give the baby to Cale, and tell the others we'll be down in a minute?"

"I hate that I have to do this, but fine," I said as I handed the baby over reluctantly. She let out a huge wail as she reached for Cale's chest, and I laughed.

"Don't think she's going to be getting food from there."

"It's been an interesting time for sure," Cale said with a dry laugh.

I gestured towards the door and Harper and I exited, leaving the happy family behind.

"I think my ovaries just exploded," Harper said with a laugh.

"I don't know what that means, but if it means that they're the cutest babies in the world, then yes, you're right."

"They are. And I hear you're going to be an uncle again."

"I guess we're getting to be that age. All of the Cages are producing the next generation."

"Why does that scare me?" she asked, her eyes dancing with laughter.

"You're ridiculous. But I don't blame you."

"Anyway, I'm glad you're here," I said after a moment, trying to figure out what I was supposed to do with my dead best friend's little sister.

Because what I wanted to do was push that lock of hair that kept falling in front of her face behind her ear. And then maybe feel the back of her neck and finally figure out if her skin was as soft as I thought it was.

But what the hell was I thinking? She was too young. And off limits for more than one reason. She probably thought I was a damn creeper.

Since my attention was on Harper and not the stairs in front of me, I took a step too quickly, and my thigh and knee twisted wrong. And when I tried to move backward, overcorrecting, the scars on my side stretched.

"Fuck," I grumbled as I leaned against the wall, trying to catch my breath.

Harper was there in an instant, one hand on my side, the other on my thigh. "Dorian. What's wrong? Do I need to call someone?"

What's wrong? Her hand was less than a foot away from my cock. What was I supposed to do? How was I supposed to think? Instead, I just let out a deep breath and tried to ease my way through the pain. Because now I was going to get a damn erection with Harper so close, and that would be the most idiotic thing to do. Especially since I wouldn't be able to hide it as her face was damn close to it since we were at an odd level on the stairs.

"Seriously, let's get you sitting down."

I shook my head, but I didn't shake off her hold. "I'm fine. Really. Just took a step wrong because I wasn't thinking."

Because I was thinking about you.

No, I wasn't going to say that out loud.

She looked up at me then, studying my face, her hands still on me, and neither one of us said a word.

"So, looks like I'm interrupting," Hudson said from the bottom of the stairs, and Harper lifted her hands quickly as if she had been burned, and I cleared my throat.

"Just took a step wrong."

"If that's your answer. I thought you should know Mom's here."

I blinked as Harper stiffened, and then I knew tonight was going to go downhill from here.

Because why the fuck was my mother at a place where she wasn't welcome? And why the hell did I feel I was the one who had to deal with it?

Chapter Seven

HARPER

"*MOTHER.*"

I had known the Cages for most of my life. But I had never heard Aston Cage's voice in that chilly tone before. Not once. Not even when his persona had been the icy asshole that people didn't truly understand. Perhaps he had always been a little growly, a little standoffish. And perhaps it had been Blakely who had brought him out a bit.

Only I had always thought he hadn't enjoyed small town gossip and shied away from it. It made sense to me. And yet, I had never heard him sound so glacial.

Melanie Cage narrowed her gaze. "I see you're still working through the will's dinners. Good for you. You always were like your father and keeping up with promises."

I wasn't sure I had ever heard so many wrong things spoken at once. Because Aston was nothing like his father, and for a man who had not only cheated on his wife but made sure he had done it in the most complicated way possible, I wasn't sure that Dorian's father was good with promises.

"I wasn't aware you cared."

Melanie Cage glared at her eldest son before turning to take in the others in the room. Sophia, Cale, and the babies were still upstairs, and for that I was grateful. From what I knew about the older woman's relationship with her children—at least from Isabella's take—they didn't have a relationship currently. Meaning I wasn't even sure she had met the babies who might not be her grandchildren, but through the tangled lines of their lives, were as close as.

Of course, the woman with icy blonde hair, a trim and tailored baby blue pantsuit with a ruffled collar, complete with matching jacket, and boots for walking through snow, didn't look the grandmotherly type.

And while that was wrong of me because you didn't have to be wearing an apron and bright smile in order to be a grandmother, I still didn't like the woman.

Of course, I had my own issues when it came to grandmothers. I suppose I shouldn't be throwing rocks at glass houses. But my mother had been amazing. And I didn't like this current mother in front of us.

"I thought this was supposed to be family only. You seem to be inviting so many people." Her gaze caught mine, and I just gave a little finger wave. "Hello, Mrs. Cage. I'm Harper. We've met a few times."

She turned away from me as if I hadn't spoken. Dorian's hand clasped mine and gave it a squeeze. I swallowed hard and tried not to lean into exactly what this touch meant to me. Because it couldn't mean anything. He was just giving me reassurance like a good friend.

And I totally wasn't holding Dorian Cage's hand.

"Oh. I know you. Your brother tried to kill my son. You're lucky that Dorian is so kind, or I'd have ensured he sued your entire family. After all, my *son* is forever scarred and altered because of the incident. It's a pity your brother didn't make it."

It was like knives to my chest, someone squeezing my lungs as if they were trying to suffocate me, and the pounding in my brain wouldn't ease.

And as everybody spoke up at once, demanding she leave, or shouting obscenities towards her, I just moved forward, thankfully taking Dorian along with me. Melanie Cage didn't miss our connected hands, and if anything, her scowl had increased—the rage in her eyes a bare glimmer before she squashed it.

I let out a breath and lifted my chin, raising my voice to be heard over the others. "Suing me really wouldn't have helped anyone. I have no money and I'm pretty much in debt. But don't worry. I'm a big girl. I guess I can take what you lash out at me. I'm very sorry that Dorian was hurt. But if you ever speak to me like that again, I'm not going to be the kind, naïve, small-town girl you think I am."

Hudson whistled under his breath, and my hands began to shake because I was not the type of person who ever spoke like that to another human being.

It was Isabella who began to clap. "Bravo."

"I don't need your tone, or anything from the rest of you." Melanie scowled at Isabella, and my friend lifted her chin and glared at the other woman.

"You are rude, a liar, and I don't know why you're here. Maybe to annoy Dorian like you're so good at doing, but you're on borrowed time. You're just lucky that I'm not in the mood to deal with an assault charge," Isabella snapped.

"And that's why I love you," Weston said as he wrapped his arm around her shoulders.

"You need to go, Mom," Dorian said as he squeezed my hand.

Melanie's brows would have risen if they could have. "Dorian, I'm here to talk to you."

"I don't care. I told you last time I saw you that I didn't want to speak to you. How dare you talk about my best friend like that. If I ever hear you speak to Harper like that again… I don't care that you're my mother. Do you understand that? You don't get to speak to *anyone* like that. Especially not Harper." He let go of my hand as he moved forward, his brothers each taking a step with him, along with Cale who I hadn't realized had entered the room. Sophia must still be upstairs with the babies.

Dorian leaned forward, his words a breath above a whisper. "Don't forget, Mother, there's a reason that you like to hover around me. And I'm not in the mood to deal with being your trained little soldier anymore. So leave."

"I need to talk to you and ensure that you are all complying with the will. It's my money too."

"Money. All you care about is money." Aston shook his head. "Go. This is my home. Not yours. You have three very pleasant homes that are outside of the ridiculous terms of dear old dad's will. So go there and pout or do whatever you want to do. But if this family keeps to the will, it's because we want to."

"Because unlike how we feel for you, we actually like each other," Dorian put in. He shrugged as he said it, and Melanie took a step back. "We're here because we want to be. And because we care about the people of this town and our companies. You'll get your money. But you don't get us. You're already tiring me. So go."

She reached out for a moment, and I took a step

IF YOU WERE MINE

forward, ready to pull Dorian back if the woman hit him. I didn't know why I thought she would, but this farce of a relationship between her and her kids weighed on me.

"Fine. Contact me when you're done."

"Done with you? Deal." Dorian reached for my hand once again, and Melanie whirled on her boots and stomped outside.

Aston slammed the door behind her before he pulled out his phone.

"I'm going to make sure security escorts her out of town."

I blinked. "You have security?"

Hudson cleared his throat. "Ford owns a company. And we have someone here in Cage Lake because we've had a few incidents."

I held back a shudder, remembering those incidents. Since Isabella leaned into Weston, I had a feeling she did too.

Sophia ran down the stairs and into Cale's open arms.

"She didn't even ask about you guys. Didn't even ask about the babies. I know she's not their real grandmother. But I don't know, it just feels weird."

I rubbed my temples. "For a few moments earlier, I had to remind myself that she wasn't actually their grandmother." I shook my head. "Sorry. Not my business."

Dorian squeezed my hand again, and I was grateful he hadn't let go. "We're a confusing family. But hell, I talk to Constance more than I do my own mom."

"I do love Constance," Blakely said with a smile. As she had known that side of the family longer than she had known Aston, it made sense.

"Mom has really stepped up to the plate recently. And though we butt heads, she's a great grandmother," Isabella said as she reached for Sophia's hand.

"She's an amazing grandmother. And I do know that once she hears about Ford's upcoming baby, she'll be knitting for that one too. So while Grandmother Melanie will never be a thing in my eyes, I suppose Constance gets a whole slew."

Dorian let go of my hand, and I immediately felt the cold, but when he rubbed the back of his neck, I realized that he had something going on in that brain of his that he wasn't telling anyone else.

"Ford would appreciate that." Dorian sighed. "Sorry for her following me up here. I keep ignoring her calls and she doesn't care."

"Mom's a bitch. And I cannot believe I said that out loud because I don't ever use that word unless I'm talking about you," Ford said as he winked at Dorian.

Dorian flipped off his brother, and the light chuckle that filled the room eased some of the tension.

"She's not welcome in any of my homes, and we'll make sure she stays away. Now," Aston said as he gave his brother a look, "are you to tell us what that underlying tension was between you two, Dorian?"

"You know how she acts like I'm her favorite. Used to be cute when we were kids, till I realized that she was insane." He tried to laugh it off, but nobody in this room truly believed him.

Instead, Blakely forced us all into the dining room, where we sat down and ate our dinner. I sat between Cale and Dorian and tried to pay attention. They spoke of upcoming work and when the next dinner would be. I had a feeling Dorian and the others wouldn't be part of it. Since I knew that Aston and Isabella had been part of so many recently, maybe it was time for the other Cages to step up.

Or maybe it was none of my business.

"Are you doing okay?"

I turned to Cale and smiled softly. "I am. Thanks for asking. How about you?"

He shrugged, though there was concern in his eyes. "I'm fine. I don't really know that woman. But what she said to you? That was bullshit."

"Did *The* Cale just curse?" Dorian asked as he sipped his water. "I'm shocked."

The other man winked. "I do it sparingly just to surprise you."

"As long as you don't curse in front of the babies," Sophia said, her eyes dancing.

Cale took her hand and kissed the back of it, and I couldn't help but hold back a sigh.

I was jealous, and I hated that.

"But what Cale was saying is right." Dorian whispered. "I'll never forgive her for what she said to you."

I met his gaze, my chest aching. Though I knew it had nothing to do with emotion and everything to do with my long walk since I had overexerted myself. I hated my lungs, and I knew they hated me right back.

"It was nothing. She's hurting, lashing out because she can't seem to hold on to any sense of her reality. So it's easier for her to hate anyone who dares hurt her family rather than herself who's hurting them right along with them."

Dorian raised a brow. "When did you get so wise? I didn't know you were old enough to have those kinds of thoughts."

I scowled as others laughed. "Okay fuck you. And I'm glad the babies aren't in this room because I'm going to curse again. Fuck you."

"I'm going to wash your mouth out with soap," Dorian grumbled.

"I'm an adult. I own a business. I'm going to curse,

and sometimes I have sage wisdom. Shocking. And really," I began as I looked around the table, "I'm fine. I've already been through hell, and I know you guys have been through your own versions. I really don't care what that woman says. That may be wrong of me in some ways, but I don't care. Joshua taught me that, at least. How to stand up for myself."

Dorian reached out and squeezed my knee, and I let out a deep breath, trying not to lean into the contact.

He must have realized what he was doing because he let go quickly, as if I had scorched him.

Well, same, Dorian Cage.

Thankfully the subject changed again, and by the time dessert rolled around, I was exhausted, and my lungs did indeed ache.

"I should head home. I know it's going to get a little bit colder later, and I want to make sure I get home quickly."

"Did you walk here?" Dorian snapped.

I shook my head. "Not all the way. Ivy dropped me off partway, but I needed a walk." So I could clear my thoughts about Dorian. And yet it hadn't helped at all.

"Harper, it's freezing out," Isabella chided. "Dorian, will you drive her home?

"It's not like she's going to have any other choice," Dorian grumbled as he stomped past me. At least he wasn't limping, so I knew he wasn't in that much pain. Or he was getting better at masking.

He walked out without a goodbye, leaving me alone with his family staring at him—the worry etched on their faces matching the same in my heart.

I let out a shaky, painful breath and looked at all of them. "Well, thank you for dinner."

"We're sorry for the drama," Aston said as he gave me a hug. I hugged him back, before doing the same to others, leaving Hudson for last.

He lifted my chin with his finger and glared at me. Or maybe he was just staring at me. I was never sure with Hudson.

"Be safe. And thanks for taking care of Dorian."

I rolled my eyes. "I'm pretty sure he thinks it's the opposite."

"He can think what he wants," Hudson snapped before he went upstairs. Most likely to see the babies. And I couldn't help but smile at that thought. I would have to tell Scarlett just to annoy her.

Dorian was already waiting for me outside by the time I got out there. The temperature had dropped dramatically, and I realized I had been an idiot thinking I could walk. No wonder Ivy had looked at me like I'd lost my mind.

"Text Ivy and the others and let them know you're leaving," Dorian ordered.

I scowled at him as I got to the side of his truck.

"You could say please."

"I could. Come on, let me help you up."

I scowled. "Excuse me? You have runners. I can climb up." Probably better than he could, but I didn't say that. It would be rude to both of us because I knew he had to be hurting.

He didn't listen to me however, because he never did. Instead he lifted me by the waist, and I let out a squeak as he set me inside the cab of his truck.

"Bossy," I mumbled.

"Always," he said with a sigh before closing the door behind him. He moved quickly around the front of the truck before getting in, and I didn't see a wince on his face. He was healing, and I was grateful for that. But I hated that he didn't take care of himself.

Of course, my lungs hurt, and I was slightly light-headed, so I couldn't really complain too much considering I was in the same boat.

"Do we need to pick up Lucky?" he asked, his gaze on the road.

"He's having a sleepover at Ivy's tonight. Apparently, Ivy wants to play dog mom for a night and see if she's ready for one on her own."

"With how much she travels, I don't know if that would be a good thing."

"We could make it work, especially since she drives often. But you're right, she isn't quite sure yet."

"And not every dog can be as good as Lucky."

That made me grin. "He's the best."

We sat in silence as we made our way to my apartment. I hated this awkwardness. Things had always been different with us, even when he had just been my brother's best friend. Now he held so much guilt, and I didn't know what to do with it.

Before I could say anything though, we pulled into the back of the bakery, and he shut off the engine.

"I'll walk you up."

I swallowed hard, my hands tingling. "I'm a big girl. I can do that on my own."

"You don't have Lucky at home. I'm walking you up."

With a sigh, I stomped my way upstairs with him following me. I didn't know why this was so awkward, but maybe it would just be normal. Like the fact that he would be in my apartment. Alone. At night. With no dog as a chaperone.

Or maybe I was losing my mind.

"Can I get you some coffee? Or a baked good?" Not quite what I wanted to say, but I couldn't help rambling. I didn't know what he saw when he looked at my apartment. It wasn't large nor was it my forever home. But then again, it was better than the little room I had at my grandparents' house.

"Your house always smells like sugar and flour."

"That wasn't an answer to my question," I said, my lips twitching.

"I could eat," he said, surprising me. He slid his hands into his pockets, and I swallowed hard.

"Okay. Why don't you go take a seat on the couch, and I will get you some cookies or something."

"Or something," he mumbled.

Not sure what he meant by that, I made a plate of blonde brownies, a couple of cookies, and a fruit tart I had made earlier. I was constantly practicing with recipes, and I was grateful that I had friends to hand them off to.

I quickly brewed two cups of coffee and made my way into the living room. He had a book in his hand as he laid on my couch. He had his hurt leg up on the ottoman, and I held back a wince. Because if he was showing any form of his supposed weakness, he had to be hurting.

"Are those tarts?" he asked, his eyes widening.

"I'm sure there's a joke in there somewhere."

His cheeks pinked, and I thought it was the cutest damn thing. "I'm not calling you a tart. But I will take whatever's on that plate."

"That I can do."

I had set everything on a tray, and he had tried to get up to help, but I was quicker than he was and set everything down in front of us. He lowered his leg, and I took a seat beside him.

"Do you want me to massage your leg?" I asked, and he blinked.

"What?"

"Well. You seem to be in pain. And I don't know, if you need someone to massage your leg, I'm here."

I had no idea what I was saying, or why I had even blurted it. He was probably going to laugh at me, pat me on the head, and walk right out with a fruit tart in his hand.

Instead he met my gaze and swallowed hard. "Okay."

The silence in the living room was deafening, but before either one of us could think better of it, I reached forward and slid my hand over his thigh.

His throat bobbed as he swallowed again, and I slid my other hand closer before massaging gently. I had taken a semester of massage therapy, mostly because I had been in enough pain as a teen that I liked knowing how to take care of a body. But I knew I wasn't remembering a single one of my lessons in that moment.

His thigh hardened underneath me, and I did my best not to go too high. Because if I did, I'd accidentally glance at the zipper of his jeans, and all would be lost.

I didn't look up, didn't want to see his face.

When he slid his hand over the back of my neck, his thumb sliding through my hair, I gasped.

He didn't stop touching me. Instead I moved my hand up and down his thigh, trying to ease the aches. He groaned, and we both stiffened. I looked up at him then, at the way his mouth parted, at his widening pupils.

"Where'd you learn that?" he asked, his voice breathy.

I licked my lips, and his gaze went right to them. "I took a semester of massage therapy." It was to help my own health issues, but I didn't tell him that. I couldn't break this moment.

"Well, good job." He coughed.

And without thinking, I did the one thing I shouldn't. I leaned forward and brushed my lips against his.

He froze for an instant, and I nearly pulled back, wondering what the hell I was doing. But then his hand went to the back of my neck again, and I was lost. My lips parted, our tongues sliding against one another. When he groaned, I arched slightly, my breast pressing against his arm and chest. He slid his other hand over my side, squeezing my hip, and I put my hands on his chest, aching for him. He deepened the kiss, both of us gasping into one another. He tasted of sugar, coffee, and Dorian.

I had dreamed of doing this before, of wanting this. And yet I hadn't thought it was possible. Instead, it felt as if everything was frozen in time, and it was all I could do to hang on to him. Because as soon as this kiss ended, reality would settle in and it would be over.

And it seemed he had listened to my thoughts, because suddenly he was on the other side of the couch, his chest heaving, and his eyes wide.

"I shouldn't have done that."

I licked my lips, knowing they were swollen, and I lifted my fingers to them.

"I didn't push you away," I said honestly.

"Wellesley."

But before he could say anything, I gasped, my chest seizing. I bent over, hands on the couch, as I tried to catch my breath.

One. Two. Three.

I just needed to count, to catch my breath. This had happened before. I had just overexerted myself today.

"Wellesley? What the fuck?"

And then I was in his lap, and he was rubbing my back as I tried to catch my breath.

"What's wrong?"

"I'm fine. I just lose my breath sometimes."

He scowled, as if trying to connect the dots of

exactly when this could have begun, and I didn't know what he knew. After all, Joshua hadn't told him everything from the time we had been separated. But instead, he ran his hand over my back as I finally caught my breath.

"I'm okay," I gasped.

"Stop talking," he ordered, his voice a rasp.

He just held me, as I took in deep breaths, finally allowing myself to breathe again.

This wasn't how I imagined my first time in Dorian's arms, with his rigid cock beneath me, and both of us holding onto one another, but all I could think was he was caring for me.

Because I was weak. And too young.

And my damn lungs were once again betraying me.

Chapter Eight

DORIAN

"WHY AM I INVOLVED IN A TOWN MEETING?" I grumbled as Isabella and Weston just chuckled beside me. I zipped up my coat a bit tighter, that icy wind deciding to slide right down my Henley. It was nearly February, and we had already gone through our false spring. A three-hour period of warmth where people could take off their coats.

The tourists had been so confused.

And now we were dealing with a possible snow-storm, ice, most likely sun to melt that ice, and then more frigid air to create black ice. Because why not? It was Colorado after all.

For now though, even though there was a frigid chill seeping into my bones thanks to the weather, it was still sunny out. I hated it.

Or maybe I was just grumpy because I could not get the thought of Harper Wellesley out of my head. Or her taste. Or her feel. Or the fact that I nearly pushed her down on the couch and slid deep inside her. It didn't matter that we had been nowhere close to that, it had sure felt damn close.

There was something wrong with me.

I was not allowed to have feelings for my best friend's little sister.

My *dead* best friend's little sister.

There were rules beyond rules for this. I knew this. My friends knew this. The world knew this.

And I was going to hell.

At least it might be warmer there.

"You damn Cages own this place, it's about time you attend a town meeting," Weston grumbled.

I flipped him off and winced as Ms. Patty walked by.

"Mr. Cage. I thought you were raised better than that." She frowned and shook her head. "Okay, I thought the town raised you better than that. I won't say anything ill about the dead, or your mother, but well, Mr. Cage."

The mayor's wife shook her head solemnly, and I tried not to laugh.

"Sorry for the gesture. However, are you calling me Mr. Cage because you can't remember which one I am?" I teased. The smile on my face felt forced, and yet part of me felt as if maybe this was the old side of me. The joking one that made women around me smile and swoon.

If anything, her eyes brightened, and she waved me off.

"You're a menace just like you always were, *Dorian*," she emphasized.

"See? A menace," Weston added.

"You say that as if you're not a menace too," Ms. Patty put in.

"Have I ever reiterated how much I love you, Ms. Patty?" Isabella said as she reached around me to squeeze the older woman's hand.

"I do love hearing it. Just as much as I love the fact that you're bringing these strapping men to this town hall meeting."

Isabella gave me a look that I couldn't read. "Are you saying that because you like looking at them, because one of those is my brother so I'm going to have to refrain from an opinion. And well, I get fighty when it comes to protecting Weston's virtue."

"Virtue?" I scoffed.

Weston reached around my sister and slapped me on the back of the head. I noticed Ms. Patty didn't admonish him for that. Well at least we knew who her favorite was.

And frankly it wasn't a Cage.

"There might be some manual labor later, though we wouldn't make you do it, Dorian." She patted my arm, the sympathy in her tone grating. I knew she meant well. Honestly, I'd been in a fucking plane crash and was lucky to be alive. So yes, she was being kind. Only I didn't want kindness in that moment. I just wanted to forget. However, the pain in my thigh that was slowly getting better, as well as the burn scars on my sides didn't feel as if I could truly forget.

"Anyway, I'm just grateful that you Cages are starting to show up again. I know Aston comes when he's in town, just as I know trying to get Hudson anywhere near a function like this is probably like pulling teeth."

"Why does Hudson get out of this then?" I grumbled, sounding petulant.

"Because it's your turn," a familiar yet unexpected voice said from behind me. I turned, ignoring the pain in my side, as Flynn walked forward.

I hadn't seen him in a while, which was mostly on my shoulders. While I had once been the brother who joked around and didn't stay single for long, Flynn flirted like nobody's business. He was a people person, just like I had been. We were probably the most alike out of the siblings I had grown up with. Although from what I knew of Emily, she was like us as well. I ignored the twinge that told me I should probably call her. Or start a group chat with the Cages I hadn't grown up with. Getting to know them would probably be something that Harper would tell me to do.

Not that I would do something just because Harper told me.

Maybe.

"I didn't know you were coming up here," I said as I wrapped my arm around Flynn's shoulder and squeezed.

My brother just grinned. "I'm here to annoy my twin, and make sure that Isabella and Hudson have everything they need from me."

"You always did take care of us, Flynn," Ms. Patty said as she went to pat his cheek. In turn he leaned down and kissed hers.

"I'm going to miss coming up here often. I know Aston took over for a little bit, as did Hudson, but you dealt with me for a lot longer."

"There's no dealing with you, Flynn." Ms. Patty grinned.

I met Isabella's gaze, and we both rolled our eyes.

Flynn could do no wrong.

He was also the vice president of Cage Enterprises, and I wasn't sure when he slept. He was the one who had handled most of the paperwork and went through Aston for certain Cage properties. And had given over the face-to-face time to Hudson. Isabella was taking over, and though I was here for a short time, I hoped to hell I wasn't going to be given that responsibility. After all, I had enough businesses to take care of outside of the main Cage enterprises. Though my managers were doing a damn fine job without me.

I probably shouldn't feel slighted at that. I trained them well.

Maybe it was time to open up another business, something to keep myself busy once I finished this house. The unending home.

Because if I didn't keep my hands on my work, they would end up on Harper, and then Joshua's ghost would haunt me.

And I would deserve it.

"I would love to know what's going on in that head of yours," Flynn muttered.

I resisted the urge to flip him off because Ms. Patty was close by, instead I followed her into the large barn that was town hall.

There were rows of seats on either side, and it looked like a wedding venue if anything. Ms. Patty's husband, the mayor, stood up front at the podium, though he hadn't begun yet. He spoke with a few of the town businessmen, including Scarlett. Though she didn't own anything in town, she was the manager of the highest grossing establishment.

"Well I'm glad Hudson isn't here, because then I would have to deal with his whining," Weston mumbled under his breath.

I smiled as Flynn barked out a laugh.

"I do not understand him. I would say he should just ask her out already, but she's taken." Isabella shook her head.

I choked on air, and I stared down at my sister as we took our seats. "He doesn't have a crush on her. This isn't kindergarten where you growl and pull the girl's pigtails. They honestly just don't get along."

"If you say so. But I don't know, maybe Hudson just needs a girlfriend."

I shook my head, my shoulders dropping. "I don't think that would help."

Isabella paled and cursed. "I hate not knowing everyone's family history. I'm going to step in it one day."

"You won't," Flynn said softly as he reached across me to pat her hand. "Because if you do accidentally, we know that you're not being malicious. And Hudson's secrets are his own. To the fact that I don't even know all of them and I'm his twin. I don't think he needs a girlfriend, but maybe just to get laid," he added, trying to lighten the mood.

Isabella rolled her eyes, as I fist-bumped both Weston and Flynn.

"Oh Dorian, it's so good to see you," an older woman said as she came forward. I couldn't remember her name but I knew she worked at the restaurant. I didn't bother standing up because all she did was squeeze my shoulder and pat my hand and repeat that she was so glad that I was healthy and coming back to Cage Lake after so long.

Tension rode my shoulders as one of the bartenders of the local dive bar came over and said the same thing, as well as a woman I knew worked at a knitting store or something like that. A craft store? I didn't know. The Cages didn't own it, and it wasn't like I knew how to knit.

However, by the time the seventh person came over to make sure that I was okay and didn't need anything, and were so happy that I had survived, I was done. I could not take one more platitude, one more worry.

Because the problem was, they weren't faking it. This wasn't undue pity.

They were mourning Joshua. Maybe not like I was. Definitely not like Harper. But they were missing the town's son. And they almost lost me too.

And I was done.

"Harper!" Isabella said, cutting through what I hoped to be the final person coming over to check on me.

My shoulders tensed again, and I glared at my

sister, scooting over one seat so there was an empty space between us.

This woman was diabolical, and I wasn't sure if she was aware she was doing it.

"Come and sit next to me. I need a familiar face between all this testosterone."

I turned, throat tight as Harper walked over. She'd cut bangs into her hair since I had last seen her, and it hadn't been a full twenty-four hours yet. They just framed her face even more, and dammit, she was so fucking sexy.

Why the hell was I even thinking that?

No, she was off limits. Definitely off limits.

"The place is busier than usual so I'm grateful for the seat." She walked past Flynn and I without looking at either one of us as she took a seat next to me. "I love the bangs. Should I be worried you have bangs? Or just enjoy them?" Isabella asked.

I had no idea what she was talking about. Why would someone be worried about bangs?

But from the way Harper's cheeks pinked, maybe I should be worried about bangs.

"It was time for a hair change. You know me, I've had three different hair colors since you first saw me."

"That is true. They do wonderful things for your face. Don't you think, Dorian?"

That was it. I was going to have to murder my

sister. Nobody would know. Maybe Weston, but he would get over it.

Harper turned, and I swallowed, trying not to growl. Of course my dick took that moment to stand at attention, and I shifted, hoping no one would see.

However, from the way that Flynn chuckled beneath his breath beside me, I was going to hell. I just needed to bury myself into a deep hole, and no one would be able to find me.

"They look fine," I said, and Harper laughed as Isabella slapped me on the shoulder over Harper. Flynn and Weston threw their heads back and laughed, and I realized that I was an idiot.

Although this wasn't the first time I had realized that.

"Your praise soothes me. I don't know if I could truly be able to walk underneath the weight of it," Harper said dryly.

"You're always beautiful, Wellesley. No matter what hair you have. I like the bangs." I shrugged as Harper smiled, and Isabella clapped softly behind her. Weston just shook his head as Flynn continued to laugh behind me.

I ignored them all.

When the mayor finally brought the meeting to attention, I told myself this wouldn't be too long. I could sit next to Harper, her thigh pressed against mine, and handle this. We had sat together countless times.

Though I hadn't known what she had tasted like before then.

Of course I only knew what her mouth tasted like, and now I needed to know what her pussy tasted like.

No, no, no. Those were bad thoughts. Very bad thoughts.

I was going to end up with a perpetual hard-on. I knew it.

"Now that we have the initial meeting notes done, my lovely wife is going to take my space, and we're going to discuss her upcoming Valentine's Day events. I know we've gone through this multiple times, but we're nearly two weeks out."

I leaned over to whisper in Harper's ear. "How many Valentine events will there be?"

She leaned closer, her breath warm along my neck. I had to swallow hard, telling myself that it would be wrong to turn and capture those lips of hers.

Wrong for so many reasons, including the fact that we were in public.

"Way too many to count. It's Cage Lake. We like parties. And different flowers for different seasons, and flags, and celebrations. It's what we do."

I shook my head, trying to remember some of the summer activities that I participated in. Not many because I usually hadn't been paying attention or was trying to be a petulant teenager.

But if I was going to stay in Cage Lake for a little bit, at least fixing up the old place, I should probably learn what these were.

"Now, we will start with the decorations of the gazebo tomorrow, as it will be February 1st, and prep for each of the parties that we will have during the day that begins with our under-twelve, our teenagers, and then our adults eighteen and up." Ms. Patty continued on asking for volunteers and chaperones. I wasn't quite listening but figured if Isabella had signed me up for anything, I would shout at her, and then just do what she told me. Honestly, my sister scared me.

By the time it ended, my leg hurt, and my temples throbbed.

It hadn't helped that Harper had been so close to me the entire fucking time.

"I need to talk with the mayor, and then head back," Flynn said in lieu of goodbye.

"You just got here," I countered.

"I don't have a lot of time. I really just wanted to annoy Hudson, which I'll do on my way out. It's good to see you, Dorian." He studied my face, and I held back my curse.

"Was it your turn to check up on me since you missed family dinner?"

"Isabella's here for that, but it was a side benefit. You'll tell us if you need anything?"

"Sure," I lied.

Flynn just shook his head and made his way towards the mayor.

Isabella and Weston had moved off to the side, speaking with another business owner, and I figured I would just head back to the old place. Maybe I would get some wall work in. Although I knew I wasn't going to be able to handle everything on my own. I would hire people just like I always did, but I could at least get some of it done.

I looked down at Harper as she shook her head, staring at her phone.

"What's wrong?"

"Two of my workers are out with the flu, and I was only able to come here because of a friend, but I'm going to be short-handed. And we're going to have the afternoon rush from this meeting. I have to go."

"I can help," I blurted without thinking.

She blinked. "What?"

"I don't know how to bake, but I know how to make coffee." At least her drip coffee. If I had to go to the actual barista, I had no idea what I was doing. "Put me at the register or something."

"You want to help."

"Wellesley. Of course I want to help."

She stared at me for a moment, before she finally nodded and turned towards the door. "Okay. Thank you."

And then I was following her, knowing that we didn't have far to walk. My leg would probably hate me later, but it usually did.

An hour into this ordeal, and I realized I was an idiot. Because Harper worked more than anyone I thought possible. Even Aston.

She was twenty places at once and did her best to help keep every interaction perfect and unique. Personal.

Although I did notice she tried to stay in the back as much as possible. That hadn't always been the case. Or maybe I was just reading too much into it. Maybe she was only staying in the back to catch up. Not avoiding people.

I went to ring up another order, smiling slightly when I realized that I didn't fuck it up, and handed over her change.

"Here you go. Thank you for coming to Rising Cage."

"And thank you for being here, Dorian," a woman with chestnut hair purred.

I knew when I was being hit on, it wasn't anything new to me. But when she leaned forward, her breasts practically falling out of her tight workout zipped-up jacket, I just leaned back.

"Is there anything else I can get you? Your order should be up soon."

Her face fell, and she shook her head. "No, if that's the only thing you're offering, I'm okay." She winked as she said it, and I turned towards the customer behind her.

The old Dorian probably would have done something.

And yet, I hadn't.

What the hell was wrong with me? I should just flirt with her, make sure Harper knew that we weren't going to be a thing.

And yet there was no way that I was going to do that.

Harper merely raised a brow at me, and I turned away, hoping she couldn't read my thoughts. Because it wasn't as if I knew what those thoughts were.

By the time there was a lull, I was exhausted, my leg ached, and I realized that I would suck if I had to work here full time. I didn't know how Harper did it.

"Oh, Dorian, I'm so glad that you're here," Melody said as she came forward. She was an older woman I had known for years who worked for Harper now. And I knew she was supposed to be off today.

"Melody."

"Melody, you're here!" Harper said as she threw her arms around the other woman. "I could kiss you."

"Well, I'm sure you want to be kissing someone," she mumbled, and I glared at the other woman.

Okay, maybe I didn't like her.

"I got back to town early, and that means I can take over for a bit and you can go bake. I know you had to be tired if you had to get Dorian to help."

"I feel like I was just kicked."

"Oh, shush."

She winked as she said it, and Wellesley just smiled.

"I'm so grateful that you are here to help. Dorian is doing fantastic though."

"It's a cash register, and the goods are already made."

"And you only messed up twice."

Four times, but I wasn't going to tell her that. "Will you two go to the back and take your break? I can handle this. You both look like you could use that break."

I did not like what that other woman saw, but I ignored her as I followed Harper to the back. "You can take your break, I need to work on the next set of brownies."

"Take a seat, Wellesley. You should actually put your feet up."

She just laughed. "I will later. At least after I pick Lucky up from Dog Gone It."

I blinked. "Is that the name of the doggie daycare thing?"

"Yes. And it doesn't have Cage in the name."

"Shocking."

I leaned against the wall, arms crossed over my chest as I watched her work.

I wasn't about to step in and help because I would just fuck it up, but I really liked watching her work.

And that was a problem.

"I'm sorry," I said after a moment.

She stopped in the act of cutting out brownies and blinked. "Sorry for what?"

"For kissing you."

I hadn't quite meant to say it like that, but there was no coming back from that.

Her face fell, and I hated myself. But this was for the best.

She set down the knife and wiped her hands on a towel before heading towards the sink. Without another word, she washed her hands, wiped them on another towel, and let out a breath.

"Because it was wrong?" she asked, not looking at me.

"Yes. No. Fuck. I don't know, Wellesley. I'm just sorry."

"Okay." She turned and looked at me then, chin lifted. I loved the way that she always stood up to me. Even when we had been younger. "Did you want to kiss me?"

Yes.

No.

Fuck yes.

"I shouldn't."

"That's not what I asked," she whispered.

"When did you get so good at this?" I asked softly.

"Good at what? Speaking up for myself? Dorian, I'm not a little girl."

I snorted. "You're not. But you're still too young."

"No. I'm not. I'm younger than you, but I'm not too young."

"You are."

"I wasn't too young for you to kiss me back last night." She tilted her head as she stared at me defiantly. I hated that I liked that look.

I hadn't even realized I had moved forward, so now there were only a few steps between us.

"Wellesley."

"What are you going to do? Apologize again? Run away?"

"Fuck." I growled, and then I moved forward, cupped her face, and crushed my mouth to hers.

She gasped into me as sin wrapped its way around

my soul. But it tasted of sugar and coffee and glory. So maybe sin wasn't so bad. Just tempting.

I finally pulled away, knowing this was wrong.

"I'm not too young," she repeated, her breath in pants, her lips swollen.

Without another word, I whirled and slammed my hands against the back door, needing oxygen.

I stood there, chest heaving. Joshua would hate me. I would hate me. This was *Wellesley*, for God's sake.

Wells.

This was so wrong.

And yet I turned back into the kitchen anyway. She had moved back to her brownies, back to work as if nothing had happened, and yet everything had.

"I can't let you down."

"You never have," she whispered.

I sighed and went back to the front of the bakery, knowing Melody needed help.

Because if I didn't, I knew I was going to kiss her again. Maybe not right then, but soon.

And sin would just have to be my friend.

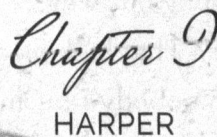

Chapter 9

HARPER

MUSIC PLAYING, FEET TAPPING TO THE BEAT, I
ignored the rest of the world as I focused on the task at
hand. The scent of sugar, flour, and rising dough filled
the air, reminding me of home. That stray melancholy
thought circled within me and rather than pushing it
away as I tended to do these days, I latched on to it.

We'd been the fearsome four growing up. My
parents loving, open, and vibrant. My dad had loved to
fish and while Joshua had been squeamish, I'd been
the one at Dad's side, learning how to cast a line. I
learned patience—though I still fell short in that arena.
Dad had sports, hiking, caving, kayaking, and so much
more with Joshua. And I'd never felt the lack.

Mom had baking and gymnastics with me. We'd
tumble around the yard and my dad would wolf whistle

at Mom, though I hadn't known what it had meant at the time. Joshua had been older and had blushed, rolling his eyes. But he—and sometimes Dorian— would cheer me on during summer events when we'd all been children finding our ways.

Baking, however? That had been just me and Mom. Dad could cook like nobody's business and had taught me, but Joshua hadn't been able to boil water without forgetting the pot was on the stove. He'd been brilliant at so many things but cooking had never been one of them.

Baking had been *mine*. I'd learned bread, cakes, pastry, chocolate work, and so much more. We'd sit together and watch the *Great British Baking Show* and learn all the technical bakes together. I'd even learned to measure ingredients with a scale rather than how most Americans did because Mom and I had been so addicted to the show.

Then they'd died and my world had ended.

At least that's how it had felt at the time. Joshua hadn't been old enough to be my guardian, but my grandparents hadn't wanted both of us. I hadn't realized true hatred or neglect until I'd been torn from the only family I'd never known and forced to live with them.

I barely remembered those years, to be honest. Not that I'd repressed them—no, I remembered the beatings. The screaming in my face because I refused to eat lima beans and begged for a glass of milk to wash it down. I'd had to sit at the table and eat each bean, one by one, until I gagged and then *finally* I was allowed my milk.

They never knew I threw it up later when my body couldn't handle the stress.

They'd taken me out of tumbling and forced me to work on their farm in the evenings instead. They'd taken Joshua away from me and I'd never told him the worst of it because he'd always felt like he'd failed me.

It had taken a storm to bring the small family I'd had left back together. In an act of defiance, I'd went outside in the dark to tumble across the grass. I'd wanted to remember my mom because my grandparents refused to talk about their daughter or the fact that my father had apparently kidnapped her to marry her. That hadn't been the case of course, but my grandparents had lied easier than breathing.

When my grandpa had found me outside, he'd tied me to the porch and screamed in my face. Then Grandpa had slapped me, calling me names and my father's brat. I'd cried and begged for Joshua and the slaps came again.

They'd left me on the porch in my tears even as the storm came. I could still remember the seeping cold latching to my skin and my breath.

I didn't remember much after that.

Only the fevers, the tears, and finally, *finally*, Joshua finding me and taking me home with him. The courts couldn't keep us apart after that. No, only fate and an engine failure had done that.

I barely had nightmares about that time anymore. My big brother had saved me and had let me thrive into the woman I'd become. There had been no need to dwell on the pain my grandparents had left behind. My new terrors were the reality that remained.

It made me wonder what dreams Dorian shied away from—and why he continued to fix up that old Ackerson place as if he were running from his own nightmares.

The hand on my shoulder brought me back to reality and I screamed, whirling as I did so, tossing the dough I'd kneaded into a wasted rock at the hard chest in front of me.

Dorian blinked at me then down to where the dough rested. "So...how are things?" He drawled out the words before studying my face.

I blinked, my cheeks heating in embarrassment. "I didn't know you were here," I blurted.

He merely snorted before gesturing to the rest of the kitchen. "I would think not since your music is blaring and the rest of your team headed home for the day."

"What?" I turned to look at the clock and cursed. "How is it so late?"

"Time moves on," he grumbled. "Seriously, though. Melody only left because I was here but are you sure it's safe for you to be back here with the music blaring and so lost in your thoughts you have no idea about your surroundings?"

Annoyance settled in and I narrowed my gaze. "Don't act all big brother protective, Dorian."

"You know there's nothing big brother about me right now."

And there it was. The thing we weren't talking about. Yet it screamed at the both of us.

"Is there a reason you snuck up on me?"

In answer, he scowled before reaching out to brush a piece of my hair behind my ear. I ignored the shivers sliding down my spine.

"I came here to see if you wanted to eat dinner."

Part of me wondered if he had just asked me out on a date. But then I remembered this was Dorian Cage, and nothing was as it seemed. He was the playboy of the Cages. The number of women that I had heard connected with him over the years was insurmountable. Yes, most of it was probably a lie, made up by his groupies and admirers. But not all of it.

I wasn't even sure how many people he had been with since he and Amy had broken up. Though broken up didn't seem like the right word. Her walking away because she was spineless, that sounded more factual.

"Oh. Well. I have to pick up Lucky."

"Your dog can eat at my place too. I have a couple of things to do, figured we'd eat. Watch *Shaun of the Dead*."

My lips twitched, remembering the first time we had watched that movie. "You told me it was a comedy."

"It is."

"You forgot to mention it was a zombie movie."

"It has dead in the title."

"I didn't really think about that at the time. And I didn't see the movie poster. It scared me."

"I'll take care of you."

"You told me that you owed me a movie from that. I remember." I narrowed my gaze at him.

"You're going to make me watch *Pride and Prejudice*, aren't you?"

"Damn straight. We are going to watch both of them tonight."

"How did this turn into two movies?"

"Because I'm special like that."

He rolled his eyes, then gestured towards the dough I had ruined.

"Do you need help cleaning up?"

"No, luckily we close the bakery earlier than most

places since we wake up earlier than the rest. Do you mind picking up Lucky? I can clean up here, and then meet you outside?"

"I don't know if I like leaving you alone."

"I'm an adult, Dorian. When are you going to remember that?"

He brushed his thumb along my jaw, and I sucked in a breath. "Wellesley, sometimes it's all I can think about."

And with that, he left to go pick up Lucky, leaving me wondering what the hell I was doing.

Because I was pretty sure I was about to have a date with Dorian Cage.

Or one very long night.

"He just touched her hand. Why do you keep giggling?" Dorian asked as we sank into the couch, our feet up on the coffee table. We had been here a few hours now, the evening long past. The moon had risen into the sky, and dinner was already eaten, and the dishes put away.

And now I had forced him to watch my favorite movie of all time. Because the Keira Knightley version of *Pride and Prejudice* was the best version. I didn't care what anybody said. For the hand flex alone, I would fight for that right.

"You know why it's so wonderful? Women didn't touch men like that ever. Especially without gloves. And then she's so surprised that he touches her at all, and he has to flex his hand when she's not looking because he can still feel her warmth." I put my hand to my chest and let out a dramatic sigh. "Between that and Bingley reaching for Jane's ribbons on her dress at the dance, so many women love this movie."

"I will say, I love watching you watch this movie. It makes the fact that I'm watching this damn movie worth it."

"You love this movie too. Don't lie to me."

"It's okay."

"I promise that we'll watch *Shaun of the Dead* after this."

"Oh, we will be. I don't care how late it gets." He looked at his watch and grimaced. "It may be a midnight movie, but then you're just stuck with me all night." As soon as he said the words, a silence echoed between us, and I cleared my throat.

"Lucky is all settled on the dog bed that you bought him, so I wouldn't mind that."

What the hell was I doing? Was this me hitting on Dorian again? Well, fuck yes it was. But I had never been good at this, especially with the one person I'd been crushing on since I had turned eighteen.

"If you can take *Shaun of the Dead* that is," he said dryly as he nudged me with his elbow.

Laughing, I leaned into him a bit more, resting my head on his shoulder. He adjusted, wrapping his arm around me, and I sunk into him. He smelled like Dorian, that sandalwood and cedar scent that just did things to me. My toes curled, and I told myself that it was just the movie. The ambiance.

We were just good friends, cuddling on the couch and watching *Pride and Prejudice*.

"Back in the day, I would sit on the couch with friends, take an edible because it's Colorado and it's legal here, and watch movies until the sun came up. Then I'd go straight to school, kick ass, and at some point, sleep. I have no idea how I made it through college."

My lips twitched as I thought about Dorian in college, most likely with my brother, not sleeping.

"I've only had an edible once, and while it was fun to be relaxed, they mix with my meds now." I hadn't meant to say that, so when Dorian looked at me, worry in his gaze, I swallowed hard.

"I got sick when I was younger. Do you remember that?"

Anger clouded his features, and he leaned forward

and paused the movie. I looked over at Elizabeth Bennett as she stared into the distance, one of the most beautiful shots in cinematic history, and swallowed hard. Because I didn't think I'd be able to ever visit that place. That I'd be able to make that hike.

"I remember your brother said that you got sick when you were younger, and then you came to live with him. But he didn't give me the details. Only that he was fucking scared."

I swallowed hard and began to play with the seam of jeans on his outer thigh. He didn't wince, and I was grateful for that. But I knew this was the leg that always gave him trouble. The knee that had required surgery after the plane crash.

"I got pneumonia because my grandparents were abusive assholes that didn't deserve to have a child, and it was no wonder that my mother had left them when she did."

I explained the story in detail, how once my grandparents had found me on the porch the next morning, and finally let me inside, I'd spiked a fever. But they didn't give me medicine, didn't take me to the hospital. Instead, they waited it out because they knew better. They didn't trust modern medicines and vaccines. My parents had given me enough vaccines as a child though, so I had a better immune system than my grandparents would've let me have to begin with.

"I ended up in the hospital when I stopped breathing, and my grandmother finally got worried that she couldn't handle it on her own."

"If your grandparents weren't already dead, I'd kill them myself," he snapped.

I squeezed his hand and then leaned farther into him so I wouldn't have to meet his gaze.

"I nearly died. They intubated me, and I don't remember much of it. All I do know is that by the time I recovered, I had reduced lung function. To the point that I will always have reduced lung function. At one point, they were worried that it would turn into COPD, but thankfully my meds and genetics helped me heal. I'm never going to be able to run a marathon or climb a mountain beyond where we already live. Gymnastics are so out of my hands at this point, even though I'm not quite as flexible as I used to be."

I tried to make a joke of it, but he didn't laugh.

"You're really okay?" he asked as he shifted me so I was sitting on his lap, straddling him.

I froze, meeting his gaze. I wasn't quite sure why he had done it. And damn it, I wanted that to. I slid my hands through his hair, playing with the ends of it as he ran his palms up and down my back.

"I'm fine. I promise. Sometimes I get a little dizzy, and I have to pause. But I do try to take care of myself. I promise."

He scowled, and I rubbed his temple, making the wrinkle go away.

"I promise I'm taking care of myself. Can you say the same?" I asked, honestly worried.

Instead of answering, he sighed, squeezing my hips.

"Dorian."

"I do my physical therapy. And frankly, I know how lucky I am. I'm always going to have some scars on my side, and my knee will sometimes let me know when the weather's about to change, but one day, I'm not going to walk with a limp. And one day I'm not going to twinge every time I sneeze because I stretched the skin at my side. It's not perfect, but I'm okay."

"Good. Then so am I."

Because the thought of Dorian not being okay would break me. It scared me how much I wanted him, how much this feeling of being close to him felt right. I hadn't thought this moment would be possible, and yet here I was, in Dorian's arms.

And we weren't talking about it.

Instead, his fingers slowly played with the edge of my jeans, and I sunk my teeth into my lip.

"I would love to know what you're thinking right now, Wellesley," he whispered.

"I really want you to kiss me again. Is that okay?" I asked, my voice soft.

"If I kiss you, Wellesley, I'm not going to stop. This

isn't going to be one of your high school or college boyfriends that are so sweet and caring. Not the ones that you can walk all over because you are so powerful. I'm demanding. I'm an asshole. I'm going to take care of you, Wellesley. But if I kiss you again, it's going to be because I want you. Because I want to fuck you. I want to feel that tight pussy around my cock as you come and call me yours. I want to know exactly what color your nipples are, I want to know what you taste like. And I know that my wanting this is so far beyond wrong that it makes no sense. But in this moment, I don't fucking care. I can feel your tight little cunt all hot over my cock right now and we're both wearing jeans. But I can stop. I can walk away if I have to. But I don't want to, Wellesley. There's just something about you. It scares the fuck out of me."

I had never heard him be so honest, so open. And I could imagine every single thing he wanted to do with me. Because it was only imagining. I had never been with a man before. Never let a man touch me like that. I hadn't had the need, the time, or desire. Because some part of me, ever since I was old enough to know, had known I wanted it to be Dorian—even though the idea was so far-fetched it would never happen.

And yet here I was, in his arms.

"Kiss me," I whispered.

"Damn it, Wellesley." And before I could say

anything else, his mouth was on mine, and I gasped. He slid one hand up to my hair, tangling it in his hands as he tugged hard. The slight pain shocked me, but I arched into him, my breasts pressing to his chest.

"That's my baby girl. You like that, don't you?"

"I don't, maybe, Dorian."

"I already have you flustered. I'm barely even touching you."

He tilted my head so he could kiss me harder, and I went silent, not wanting to break this moment. I was so afraid that at some point he would realize what he was doing and walk away.

This was my brother's best friend. And yet, maybe in this moment, I was just Wellesley. I wasn't Harper in this moment.

Lost, I let Dorian take over. I had no idea what I was doing, and I didn't want to make a mistake, but then again, I just wanted to touch him. I let my hands slide over his shoulders, down between us over his chest. His hand tightened on my hip, and then he let out a moan that went straight to my core.

"I am going to take you to the bedroom, because I know my knee's not going to last long if I take you on this couch."

The vulnerability in that statement nearly broke me, but instead I just kissed him softly on the lips and nodded. I scrambled off him and reached out to help him up from the couch. In answer, he rose to his feet and picked me up against his chest.

"Dorian!"

"I can carry you. I just know that if I bend you over the couch and fuck you hard from behind, I might hurt my knee. And I want to last a long time. Call me greedy."

I let out of squeal as he tossed me into the air and caught me, and I couldn't help but laugh. Somehow, I was laughing in this moment, this moment that felt like a dream.

Because this sure as hell wasn't real.

Suddenly we were in his bedroom, and he laid me gently on the bed.

Breath coming in pants, I watched as he stripped his shirt over his head with one arm and I couldn't help but study the man in front of me.

All hard planes and muscle, the tattoos running down one side of his body. The other side, the ravaged scars were no longer red and puffy, instead they looked to be healed, only not quite settled.

He didn't say a word, just studied my face. I sat up and reached for him. When he didn't move back, I swallowed hard and gently brushed my fingers along the burns.

"Will you tell me if I hurt you?" I asked, keeping

my voice steady. He slid his thumb over my lips and nodded.

"As long as you do the same." And then he slid his thumb against my mouth. I opened for him and sucked. I had given a blowjob before, though I hadn't been very good at it. But with the way he slid his thumb in and out of my mouth, I couldn't help but wonder what I would do if I was on my knees in front of him. Eager, I tried to move so I could do so, but he shook his head before reaching down and tugging on the bottom of my shirt.

"Arms up."

"You're very bossy."

"And you're just realizing that now?"

He leaned down and took my mouth before he tossed my shirt to the side. For some reason, embarrassment slid over me, and I was suddenly shy.

Dorian seemed to understand, and he leaned forward and took my lips. Then his hand was around my back again, undoing the clasp.

My breasts fell heavy, and I swallowed hard, wanting to cover myself. But instead I just sat there at the edge of the bed as he tossed my bra softly to the side and studied me.

"Such a pale pink. I wouldn't have guessed that. And I've been thinking about your nipples for a long time."

My entire body blushed, and when he gave out that rough chuckle, I had a feeling that's exactly what he wanted. He reached forward and ran his knuckle down my breast before pinching my nipple between two of his fingers.

I gasped with the sensation, arching my back and pressing my thighs together.

"So sensitive." He leaned forward, licking my other nipple. "So reactive."

I let out a breath, and then I couldn't think of much else.

I was on my back, and he hovered over me, licking and sucking and biting at my breasts to the point that I writhed beneath him.

He slid his thigh between my legs, and I shifted my hips, riding him.

"That's it, I want you to come for me. Do you think you can come with just that friction? With my mouth on your breasts?"

I couldn't say a thing. Instead, I just slid my fingers through his hair, rocking my hips against him.

He let out a rough chuckle, before he continued to lap at my breasts. When he twisted one slightly harder than before, I sucked in a breath, and he shifted his thigh so the seam of my jeans hit my clit just right.

And in that moment, I burst. Stars shattered

beneath my eyelids as I came, arching my back and making a gasping sound that bordered on obscene.

Dorian just leaned over me on one arm, his hands lazily playing with my breasts as he stared down at me.

"So fucking beautiful."

"Dorian," I whispered as I reached for him.

In answer, he kissed me softly before he shifted down to the edge of the bed and worked on my pants.

I licked my lips as he undid the button and unzipped them slowly.

"Ass up," he ordered, tapping my hip. I planted my feet on the edge of the bed and lifted my ass as he pulled my jeans down my legs. He took my panties with them, and I blushed, realizing I was bare before him. Naked in front of a man for the first time in my life.

Some part of myself told me I should probably tell him, but I didn't want to break the moment. Instead I laid there, my thighs pressed together, feet planted on the bed, and naked before Dorian.

"Don't be shy. Let me see that pretty pussy of yours."

I shook my head, teasing, even as my hands went to my breasts.

When he slapped my thigh, I gasped, my knees falling to the sides.

"Don't be embarrassed or shy in front of me. Wellesley, I'll take care of you, I promise."

And then he was on his knees, hands on my hips, and pulling me towards his face.

"Dorian!" I shouted, embarrassed.

"Look at that beautiful pink pussy. Your clit is all swollen and practically begging for my mouth."

He slid his thumb up and down my swollen folds, and I wiggled, the sensations so different than when it was my own hand.

"Look at you. Just so beautiful. And this tiny patch of hair that you shaved into a triangle? So fucking beautiful. And sometimes I forget that you're naturally blonde," he whispered before he tugged at my curls.

I gasped, my back arching, but before I could say anything, his mouth was on me, and I couldn't focus on anything else.

He used one hand to spread me as he licked at my clit, and then the other one he used to reach up and play with my breasts.

Dorian Cage was eating me out on his bed, and at some point, I was going to wake up from one of the best dreams of my life.

But for now, I was just going to lean into this reality. Even though it had to be fake.

When he teased my entrance with his finger, I stiffened.

"I'm not going to hurt you, Wellesley. I promise."

I swallowed hard, nervous, as he slowly began to slide his finger inside me.

"You're so tight," he growled as he worked his way in and out of me.

Panting, I leaned into the movement, loving the way that he was so gentle with me.

Then his finger found that bundle of nerves that I had never found on my own before, and my toes curled.

"That's what I was looking for," he whispered, and then his mouth was on me again.

I couldn't think, couldn't breathe, instead, I just let him have me. The man I was slowly falling for, or perhaps not so slowly, licked and sucked and worked towards my pleasure. When he inserted another finger, I twinged at the pain, then relaxed in the most lucious way, as he found my G-spot once again. When he worked his fingers harder and faster, the wet sounds of my own desire filling the room, I should have felt embarrassed. Instead, all I could feel was wanting to crest over that peak.

I looked down between my legs, at the sight of his head, ensuring my pleasure, and I couldn't hold back any longer.

"Dorian!" I called, and then there was nothing, just heat, a growl, and then I was coming on his face. My wetness slicked my thighs, and his face, but I didn't care. I could be embarrassed later.

When I came down from my high, I hadn't even realized that Dorian had moved. I looked up at him then, as he ran his knuckles down my cheek.

"You are so fucking wet that I know I'm not going to last very long."

"I feel like I should be embarrassed or say thank you," I whispered, but I couldn't really move. Instead, I just lay there, limp, as Dorian chuckled.

He moved to the nightstand and pulled out a condom.

Everything crashed into reality again, and I realized this was real.

There was no going back.

"We can stop," Dorian said quickly as he leaned forward and brushed his lips against mine.

I could taste myself on him, sweet and tart, and I couldn't help but want every inch of him for myself.

"Don't stop," I said in answer.

He nodded after a moment of studying my face and then went back to the edge of the bed. He undid his pants and shoved them to the floor.

I only had a few moments of looking at him before he was sheathing his long, hard cock in a condom.

He was thick, with the tip of his dick angry and red, that vein pulsating. His balls were heavy, and while I had seen plenty of dicks before in porn, it was very different when the dick was facing you, and about to touch you. Yes, I'd given a blowjob, but this was different.

Dorian crawled over me and took my mouth.

"Let's make sure you're ready for me," he whispered as he slid his fingers between us.

I ran my hands up and down his body, afraid that this would all be a dream and I would never have this moment again.

Or perhaps this was all truth, but it would be our only time.

Tears threatened, and I told myself that this wasn't an only time. That he wasn't just taking care of me because he made a promise.

No, Dorian wanted me.

And this couldn't be a dream.

He played with my pussy again, sliding in and out of my folds with his fingers, and when I was nearly ready to come again, he pulled away. Whimpering, I squirmed beneath him but Dorian just smiled down at me.

"It's okay, you might miss my fingers, but my cock will take care of you."

I couldn't help but laugh, and Dorian winked. That was the Dorian I knew. The one who could make me laugh even in the oddest of situations.

He knelt between my legs and pressed the tip of his cock to my heat.

"Look at you all wet and ready for me. Your pussy's practically sucking the tip of my dick in right now. Lean up on your forearms and watch. I want you to watch as I enter you."

This man was the hottest person I'd ever met in my life, and I hadn't even realized that I liked dirty talk.

I did as he ordered and watched as he slid into me, inch by inch.

Pain rocked me as he slowly moved deeper and deeper inside of me. I was tight, and this was my first time. I had never used a dildo or a vibrator inside. I always played with my clit alone.

I had to hope that Dorian didn't see the pain on my face. So instead, I closed my eyes and arched my back.

And when Dorian leaned over me, I realized he had stopped moving.

"Look at me, Harper."

Harper. He called me by my name. Why did that change everything?

I looked up at him then and saw the worry there.

"You have to tell me if I'm hurting you. That was the promise."

I reached up and brushed his hair back from his forehead.

"You're not hurting me," I swore. And he wasn't. "I'm just so full."

He smiled then, his eyes crinkling. "Well, then let's make it feel good."

And then he moved even deeper, and I called out.

He was seated fully inside of me, his balls pressed against my body, and I had never felt this sensation in my life. Full, and yet wanting more. I wiggled beneath him. But he refused to move. I shoved at his shoulder.

"Dorian. Please. I need…"

"What do you need?"

"I don't know."

He nodded then, and I realized I had answered the question that neither one of us had asked.

But he didn't say a thing. Instead, he took my mouth and slowly slid out of me. I reached for his arms, then his hips, needing him back.

Dorian just chuckled against my mouth and then slammed into me. He wasn't soft, wasn't sweet, not like that first moment. And yet, it was exactly what I needed.

I tried to meet him thrust for thrust, but my rhythm was off, and Dorian just shook his head and gripped my hip.

"Like this. I've got you."

And I followed his motions, tilting my hips exactly

like he wanted. And suddenly we were in sync, moving as one, as I raked my fingernails down his back.

"Fuck, yes, Wellesley."

And then he was moving faster, his hand between us. When his thumb went over my clit, I shot off, coming once again and clamping down on his cock.

"Fuck," he groaned, the word stretching.

But I couldn't breathe, couldn't think, I was all his.

And when he moved faster, and then slammed into me one last time, I couldn't help but try to catch my breath. He buried his face in my shoulder and held onto me tightly as he came, and I tried to catch my own breath.

Because I had just lost my virginity to Dorian Cage. He was still deep inside me. And there was no going back. I held onto him, ignoring the tears that threatened.

This was the most magical moment of my life. And I still had no idea why it had happened. Or if it would ever happen again. But damn it, I was going to fight to make sure it did. Because I wanted Dorian Cage to be mine. I just had to prove to both of us that we deserved it.

Chapter 10

DORIAN

"THE AIR FEELS GOOD TODAY, DOESN'T IT?" JOSHUA tilted his face up to the sky, the sun bouncing off his blondish curls. The man usually had dark brown hair, but sometimes, after spending far too much time in the sun, and under just the right light, his hair went full surf boy.

"The wind feels pretty good," I said in answer, but I couldn't feel the wind. I couldn't feel much of anything. Perhaps though, I just wasn't sitting under the right slice of sun. I moved forward, though my limbs felt sluggish. As if each movement took a little too much time.

"Feels better than that. Here, put your arm out the window."

I frowned and realized we weren't standing on the

flight line like I had thought, with the sun shining ahead of us and that cool breeze sliding over our skin. Instead we were in the cockpit of a plane, with the windows open as if we were driving down the highway in my Jeep, the doors and roof completely off.

When I had been in college, I'd dug into some of my trust fund because I couldn't help myself. I bought a sports car, because everybody did. And I liked going fast. I'd take the top off and just let the engine purr. Joshua and Wellesley would be in the car with me, with Joshua egging me on, begging to drive, and Wellesley just in the back seat, arms above her head, screaming in happiness.

Then I got the Jeep, a used one that had seen better days, but the engine and tires were perfection. We'd go off-roading, get stuck in the mud, and laugh at each other as we tried to get ourselves out of whatever situation we ended up in. Wellesley would sit back and take photos, and Joshua would flip her off, before she'd pull out some homemade baked good to make us smile.

But I don't think I'd ever been in a plane with the windows open before. It was nice, though getting a bit cold. Even with the sun beating down on us, an icy chill settled over me, and my teeth began to chatter.

"Don't you think we should close the windows? We're a little high up, don't you think?"

"It won't matter soon. It's just a damn good day. I

love flying. I know this isn't my plane, but one day I'm going to be able to get one on my own. I'm going to be able to go anywhere I want, with no responsibilities, no looking back."

"What about Harper?" I asked, frowning when I realized I was using her name. I usually just called her Wellesley, but that was between us. And for some reason I didn't think I should tell Joshua that there was anything else between us. That would be wrong. Wouldn't it?

"Oh, don't worry, she can take care of herself."

"That doesn't sound like you," I said dryly.

"Too true. But you've got her. Whatever I can't handle, you're there. That's why you're my best friend."

Guilt settled into me, but I didn't know why. It wasn't like she was in the plane.

Then a small hand gripped my shoulder, and panic seized me.

"How did you get in here?" I asked, knowing what was coming next. I looked over my shoulder at a smiling Wellesley. Her hair was back to that reddish hue that she'd had once before. And she no longer had bangs. Instead her hair was piled on the top of her head, and she grinned at me with that gorgeous smile of hers.

"You shouldn't be here."

"I'm where you are. I trust you."

178

Guilt warred with horror as I turned to Joshua. But my best friend wasn't looking at me, instead he faced forward, his eyes vacant.

"I wasn't ready to die."

I swallowed hard, my throat tight. "You shouldn't be dead, Joshua."

"It sucks. I had all these plans. I was going to go out and take over the world right beside you. We were going to open up a bar together. You remember that?"

I nodded, unable to speak. Though Joshua couldn't see me. He couldn't see anyone.

"You were going to fly with me, and if I couldn't find a way to save to buy a plane of my own, I was going to trick you into doing so."

He winked and blood began to seep out of his ear. I reached forward and tried to wipe it away, but it wouldn't budge.

"I would've bought you anything. Even though I don't think I can ever get in a fucking plane again."

"You don't have to. I don't need the plane anymore. You're taking care of my sister though."

He turned to me, his eyes gaping holes instead of that blue gaze of his.

I tried to move back, but the plane just continued to get smaller and smaller, and I couldn't escape him.

"Joshua."

"I'll be okay. Wherever I am. I'm long dead. Worm

food if you buried me. Or that dust that gets stuck in your throat because you fucked up."

"You weren't supposed to die."

"I know. But I'm gone. And now you're fucking my baby sister."

"It's not like that," I whispered, my hands fisting at my sides.

"Maybe. Maybe not. I told you to take care of her. Maybe that was the thing that you had always planned to do."

I ran my hands over my face, but I couldn't feel anything. I wasn't sure you were supposed to feel anything in a dream other than horror.

"I know it sucks. But I'm gone. You don't have to feel guilt over that. I'm dead. I can't feel that guilt anyway. You didn't kill me. I'm the one who wanted to get on a plane. But I saved you, didn't I? You didn't die. So at least I did one thing right."

"Joshua, I didn't want you to die. Part of me wishes that I would've burned up right next to you."

"If you would've done that, you wouldn't have been with Wellesley."

"I'm not good enough for her."

"Damn straight. No one's good enough for my baby sister. And I realize that I'm probably just a figment of your imagination and your dreams, and I could say anything you want me to say. Or maybe I'll just haunt you until the end of your days. Either way, don't fuck things up with my sister."

"I don't want to hurt her."

"Then don't."

I opened my mouth to say something, anything. How I cared for Wellesley, but I didn't know how to make that work. Or to be worth that. To tell Joshua I promised I wouldn't actually break her like I broke everything else. But there was nothing for me to say. Instead a whirring sound echoed in my ears, and the screeching of metal against metal, and the blood-curdling screams of Harper behind me as Joshua pushed us down into a nosedive, shook me right down in my bones. But I couldn't wake up.

"Dorian!" Wellesley screamed.

I reached for her, but my fingers slid through her like smoke.

"Wellesley. Wellesley!"

"Dorian, wake up!"

I sat straight up in bed, my entire body shaking as bile coated my tongue. I looked down at her as she cupped my face, and I couldn't help but run my hands up and down her body.

"You're safe. You're safe."

She frowned at me as she slid her hands through my hair, the sheet pooling at her waist so her bare breasts pressed against my forearms.

"I'm safe. I'm right here. It was just a nightmare."

A nightmare where I could still smell the putrid scent of burning flesh, still feel the heat and sharpness of metal slicing into my body. I hadn't been able to feel or sense a damn thing in that dream until the end. When it became all too real. And yet Harper Wellesley had been the one right beside me, as Joshua had tried to save us, only losing himself in the process.

"You're okay," I said, and my voice ached. I must have been screaming for far longer than I thought, because it felt as if I had jagged shards of glass in my throat every time I swallowed.

"I won't ask you what you were dreaming about," she said softly, sliding her arms down my body, as if checking me for new wounds. When her hand went to my side, I didn't flinch. Instead she leaned her forehead on my chest, and I just wrapped her in my arms.

"Sorry for waking you."

"It's okay. I have dreams too."

I opened my mouth to say something, to say anything, but thankfully Lucky took that time to slide his wet nose against my back. I yelped as Harper's shoulders shook.

I scowled down on her. "Really?"

"I need to take him out."

I shook my head, as I pushed her back slightly so I could run my hands through her hair.

"No, I've got it. You don't know the land out here."

"I've been living in this town longer than you, Dorian."

"And you don't know this property. Just let me take care of him, okay?"

She studied my face, as if looking for answers I didn't have. "Okay. I can do that. I'll make breakfast."

"You don't have to do that."

"Maybe I want to."

I studied her face for a moment before finally nodding and getting out of bed.

I didn't bother to wrap myself in a blanket, and I could feel her gaze on me as I walked naked to my dresser. My cock stood on end, just the feel of Wellesley touching me was almost a little too much. But I shoved my legs into gray sweatpants and pulled on a Henley. I'd have to wear a jacket as well, since it seemed to be a little frigid outside, but hopefully the cold would bring down my hard-on. The two of us needed to talk, but maybe I should get my thoughts in order first.

Lucky pranced around my legs, and I couldn't help but smile down at him.

"Okay, let's go for that walk. I need to stretch anyway."

My leg hurt like a bitch, and I knew I had overexerted it last night. But frankly, if I was going to hurt myself, I might as well do it that way.

I wasn't going to think about the fact that it had been the best sex of my entire life, and I had no idea what to say about that.

Lucky shot off into the backyard, and I nearly fell off the stoop as I realized the dog was way more awake than I was. Thankfully I had him on a leash, and we made our way down the path for a short walk. Lucky took care of his business, and I cleaned up after him. It didn't matter that this was my property, and we were out in the forest, I wasn't about to leave dog shit all over the place.

The cold mountain air woke me up fully, and I was grateful for it.

I loved living in Denver. I loved my jobs. I loved my businesses and working with people.

Even after the crash, I loved it.

But taking these moments when the air was fresh, clean, and crisp? I loved this too.

I didn't know what I would do when I finally finished this house, when I needed to go back to reality.

I was going to take this moment. And I was going to talk with Harper. Because we both had some explaining to do.

By the time we got back into the house, Lucky went

straight for his water and food bowl, and the scent of coffee wafted through the air.

"I didn't think to ask, do you open today?"

"Considering the sun is up, I would think not."

Wearing one of my shirts that looked baggy and overwhelming on her, she padded forward and held out a cup of coffee for me.

"Just how you like it. And no, I'm off for the full day. I'll get in trouble with my staff if I show up and try to work."

"They're just taking care of you," I grumbled before taking a sip of my coffee. And she was right, she made it perfectly. Yes, I came in often enough that she would know my coffee order, but she had known it far longer than that.

What the hell were the two of us doing?

"I don't know if I like the look on your face right now," she whispered.

"What do you mean?" I asked, leaning down to pet Lucky as he pressed his head to my thigh. Thankfully it wasn't the leg that hurt today, but for Lucky, I'd have taken the pain. He was Wellesley's after all.

"Are you going to say that last night was a mistake?" she blurted, surprising me. Of course she shouldn't have surprised me. This was Wellesley.

She spoke her mind, even if sometimes I knew she wanted to hide behind her own fears. She stood up to my mother, and frankly, stood up to most people. Maybe I needed to be the smart one and stand up for her.

"You were a virgin," I said, knowing it was the truth. We hadn't had a fucking conversation. We should have. We should have said anything before just falling into one another. But I had a feeling if either one of us had, we would've backed away. Not because it was wrong. Because I couldn't have those kinds of regrets, but because it would've been too much.

"Yes. I was a virgin." She took a sip of her coffee, her gaze right on mine.

Out of the corner of my eye I saw she had begun working on biscuits, flour spilling over the cutting board, with a bowl filled with whatever ingredients she'd found in my kitchen that I rarely used.

"You didn't tell me."

She shrugged again, before going back to the biscuits and not looking at me.

"Virginity is a construct. Yes, you are the first person that I've slept with. I wasn't waiting on anyone. It just happened that way. But you sure as hell weren't my first orgasm. Or the first person I've ever had any sexual contact with. You were just the first person to enter my vagina."

I blinked at her, laughter threatening. It was getting

far more difficult than it should be for me not to fall for this woman.

"It makes me a fucking monster. It may be a construct, but it wasn't mine to take."

"You didn't take anything. And I didn't give you anything. Other than an orgasm." She winked over her shoulder, and I chuckled. I couldn't help it. This woman. She was just too much.

But then she always had been.

"Seriously, I am a damn monster."

"No you're not."

"It makes me feel like one because right now all I can think about is the fact that I fucked you and claimed you and I'm the only one who has. I'm the only one that's been in that tight pussy of yours. And how fucked up is that?"

Her eyes widened, before she painstakingly and methodically went to the sink to wash her hands.

"Oh? Is that what you're thinking about right now?"

"Damn straight."

"So, you have been the only one there. Is that going to be a problem for you?"

"It should be. But we both know it isn't."

"So what are you going to do about it?" she asked.

"What do you want me to do about it, Wellesley?

Because we both know I want to do this again. That you want this again."

"Oh? You think I want this again?"

I looked down at her, at her parted mouth, her wide eyes.

"Of course you fucking want this again. But that doesn't mean it should happen."

"Because you don't want it? Or you think I shouldn't want it."

"I'm only going to hurt you," I said point-blank, thinking of Joshua's words.

"Then don't hurt me. It's not a full-on promise that you will. Just try not to be an asshole."

"Baby, I am an asshole."

"Okay, try not to be the asshole that breaks my heart."

I set down my coffee cup and sighed.

"I don't promise forevers, Wellesley."

"I wasn't aware I asked you for them."

"So what do you want out of this?"

"If you want to have that talk, I guess the answer will be your cock then."

"You talking dirty is just getting me hard."

"I can see that. You're out here wearing male lingerie with those gray sweatpants."

That made me bark out a laugh.

"If I fuck you again, that could be the end. That

could be all we are to each other. Because I am not in the right head space for forevers. For a relationship."

"Again, I wasn't aware I asked you for one."

"You have relationship written all over you."

"Maybe. But then again, you're the one who came inside me last night, so maybe I have *you* written all over me."

"You're ridiculous."

And I was falling for her. And that was the fucking problem.

"Dorian. We're friends. Before anything else, we're friends. I'm not asking you for forever. I'm just asking you not to hurt me."

She faced me then, so I reached forward and cupped her chin.

"I never want to hurt you, Wellesley."

"Then don't."

"But if I fuck you again, you don't get to fuck anyone else. While we're together? This pussy is mine."

I reached between us and cupped her over her panties.

"Oh," she gasped.

"That's right. When we're together like this? You're mine. Your pussy is mine, your orgasms are mine. Everything is mine. I'm not a nice man. I'm possessive as fuck."

"Then same goes for you."

She reached forward and gripped me over my sweatpants.

"You're going to say that my cock is yours?"

"Damn straight," she said, her voice shaking.

I grinned before I slid my thumb over her lips. She opened for me, and I let her lick at my thumb, imagining what it would feel like when that mouth was on my cock.

"Just you and me then."

Until we fucked this up.

In answer, she went to her tiptoes, and I let my hand fall. When she pressed her lips to mine, so soft and sweet, I couldn't hold back. I groaned into her, needing more.

The kiss was slow, tempting, as we explored one another.

I had wanted her before. When I had seen her thrive in her shop and show the world that she could do anything. When I had realized that she was one of the most beautiful people I'd ever seen in my life.

When she had been Joshua's sister, and I couldn't have anything more. But now she was on my tongue, her body pressed against mine. And I needed every ounce of her. I pulled away, my breath coming in pants. Before she could say anything, I twisted her so she faced the sink.

"Grip the edge of the counter," I ordered.

"Dorian."

"Do as I say, Wellesley. And if you're a good girl, I'll let you come on my face."

In answer, she pressed her ass back against my crotch.

Groaning, I went down to my knees and slid my shirt she wore up over her hips.

"Seeing you in my shirt nearly made me come in my sweats. You're so fucking hot."

"You in gray sweatpants pretty much did that for me."

I pulled her panties down softly, gently, and she stepped out of them. And now, the feast of a lifetime stood before me. I spread her ass cheeks, looking at that beautiful pussy and her tight little hole.

"One day I'm going to fuck this part of you too, what do you say?" I asked, tracing the rim with my finger.

"Oh. Well. I don't know."

"I'll make sure you're ready for me. Eager. I promise."

Before she could say anything, I leaned forward and kissed her there, and she shivered.

Smiling, I lowered myself slightly and licked at her cunt. Her knees went weak, and I gripped her thigh with one hand, keeping her steady, but used my other to keep her spread before me. She groaned, pressing her ass to my face, and I just grinned, lapping up her sweet juices. She wiggled her ass against my face, and I kept going, sucking and licking until she arched for me.

She was like sweet mango, all lush and soft and ready for me.

When I shook my face between her cheeks, she let out a gasp, and then she was coming on my face, her juices spilling down my chin as I tried to lap up every ounce of her.

She was the hottest thing I had ever seen in my life.

I loved going down on women. I loved their tastes, their feel. I loved the way each of them arched differently whenever you found that perfect spot.

But Harper Wellesley bending forward so she could press her ass to my face as I ate her out?

The best breakfast in the history of mankind. There was no way I would ever top that.

Body humming, I finally stood back and palmed myself over my sweats, squeezing and tugging on my dick. She tried to turn from me, but I pushed at her lower back, keeping her facing away from me.

"I don't think I can even stand much longer. Wow."

"I'm going to love eating you out every morning. Just saying."

"And I'm not going to stop you," she rasped. "Except, why won't you let me taste you?"

I groaned, squeezing the base of my cock so I wouldn't come right then and there.

"You will. But not right now. First, I need to go get a condom though."

"I'm clean. I just had all of my tests, and I have an IUD."

She looked over her shoulder at me, her eyes dark with desire. In answer, I licked my lips and looked down between us. At the way her ass pushed slightly towards me, begging for my cock.

"I'm clean too. I can show you my papers. And dammit, I should show you my papers."

"I trust you."

I cursed under my breath again, before I leaned back and shoved my shirt over my head.

"Pull your shirt up, I want to see your tits move as I fuck you from behind," I ordered.

Eyes wide, she did as she was told and pulled her shirt completely off. I reached forward and palmed her breasts, loving the heaviness in my hands.

"Next time I'm going to fuck these tits too. And then I'm going to come all over them, painting them. What do you think?"

"I think I can feel my wetness sliding down my thighs."

With a rough laugh, I shoved my sweats to my knees and positioned myself at her entrance. She was so wet she swallowed up the tip of my cock before I could even move.

We both froze, and I let out a shuddering breath.

"I've never fucked anyone bare before, this may be over quicker than we want."

"Okay," she said, and before I could take over, she pushed back, taking me to the hilt.

"Fuck," I growled, drawing out the word.

I gripped her hips, keeping her steady, as I was buried to the hilt, my balls pressing against her.

"You are trouble."

"If you say so." She tried to wiggle on my cock, and I leaned forward and pinched her nipple.

"Dorian!" she squealed.

"Watch it, minx."

She wiggled again, so I pinched her nipple once more. But before she could even squeal in surprise, I slapped her ass.

"Oh," she said, this time a moan.

"Well, that's interesting," I muttered before I pulled out slowly. I looked down between us, at the wetness she left on my dick, and I had to count to ten before I moved again.

She whimpered for me, wiggling her hips over me since the tip of my dick was still inside. In answer, I slammed home in one movement. She froze, her knees shaking, so I leaned forward and kissed her shoulder.

"Do you want it slow? So I just tease you over the edge? Or do you want me to fuck you so hard that you practically fall to the ground, bruising your knees?" I growled before I nipped at her earlobe.

"Yes please?" she said in answer. She tasted of coffee, and of Harper, and I knew that walking away would be the hardest thing I ever did.

So I wouldn't do it yet. Instead, I pulled out of her and then slammed home once again. It was hard and fast, her breasts bouncing with each thrust. I threw my head back, leaving myself to abandon as both of us arched from one another, finding a rhythm that was far too much and yet not enough all at once.

And when she finally came again, her pussy fluttering around my cock, I pulled out of her and twisted her around.

"Dorian," she whined, but I didn't say anything. Instead I slid two fingers deep inside of her and fucked her hard with my hand, loving the way that her juices filled my palm and trailed over her legs.

When she came one more time, I knew it was my turn.

I lifted her by the thighs, set her on the edge of the counter, and met her gaze before I rocked my hips forward. It was hard and rough and too much for a virgin, and I knew she would be sore. So I would take care of her soon. Pamper her the way that she deserved. But for now, I took her mouth, as I took her.

When I came, filling that precious cunt with my cum, I didn't pull away. Instead, I filled her, wanting her to scent of me, to feel of me, to be marked by me. I kissed her again, loving the way that she gripped me, not wanting to let me go either. And I knew I was in so much fucking trouble—I had no way of getting out of this.

And yet, with her cunt keeping me in place, my cum filling her, I didn't want a way out. And that was a fucking problem.

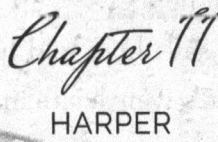

Chapter 11

HARPER

Zero texts. Nothing. Zip. Nada.

How did I have zero texts at this moment?

Yes, I was meeting my friends at the resort in a bit, that way we could have girl time while Scarlett still kept an eye on the place, however, I didn't have any other texts.

A slight pang hit me, remembering the random texts that Joshua would send me throughout the day to check in.

Big bro: Have you had your milk yet? You need to be big and strong.

Big bro: When are you going to change my name in your phone? I don't think I've ever heard you use the word bro.

Big bro: Are you wearing your sunscreen? You're paler than I am.

Big bro: I love you, bug.

Big bro: I haven't had a photo of Lucky in three days. I'm missing my nephew. Send photos.

Big bro: Dorian says hi. I told him to just text you, but he got weird. He's weirder than you are, and that's saying something.

Big bro: Take a look at this view. Yes, I'm the co-pilot this time, so I can take a photo through the airplane window as the pilot does his thing. I'm safe. Promise.

Tears slid down my face as I went through the long texts, realizing that he was never going to respond again. What would happen when somebody got his number?

I was afraid to call and have someone pick up. Or to text, and someone say that I had the wrong number. It was odd that life could end so abruptly, and yet memories of it ebbed in waves long afterward.

Because the paperwork and solace of death never truly catapulted into nothingness. I still had to deal with lawyers and other stacks of papers when it came to Joshua. I still ended up with emails from his old boss, making sure I was okay. Though I had a feeling he was also trying to gauge if I was going to sue him.

I would never. And I knew Dorian didn't have any

plans to either. It had been a true accident. And the company had not been at fault. Those maintenance logs were detailed, and it had just been an act of God according to some.

I would like to think that whatever God you believed in wouldn't want it to be an act on their accounts, but what did I know?

I was just the person left behind.

I set my phone down, as I was afraid I was going to text someone, and maybe not even Joshua.

Because Dorian had not texted me today. Or yesterday. Or the day before.

I had left the next day, my body sore, my heart full to capacity, and he had promised he would get back to me soon. And then he'd needed to focus on a few work things and get through the rigors of rebuilding part of the house.

I'd been up to my eyeballs in baking issues, as well as two wedding cakes for the resort since sometimes the pastry chef for the Cage Lake Resort was a little testy, so I stepped in.

I had been just as busy if not busier than Dorian, and he hadn't texted.

Of course I should probably text him, but he had been the one to say he would reach out.

Hadn't he?

I ran my hands over my face and growled.

Lucky yipped at me, and I slid my hands through his fur.

"I am not good at this whole relationship thing. I don't even know if this is relationship. Can you tell? Lucky? I feel like you should be able to tell."

He tilted his head at me, and I rolled my eyes.

"I'm sorry for putting the burden on you. I know you don't understand Dorian any more than I do. I barely understand myself at this point."

With a groan, I slid my phone into my purse, then went to get ready.

We were just having dinner at the restaurant at the resort, but the place was higher end than my living room. Meaning I wanted to look somewhat fancy, just not altogether overdone.

And why hadn't he called?

I just needed to put Dorian Cage out of my mind for a moment. I didn't know what was happening between us, other than the fact that we were exclusive. Exclusive to just sex? Or dating? I didn't know.

This was the point in my life when I realized that I should probably have tried to have a little more experience.

I'd never really had a serious boyfriend. There hadn't been anyone in high school that I wanted to spend time with, and I had moved during an inopportune time thanks to my grandparents' neglect, so making friends had been difficult. Most of the people in Cage Lake had been here since birth, and they all knew each other. And while I had known them when I was younger, and now later, that gap had been right during the time of puberty where everything was that much more difficult.

So falling for a boy just really wasn't in the cards.

And in college I had been working on setting up the business, and there hadn't been time for falling for anyone.

Not to mention Dorian had been on my mind then as well—even though he had been so far out of the possibility, it wasn't even funny.

Now I had a situationship or whatever the kids called it these days with Dorian, and I needed to tell somebody.

I couldn't help but wonder what my brother would have thought of all of this. I cringed as I slid my feet into my shoes, imagining my brother being his overprotective self.

He had loved Dorian like a brother. Of course that made it a little weird. And he thought Dorian was a great man. He should have been okay with Dorian and I—well, just Dorian and me. However, I did not understand the male psyche. For all I knew, he would have decided that he needed to go all caveman and beat the ever-loving crap out of Dorian for daring to touch his sister.

"I really wish you were here to get angry or happy about this," I pouted.

But no amount of hoping and wishing was going to bring my brother back.

I had to live for the now. Even though I had no idea what that truly meant.

"Okay, you be a good boy, and I promise I will come home early. I'm not spending the night at Dorian's. Promise."

Lucky licked my palm, and I smiled.

No, I would not be spending the night at Dorian's. Because that would require him to actually text me and want to get ahold of me.

Damn that man and everything he stood for.

Or maybe I needed to just calm the hell down.

I grabbed my purse and said goodbye to Lucky one more time, letting the dog mom guilt settle in. I didn't leave him home often, as I usually took him with me or left him at doggy daycare or with friends. But he could spend a couple of hours on his own. And I would make sure I made up for it later.

I got in my small compact car with amazing tires thanks to Joshua and Hudson because even that Cage wouldn't let me go around town without taking care of myself. The drive east of town was laidback since Cage Lake wasn't that large.

I enjoyed the scenic views, and the fact that I knew most of the people walking around. Yes there were some tourists, but tourists tended to stay at some of the cabins on the lake, rented along the rivers, and against the mountain ridge, or were at the resort itself. These long winding roads to the resort were for locals.

I pulled into the parking lot and bypassed the valet. Though Scarlett had told me repeatedly that I was able to just use the valet on her card, I refused. Then Isabella had said the same thing, and Hudson. So eventually I was just going to have to give in. But not now. Now I would just be myself and not rely on Cages or those close to them.

By the time I got into the restaurant, I seemed to be the final one there.

Isabella, Luna, Scarlett, and Ivy had a large table in the corner and waved me over as soon as I walked through.

"Luna! I didn't know you would be here," I said as I hugged Scarlett's twin tightly.

"I wasn't sure I would make it either, but I'm glad I did. You look amazing. So bright and happy."

"You do look amazing," Scarlett said as she narrowed her gaze. "Hmm."

"Well, I just, I'm glad I'm here," I sputtered,

wondering if I had a sign on my forehead that said *'recently devirgined by Dorian Cage's cock and I love it.'*

No, that sounded ridiculous. Of course, I was ridiculous, wasn't I?

"I'm sorry I'm the last one here. I got distracted."

"You're not the last one," Isabella said as she reached forward and squeezed my hand. "However, you just beat Sophia."

I turned as Isabella's sister walked forward, a small smile on her face and dark circles under her eyes that she couldn't quite hide with concealer.

"Sophia!" I said as I hugged the woman close.

"Sorry I'm late. We're staying at Aston and Blakely's place by the lake, and I'm still not used to driving on these roads. Even though I'm from Colorado, not living here is a bit different."

"You should have told me, I would've driven you," Isabella said as she squeezed her sister's hand.

"No, I'm going to learn it. And honestly, most of this just comes from the guilt of leaving the babies at home. I know that my husband can handle them, but I have mom guilt."

"Well, I'm glad you're here, and I'm going to need photos," I teased.

"Hell yes, all the photos," Ivy said as she reached forward and grabbed the champagne bottle I hadn't noticed.

"Can you drink? We can get the non-alcoholic bubbly too," she said before reaching for Sophia's glass.

"I'm allowed one since I'm not pumping tonight. So yes, give me the champagne," Sophia said, exhaustion evident in her voice.

"Well that's it, I'm just going to have to come over tomorrow and steal those nieces of mine," Isabella said point-blank, and I just sat back and laughed, holding my champagne glass as the two sisters playfully argued.

"We really are okay. I'm just tired. I'm always tired. I mean I was exhausted when I was a dancer with the ballet, but that was a different kind of exhaustion."

"I can't believe you were a principal dancer," I said, trying to imagine Sophia on stage and honestly it was easy. She was so graceful and beautiful. And to be honest, motherhood seemed to make it even more so.

"Looking back at some of those photos, I can't believe it either."

"To motherhood, feminism, and finding our path," Scarlett said as she held up her glass.

"Because we're allowed to kick ass with all of it."

We each clinked glasses, and I took a sip of the tart bubbly.

"So, are you going to tell us exactly why you're looking so smug and nervous?" Scarlett asked. It took a moment to realize she was staring at me, as were the rest of them.

I quickly gulped the rest of my champagne and shook my head. "What? What do you mean?"

"Well, you've been a little busy for the past few days, and I'd love to know why," one of my best friends teased, and I glared at her and Ivy. Luna looked as confused as Dorian's sisters did, and I wasn't sure what the hell I was supposed to say in that moment.

Because I wasn't about to tell everybody that I had slept with Dorian.

Right?

But this was girl time, maybe I should at least say something? Or hide underneath the table.

"Nothing. I've just had a long day. Long week," I corrected.

Scarlett narrowed her gaze, and opened her mouth to say something, before she stood up abruptly.

"Excuse me. I'll be right back. I have something to deal with."

Before I could say anything or thank her for leaving me a moment to think, she stomped off, and we all turned to see the object of her ire.

Hudson stood in the corner, growling with Scarlett's boyfriend, Ronan.

"What on earth is that about?" Luna asked of her twin.

I shook my head. "I have no idea."

"There seems to be a lot of secrets going on around

here," Ivy said as she stared at me, and I quickly reached for my water.

I wasn't about to talk to the girls about what happened. Not until I had answers. Or at least had spoken to Dorian first. What's the secret? Were we telling his family? I had no idea what I was supposed to say. After all, telling the family you were dating someone was usually a big deal. Except for the fact that I was already so entwined with his family, this made everything more complicated.

Thankfully before I had to deal with any answers, the waiter came by, and we ordered a few appetizers to share.

The subject changed to Isabella's current job, as well as Sophia's kids. Luna and Ivy went on a long discussion about Ivy's next project, and when Scarlett came back, she didn't say anything, except her face had paled other than her reddened cheeks.

Luna just squeezed her hand, and Scarlett shook her head. So there would be no questions on that front. And I understood. Because I didn't want any questions on mine either.

By the time I got home, my head ached, and I'd only had a small glass of champagne.

And Dorian still hadn't texted.

"I'm going to have to call him and annoy him later," I whispered to Lucky as we took our evening walk.

Then my phone buzzed.

I quickly answered the call, realizing I'd probably answered too quickly. "Hey there," I said as I let out a breath.

Dorian's rough chuckle filled my ears. "Sorry I didn't call you right away. There were a few issues to handle with the lawyer, and well, it's been a long fucking day. You sound like you're outside? Are you okay?"

Warmth spread through me, and I tried not to lean too much into whatever I was feeling. Because this man could hurt me more than anything, and we both knew it.

"I'm just outside walking Lucky. I'll be inside soon."

"Be safe, okay?"

"I am."

An awkward silence settled in, before I finally cleared my throat. "Are we telling anyone? I mean I just had dinner with two of your sisters, and I didn't say anything, and now I feel weird. Because they're my friends, as are my other friends in town, and I just, well, I don't know what to say."

"Wellesley, baby. You can tell anyone you want. Just warn me if you tell any of my brothers in case they want to throw fists."

"They're not going to hit you."

"Oh, they will. Because I'm defiling Joshua's little sister."

"Don't make it weird."

"I'm remembering exactly how I defiled you right before you left my house. So, not too weird. I have a hard-on, but I digress."

I burst out laughing, as Lucky danced in front of me.

"Okay."

"Stop thinking too hard. That's my job."

"You're right. You usually are the annoying one who thinks too hard."

"Ouch. I'll have to spank you later for that."

I pressed my thighs together, annoyed that this man could turn me on with just his voice.

"So. I need to go to Denver."

Reality crashed in, and I tried not to let disappointment settle over my tongue.

"Oh. Well that makes sense. You have a lot of businesses to deal with. Do you know when you'll be home?"

"It should only take a couple of days, but Wells? Do you think you can come with me?"

Elation slithered into me, but I tried not to latch on to that.

"I don't know. I'll have to look at the schedule, this

isn't a lot of notice. And I'm the owner. I have to be responsible."

"I know. I'll help with whatever I can. It won't be too long, and frankly I can make my own schedule. I know you get a full day off, so if we work around your schedule, you won't have to take off too much time or find too many replacements. We'll make it work with you, okay? I just want you there."

My lips formed into a small smile, and I told myself that I was thinking too hard yet again. Because Dorian wanted me.

And why did I feel like that might be one of the most connected and irrational feelings circling me?

"I'll try."

"I want to show you my Denver. My life down south."

Reality settled in once again. Because Dorian did not live here. And my home was Cage Lake. My business, my friends. My life.

Dorian wasn't permanent.

I had to remember that. We hadn't promised forever. We had just promised honesty.

I swallowed hard and let out a breath.

"I'll try. I'd love to go."

"Good. I want to come over tonight, but I know you have to work early. I'll see you tomorrow at the bakery though? I promise not to be gone for too long again."

"Well, if I know you're going to be there, I guess I need to make your favorite Danish."

"Okay, dating a baker who knows all of my favorite things is going to be hard on my workout routines."

He laughed as he said it, and I couldn't help but cling to the word dating.

I was so far out of my depth, but I was just going to ride whatever this was.

Thinking too hard would only break me in the end.

"So, what are you wearing?" he asked, his voice low.

And when I burst out laughing, and followed Lucky back into my apartment, I smiled.

I may not know what I was doing, but I was going to live in the moment.

And when Dorian left, because he would have to, I wouldn't break. Because I had set my own expectations.

And apparently when I said honesty was how I was going to work with Dorian, I only meant between him and me. Because I was sure as hell lying to myself.

Chapter 12

DORIAN

WHY THE HELL HAD I DECIDED TO BRING HARPER with me? Of all the things I could do to try to get my head out of my ass and maybe focus on what I should be doing, bringing Joshua's little sister with me to look at my clubs after spending far too long ignoring them didn't seem like the best way to go about it.

But there was no going back now. Here she was, in my house, surrounded by things I had pieced together over the years to try to figure out my own sense of style, and I had no idea what the hell I was supposed to do about it.

"Is everything okay?" Harper asked as she came out of the bedroom. We had taken the long drive down from Cage Lake to my house in the suburbs of Denver. Traffic had been a bitch on I-70 once we'd made past the hardest curve of the drive in the winter, and I was just grateful the pass had been open. Frankly, I probably should have hired the company helicopter to get back to the place, but I knew there was no way I could get in the air.

I would have to eventually. I used to love traveling. Used to love seeing the world and even flying on my own.

But sometimes I still woke up with the sound of an engine screaming at me. Even though we hadn't made that exact sound when we'd slammed into the ground. Joshua had been able to get us to a safer speed and distance in the end. He'd saved my life, and I knew it had only been his skill that had let me walk out of there. Or at least, crawl out.

I hadn't been able to put any weight on my legs, and the smell of my own flesh burning kept me up at night.

And if Joshua hadn't had that single piece of metal carve its way into his neck, he'd have survived. He'd had fewer burns on his body, and his limbs had all been intact, not broken.

The only true injury on his body had killed him. I'd ended up with far more injuries, far more issues, but I had survived.

And here I was, ready to defile his little sister once again.

"Dorian?"

I blinked myself out of my thoughts and couldn't help but groan as she walked forward.

She wore long black pants that flowed around her, and a crop top that showed just enough skin it made me want to bend her over that couch just to see exactly what we had together. But I already knew what her pussy tasted like, what her cunt felt like around my cock.

I was going to hell, and I was damn fine with it.

Her hair flowed around her shoulders, her makeup smoky and luscious. We were headed to my clubs for the evening, so I could check in on them, and frankly tell myself that I could do this job of mine. Then in the morning we would have breakfast at Aston's and then head back up to Cage Lake. It wasn't as if Harper could take that many days off. She worked her ass off, like I used to. And I was proud of her. The fact that she'd even taken an extra day off just to be with me? It should worry me. And yet it was all I wanted.

"Sorry, just wool-gathering."

She frowned and slid her hand over my shoulder before cupping my cheek.

"Talk to me. What's going on in that mind of yours?"

"Don't worry about me." I turned to kiss her palm, but she stepped away, scowling.

"No. Don't do that."

"Do what?"

"Don't act as if you're trying to protect me by keeping your thoughts safe. I want to know what you're thinking. We spend hours a day together, you brought me to Denver to show me your home and your businesses, we're sleeping together, I let my friends take care of my dog overnight so we could be together, and you're not telling me a damn thing. If what we have is just sex, that's fine. But I need to know ahead of time. We both know that I'm new to this, but just because I'm new doesn't mean I'm an idiot."

I cursed under my breath. "I'm not calling you an idiot."

"Then talk to me. You don't have to tell me all of your deepest darkest secrets, but I'd like to know something. Anything."

"I was wondering if I was making a mistake by bringing you here," I snapped. I could have rightly kicked myself.

Her face paled, but she raised her chin.

"Okay. Are you?"

"I'm not. I know I'm not. It just makes me think of Joshua."

"And you think he'd disapprove? Even though he was your best friend. I would like to think that my brother and his best friend liked each other because neither one of them were assholes."

"I am an asshole, Harper Wellesley," I said dryly.

"You might be an asshole, but you're not cruel. My brother wouldn't have wanted to be friends with somebody cruel. Not after my grandparents."

I cursed again and moved forward, this time cupping her face.

"I know that. And I would love to think that your brother would approve of this. I just hate the fact that I don't get to ask him."

Her eyes filled, but she blinked the tears away.

"He always knew I had a crush on you."

I froze, uncertain. "Really?"

"Yes. And he never forbade me dating you, but he did ask for me to wait until I was older to act on it."

"You're serious." My heart beat so quickly I was afraid it was going to rush right out of my chest. "He wanted you to make a move?"

She laughed, taking a step away. But she let me slide my hand over hers, so the loss didn't ache.

"I don't think he meant that, but he didn't warn me away from you. He didn't get all overprotective and growly. Why would he be friends with somebody he wouldn't trust with his own sister?"

"When you say it that way—"

"You know I'm right."

"I have a feeling that in whatever this relationship is you're going to be right often."

She beamed. "Damn straight."

"I should also tell you that I was thinking about how I didn't call us a helicopter even though I knew the roads were going to be slick, well, for the obvious reason."

Her face paled once again, and she wrapped her arms around me. She didn't squeeze too tightly, but the burns at my sides didn't hurt today. Apparently time did heal some wounds. Maybe not all of them.

"I thought about that. I just didn't want to mention it and bring back memories to the surface."

I ran my hand up and down her back and brushed a kiss on the top of her head.

"I know I will have to fly again. Maybe not as a pilot, but I'm going to have to get on a plane. Or one of the multiple helicopters the company owns."

"Of course the Cage Empire owns helicopters," she said dryly.

"We own a plane or two as well. But I don't think I could get on one."

"We can drive anywhere you want from now on."

"But what if I want to take you to Paris?" I teased.

Her eyes widened. "Paris?"

I had only said it as a joke, but right then and there I promised myself I would find a way to get on a plane and take her to Paris. I would take her anywhere that she wanted. Because Harper Wellesley deserved to see the world. And if my asshole father and his money could help that, I'd do whatever it takes.

"Let's do it."

"I might need to take a little more time off work for that," she said dryly.

"That means I should probably learn to get on a plane." I paused. "Do you think you'd be able to fly?" After all, it had been her brother with me.

She nodded, though carefully. "Yes. Because I don't have those nightmares. Not the ones that keep you up."

I swallowed hard, remembering how she had wrapped herself around me, naked, willing, but so steady for me. I wasn't used to that. Hell, the only serious girlfriend I'd ever had before had been Amy. And she'd walked out on me without a second glance. I'd been too much for her when I'd been broken.

And here I was, trying to pick up the pieces, and Wellesley was there.

Where she had always been.

And I had nearly been blind to it.

"Do you talk to your therapist about this?" she asked after a moment.

I nodded, rubbing my chin over the top of her head. "I do. And I'll get there when I get there. I might scream and cry and pass out, but I'll get there. I don't want this to stop me from anything."

"You are one of the most stubborn people that I know, and that's including myself, we can figure this out."

I threw my head back and laughed, because indeed, we both were stubborn as hell. Then I leaned down and slid my lips over hers. "Let's go head to the clubs."

"Thankfully I'm old enough to get in now."

I let my head fall back and groaned. "Please don't remind me that you're that much younger."

"Only like eight years. I'm twenty-three. I'm an old maid."

"If you call yourself old one more time, I'm going to toss you over my lap and spank you."

Her eyes darkened. "Well, I guess I'm old, old, old, old." She laughed as I chased her through my living room, tossed her over my shoulder—ignored the pain in my side—and carried her to the bedroom.

We might be a little late to the club.

IT WAS STILL EARLY YET, SINCE I WAS JUST MEETING with my managers, my staff, and getting the feel of things, but honestly it was like I had never left.

The first two clubs we had visited were my newer

CARRIE ANN RYAN

ones, and everything had worked out well. I liked
creating high-end clubs for people who wanted to dress
up, have quality drinks, and occasionally toss around
money to show off. You didn't need a Chanel bag or
Louis Vuitton when you walked inside, but those with
their Cartier's and Hugo Boss tended to puff up like
peacocks when around each other.

"I'm glad that I borrowed this from Blakely,
because I don't own anything that would fit into any of
these clubs," she teased. I slid my hand over her cashmere crop top.

"Are you telling me that I stripped this shirt off of
you earlier and it's my sister-in-law's?" I asked,
grimacing.

"No this was a gift. Don't worry, I promise you that
your brother never fucked your sister-in-law in this
outfit."

I nearly tripped over my own feet, holding back a
laugh as others gave me a look.

Everywhere we went, Harper had blown everyone
over. They'd practically fallen at her feet, wanting to
make sure she was taken care of. Maybe I was one of
those peacock guys who wanted to puff out their
chest. And whenever somebody gave her a second
look, wanting a little more, I couldn't help but stake
my claim. Maybe it was a hand around the hip, my
palm at the back of her neck. But every single

fucking person I introduced her to knew she was mine.

I might be an old creep in his thirties when she was in her twenties, but I didn't fucking care. We were both adults, and we were both making our own decisions.

And I couldn't wait to taste her pussy as soon as we got back to the house.

"There you are."

I looked up quickly as my brother Theo strolled over, his hair disheveled, his beard longer than usual.

Theo usually wavered between looking completely clean cut, or as if he hadn't slept for days. It had to be a back-of-house chef thing, but the man never touched drugs, didn't really drink, and yet still sometimes looked like he was out on a bender.

That was just Theo.

"I didn't know you were going to be here," I said, but then nearly tripped as I was shoved away.

"Harper. My favorite." Theo pulled Harper into a hug, then picked her up and twirled her around.

"It's so good to see you!" Harper said with a laugh.

I narrowed my gaze. "If you could stop trying to break her that would be great."

"What? It's just Harper. I've missed my girl." He smacked a loud kiss on her cheek, and I hadn't even realized I had taken a step forward until my brother raised a brow.

"Well, well, well. It seems the rumors are true."

"You're a menace," Harper teased.

Theo just beamed. "I am. But I had to make sure that my big brother was doing okay. And ensure that the rumor of him kidnapping you was not too untoward."

"I was a willing victim don't worry," she teased.

"Keep laughing," I muttered as Theo's shoulders shook.

"It's good to see you out and about," he said, his voice getting serious.

I shrugged, not wanting to make a big deal of it. "Sorry we're not making it to your restaurant for dinner. We have these clubs and then breakfast at Aston's before we have to go back. Wellesley over here has a job she actually likes and can't miss too many days."

Theo smiled. "I do love your bakery."

"Are you doing okay though?" I asked.

Theo nodded. "Long hours, The Teal Door is kicking ass."

"And Luke?" I asked, speaking of his business partner and best friend.

Theo shrugged. "You know."

I didn't, but if Theo didn't want to mention what was going on with his best friend, I wasn't going to ask. At least not right now.

"Anyway, I'm joining you for breakfast tomorrow."

"Really?" Harper asked, clapping her hands together. "It's going to be so good to see all of you guys. I don't get to spend nearly enough time with the Cages."

"There's only one Cage that matters here," I grumbled.

"I like this look on you," Theo teased.

"Fuck off."

"No I don't believe I will."

My manager came up to me in that moment, her smile far too knowing. "Sorry to bother you, but we have a few things for you to look at. I know we can do them online, but if you're here, it just makes things easier."

Guilt swept up my spine. "I'm sorry. I should have come down more often."

She shook her head, hand up. "No, the fact that you've trusted me to do all of this for this long? It's the best thing you could have done. You honestly never need to step foot in here again. But it's good to see that you can." She winked at Harper, as I had introduced them beforehand.

"I'll make sure he doesn't overdo it either," Harper purred.

"I knew I loved her," Theo teased.

I was going to have to kill my brother later. It

would be sudden, swift, but he wouldn't even know until it was too late.

"I'll be right back," I said softly as I leaned down and brushed my lips along Harper's.

"I'll be here with Theo."

"Damn right she will be," Theo teased as he wrapped his arm around her shoulder.

"I'll deal with you later," I growled.

The two just laughed, and I followed my manager to the back.

"It's good to see you happy."

I shrugged. "I have been, other than the obvious."

"I'm not talking about the last year. If you never wanted to step foot in here again or talk to anyone after what happened, I wouldn't blame you. But you seem lighter now. I like this girl for you."

"You've known her for all of ten minutes."

"And I'm good at my job so I see things quickly. She's good for you."

"We're just, well, it's not what you think."

Her eyes widened, then that look of pity in her eyes stunned me. I turned and cursed.

"Harper," I whispered.

She held up her hand. "Well, that is my fault for overhearing." With that, she left the room, her shoulders tight. But I hadn't missed the look of hurt in her eyes.

I pinched the bridge of my nose, my hand shaking. "Fuck. That's not what I meant."

"You better figure out what you meant." Theo slapped my shoulder.

"I love her."

My brother's eyes widened. "Then maybe tell her that, and don't try to pretend that you're protecting her by lying about what you feel to others."

With that, I moved towards the door, only to be blocked by Theo. "Joshua's not here, so I'll kick your ass if I have to."

It was another kick to the solar plexus. "Let me through. I need to fix this."

"By fix this you better not mean breaking up with her. She's the best thing that's ever happened to you, and we both know it. Don't fuck this up."

I pushed past Theo, ignoring the ache in my leg as I made my way down the hall. At the end of the hallway there was a fork, one path went to the main building, the other to a balcony that was only for certain VIPs. It wasn't late enough yet for people to be out there, but I knew she was there. Everything about her drew me to her. And I was a fucking idiot.

I moved forward and tried to figure out what the hell I was going to say.

She stood there in the moonlight, her face lifting towards the sky. It was damn cold up here, the wind whipping at her since we weren't at the ground, and I cursed under my breath. I pulled off my suit coat and draped it over her shoulders. And she didn't push me away. I had to hope it was because she wanted me there, not because she was cold.

"Wellesley, that's not what I meant to say."

Her voice didn't shake but I couldn't tell what she was feeling in that moment. "What do you think this is then?"

"I don't know what it is, but I'm not walking away from it."

She turned and looked at me, confusion on her face. "You brought me here. And yet you're trying to hide it."

"No, I'm not."

"Okay. Then what did you mean to say?"

"That I don't know what the hell I'm feeling because I've never felt this before," I said quickly, and her eyes widened. "See? It's scaring me. Not because it's wrong, I know that. But because I don't know what the hell I'm supposed to do. So when people say that they're happy for me, I freak the fuck out. Because I don't know what I'm supposed to be thinking."

"Dorian."

I kissed her softly, taking her mouth as if she were everything to me. Because damn it, she was.

"I'm sorry. All I want to do is claim you in front of

the world, to make sure everyone knows you're mine, and then the other part of me is so damn afraid of what I'm supposed to do, that I just sit here, confused as hell. I didn't mean to hurt you."

"I know you didn't mean it. But it's still hurt nonetheless."

"I'm sorry, baby." I kissed her again, needing her taste.

"I'm sorry for overreacting and running out like the kid you think I am."

"Baby, I don't think of you as a kid. Seriously. You may be younger than me, I may call myself a creeper, but I know exactly who you are."

And that's what scared me. But in the end, she wrapped her arms around me, and I took her mouth and hoped to hell I didn't fuck this up again. I was falling for Harper Wellesley. No, that wasn't right. I'd already fallen for her.

I craved her more than air itself.

And I knew with one casual cruelty, I could break her.

And yet I knew she could break me just the same.

And how fucked up was that?

Chapter 13

HARPER

Taking a whirlwind long weekend to head to Denver with your newly called boyfriend wasn't something that I had really put much thought into until it had happened.

We had spent two nights wrapped in each other, with Dorian showing me his world. The big city of Denver, which wasn't like any other large cities I had been to. It had its own flavor, its own feel. And it was such a far distance from Cage Lake that it felt nearly insurmountable.

Because frankly, it wasn't just distance.

I pounded my hands into the dough again, working on my kneading. I had a seven-plate loaf to make, and then I'd work on rolls, and a few other baked goods before I got ready for the Valentine's Day dance tonight. Because of course, it was Valentine's week.

Cage Lake loved spreading the holiday out over an entire week. Yes it was good for the town's revenue and income, but really it was for the town's spirits. Yesterday had been the child's party and fair. I had baked far too many cookies and other baked goods that had been gobbled up by everybody in sight. My hands still hurt but it had been worth it to see the smiles on their faces.

Dorian had shown up to help, ignoring the town busybodies as they had stared at him, wondering why he was standing so close to me. It wasn't like we were hiding who we were. But there were some judgments.

After all, he was a Cage. A millionaire playboy with a tragic backstory who happened to have been best friends of my older brother.

Of course, the busybodies including Ms. Patty had opinions. Even my own team had opinions, but they were doing their best not to spill them my way. At least I hoped they were doing so.

I didn't want to hear what they thought. My friends were happy for me. I was happy. I just needed to lean into that.

But this past weekend reminded me that while tomorrow was the final day of this Valentine's break, today was Valentine's Day.

Today was the dance that all of the locals attended, well, most of them. I wasn't sure a Cage had ever come, though I thought Isabella might now that she was with Weston.

She hadn't come last year because she had been down in Denver setting up Weston's new business. The two had made their forevers work by having two places, and a very organized schedule.

Dorian's life was in Denver. No it wasn't that far away, but the hours added up. And when the weather was too icy or worse, the roads were closed... And even if the roads stayed closed but the weather turned sunny, Dorian himself had said he wasn't ready to get on an airplane or helicopter anytime soon. It cost money, and emotional energy, and so much more to make that work.

My business and my home were in Cage Lake. A town with his name branded on it. My hands cramped, and I forced myself to relax.

I was fine. I had to be okay. But what was I supposed to do?

We had both said something about our feelings. Though it wasn't exactly telling the other exactly how we felt. But he said he had never felt like this for anyone else. I knew Amy was the only other person he truly dated seriously. So whatever we had wasn't like that.

But what would happen when he went back to work fully? I had seen the happiness in his gaze when he had been working. And how everybody had looked up to him. Had respected him. He was damn good at his job, and I knew he wanted to open a few more places, and perhaps even work with his brother Theo on another project. He couldn't do things like that in Cage Lake. Sure he could open up any business he wanted here, but the type of places he worked with didn't fit in Cage Lake. Maybe something near the resort, but that would be a long shot.

His home wasn't here. But I was. What was I supposed to do?

No, the more I thought about that, the more my chest ached, and the more I was just begging for trouble.

We would figure it out eventually. We had to.

And then maybe he would tell me what else was wrong. Because there was something else on his mind. A reason he was working on that old house, a reason that he was hiding. We needed to talk it out but I was worried if we popped that bubble, everything would change, and he would realize that maybe the heat we had wouldn't be enough.

"I didn't know you were still here," Ms. Patty said as she waved from the back door.

I shook my head out of my thoughts and smiled over at her.

"I have a few things to settle before I get ready for the dance. You know you're not supposed to be back here, right?" I asked. Because while I loved Ms. Patty, I wasn't in the mood to get in trouble by having a random person back here. Yes Dorian helped out a bit, but his family owned the building, and I counted that as a cheat. Honestly, while I loved Ms. Patty, I didn't want her to ask too many questions. She knew far too much. Or thought she did.

"I was just on my way to the town hall to finish getting everything set up for the dance tonight. Your Mr. Cage will be there with you, right? The town's tongues are wagging, girl. I mean, catching a Cage? You are a legend."

The heat of my cheeks burned, and I shook my head. "I don't think it's called catching. Dorian's just Dorian." I shrugged, as I set the loaf out to prove. My team would finish up everything tonight, since I had started far too early to get everything set up. I wanted a little extra time to get ready for the dance, since I was going with a date for the first time. Though now I regretted getting up so early because I was exhausted. My lungs ached, and my hands shook. I needed to take better care of myself, but taking that time off to go with Dorian, and then coming back and catching up on all of our bonus orders, meant sleep and taking care of myself had taken a backseat. I would do that later. After the dance.

"Are you okay, darling? You look a bit pale."

"I'm fine. Just getting ready to close everything up. Was there something you needed, Ms. Patty?"

"I was just walking by and saw the door open. I know you keep it open even in winter sometimes to let the steam out. You're doing such a great job. Your brother would be proud of you. Your parents too." Her eyes filled, but her lips still pressed together in a thin line. She didn't know the exact story of my grandparents and why I had come back so different. But she could probably have guessed. After all, she had known and loved my parents. And had also known we hadn't had a relationship with my grandparents until it was too late.

These were the small town things that kept me on the fence. They were who I am. Because while she knew those things, I knew small tidbits about her. About her favorite pastry, or how she always started the pay-it-forward. No matter what she was feeling that day, she would make sure that someone else would be able to have a coffee or pastry even if they couldn't quite afford it. She might love gossip, but she loved people. And she was a good person.

What would I do in Denver? I loved this town.

But I loved Dorian too.

"Well, I hope I'll see you and your man tonight. It'll be good to have a Cage at the dance. God knows getting Hudson underneath those rafters is like pulling teeth."

That made me laugh. "I really don't think getting him to a dance is ever going to happen. We could probably drag him, but he's kind of strong."

"That he is. But all those Cages seem to be strong." She wiggled her brows, and I held back a laugh.

"I won't ask you for details, just know that I'm proud of you. For many things." She wiggled her brows again, and I couldn't help it. I threw my head back and laughed.

"You're a menace, Ms. Patty."

"So, Mr. Mayor tells me. Now you go get ready as soon as you can. Though you already look gorgeous. I should be annoyed with how beautiful you look covered in flour. But you've always been gorgeous, darling. And I don't know if you heard, but Isabella and Weston won't be able to make it tonight."

My face fell. "What?" I pulled out my phone, then held back a curse when I realized I just covered it in flour. Indeed, my group chat had exploded.

"Everything's fine, but they had a minor fender bender. And while Weston will fix it, it's better for them not to chance it with any possible icy roads tonight as a storm's coming in. So, that's one fewer Cage I'm going to see. They're safe though. I'm sure you'll be able to check your chat."

She said her goodbyes, and I quickly washed my hands, my phone, and then texted to make sure everybody was okay.

If something had truly happened, I knew Dorian would show up and tell me in person. That's what he did. He took care of me.

Of course, that just reminded me of Hudson walking into the bakery, showing up to tell me about the accident.

I let out a shuddering breath. Dorian was fine. He was healing.

And I would miss my brother until my dying days.

But wallowing to the point where I couldn't breathe only made my chest ache more. And considering how hard it was to breathe at this moment, I couldn't afford any other issues.

I quickly cleaned up and made sure my team was ready to close. We'd be closing in half an hour anyway, and all of the baked goods I had made were either for the party tonight, or sweet doughs that needed to prove overnight.

I loved the fact that the team members that I was slowly adding on could take more responsibilities, and maybe I didn't need to work sixty to eighty hours a week. I'd done so the past year so I wouldn't focus on the real world, but now I wanted as much time as I could have with Dorian.

Before he had to go back to his real world.

And my world crashed.

I shook myself out of that thought and quickly ran upstairs. Lucky was inside, as he had spent the morning at doggie daycare, and then the last couple of hours in the apartment.

"Okay, big boy, time to go for a walk, and then I'm leaving you for only a little while. I miss you already."

He gave me a look that told me he didn't quite believe me, but we went on his walk, while I once again ignored the pains in my chest. It was just a little too cold out, and I was overreacting about any twinges these days.

I showered quickly, fed Lucky, and then did my best to get ready as fast as possible. I was meeting the girls at the dance, and I was excited.

While Luna couldn't make it and now Isabella wouldn't be there, Scarlett and Ivy would be. And that meant the family I was slowly building would be together.

By the time I got ready, I still hadn't received a text from Dorian. He had told me he would meet me there since he had a few things to do, and I tried to ignore the disappointment. I was a big girl. I could drive myself. Heck, I could walk there if I wanted to. And maybe that's just what I would do. Because then he could drive us home after.

Well, to my home since Lucky was here. Because it wasn't like we lived together. It was far too early for that.

And his home wasn't in Cage Lake. Now I had to stop thinking about that.

Since it was Valentine's Day, I had gone full-on pink with a pale sheath dress that clung to my curves in just the right way. It was modest enough that Ms. Patty wouldn't cluck her tongue, but I still felt like a princess. I let my hair fall in waves and pulled on a short sparkly jacket to complete the look. I'd be warm underneath my parka for the walk, and the layers would help no matter what the temperature felt like at the dance.

I said goodbye to Lucky and promised I would see him in a couple hours. The dance would be fun, but I knew keeping Dorian there for too long would strain him. He was a people person, a party guy, but small town Valentine's dances weren't really his thing.

By the time I got there, the dance was already in full swing, and I searched for Dorian. I didn't find those familiar features, and I held back my frown.

He would show soon. He had promised.

"You're here!" Scarlett said as she moved forward. I hugged her tightly, and she winced.

"Are you okay?" I asked, alarmed.

She waved me off. "I'm fine. I worked out a little too hard yesterday, and now my muscles ache."

"I should probably work out, but that would require lifting things and I'm not in the mood," I teased.

"So says the woman who lifts flour and other random things all day," Ivy added dryly. "You're just fine, ma'am."

I laughed and gratefully took the pink punch Ivy handed over. "It's alcohol-free, since there is no alcohol at the Valentine's Day dance even for adults," she added.

"That's just fine. The overwhelming amount of sugar will help me crash later," I said with a laugh.

"So, well, I'm dateless by choice, but where are both of your men?" Ivy asked, her brow raised.

Scarlett shrugged. "Ronan is stuck in the city. The roads are closed. Stupid snow and stupid mountains." Scarlett took a sip of her punch, and I reached out and squeezed her hand.

"I'm sorry."

"It's okay. We knew it might be an issue. But Ronan had that big meeting, and well, we celebrated Valentine's Day last weekend. We don't need to make it a whole week like the town does," she added dryly.

"And where's Dorian?" Ivy asked. "He is coming,

isn't he? Unless he decided this is too ridiculous for him? Which, I sort of understand," she said softly.

Blushing, I shook my head. "He said he'd be here. I should probably text him now."

"Well, if he said he'd be here, he will be," Scarlett said, though I couldn't quite read the look in her eyes.

Frowning, I pulled out my phone, and texted one-handed.

Me: Hey! I'm at the dance. Are you on your way?

I waited for those three little dots to tell me he was texting back, but nothing.

"He must be on the road." I ignored Scarlet's look and put my phone in my purse.

"What do you say we dance?" I asked, as I set my empty punch glass on the table.

"The three of us with a slow dance?" Ivy asked. "I'm totally in. Those busybodies over there are already gossiping about the fact that I didn't come with a date, and they're wondering where yours are."

"You heard them all the way over here?" Scarlett asked.

"I heard them as I was walking here, so now let's make a scene."

I rolled my eyes even though I still kept watch for Dorian. He was late. He was usually never late. Maybe something had come up, but why wouldn't he have texted?

I ended up slow dancing with Scarlett as Ivy danced behind me, and I ignored the way that some people tsk'ed at us. Others cheered, before suddenly the slow dancing turned into a pile of people laughing against one another, trading partners every third step.

Most of us had known each other since we were kids, and some were old enough to be my grandparents. It was just a fun time, full of happiness and joy and town pride.

And Dorian was nearly an hour late.

I ignored the disappointment until someone touched my hip. Whirling, ready to punch out, Dorian slid his hand over my fist.

"Sorry I'm late. The bridge is out," he whispered.

There's a small bridge at the end of his current property, one that had needed to be replaced years ago.

My eyes widened. "Are you okay?"

"I'm fine. I had to take the long way around though, and there's no service on the north side of the lake thanks to the lovely storm coming in. I'm sorry I'm late, baby. I didn't mean to be late." We stood in the center of the dance floor as couples rolled around us, and I wrapped my arms around his shoulders.

"I was going to have to come find you and kick your ass."

"I'll let you do that anytime you want." Then his

lips were on mine, his arms around my waist, and I sighed into him.

"This is a public place, Harper Wellesley!" one of Ms. Patty's friends called out, and I ignored her.

"Well, looks like I'm going to have to really show them what we can do in public," he said, his voice low.

I shivered, pressing my thighs together. "Do you really want us to get arrested?"

"I'm a Cage. It's my town. Why not?"

I threw my head back and laughed and then let him twirl me around the dance floor. The music flowed, the tempo increasing as everybody enjoyed themselves, laughing and dancing, and I ignored the odd looks they gave the two of us.

Yes, there was an age gap. Yes, this was new. But why was everyone acting like Dorian was a creeper, like a lecher?

But Dorian didn't look like it was bothering him so I wouldn't let it bother me.

We took a step off the dance floor, my chest heaving from that final two-step.

"Are you okay? You're all flushed." Dorian put his hand to my cheek and frowned.

"But your skin's ice cold."

"I'm fine," I rasped as dark circles began to flutter over my eyes. "I just need some water." At least I tried to say that, but the words wouldn't come out. Instead dizziness took over, and my lungs seized.

I clutched at my chest, trying to breathe, and Dorian reached for me, calling my name.

I tried to say something, anything, but there was nothing, only an aching of breath, and Dorian holding me, and darkness.

"PNEUMONIA? I WAS FINE. I DIDN'T EVEN HAVE A cough."

"You know you have issues with your lungs, and apparently your lovely bout of walking pneumonia was literal this time," Dorian growled out.

I had only passed out for maybe a second, but the fear on Dorian's face had nearly sent me over the edge. The music had ground to a halt, and Dorian had picked me up in one swoop and rushed me to his truck. The girls had followed me in their car, and I knew Ms. Patty was already calling ahead to make sure that the clinic was ready for me.

We didn't have a large hospital in Cage Lake, but the clinic was big enough to handle emergencies. Any surgeries though, had to be medevacked out.

I was hooked up to oxygen, and an IV, and would

be staying overnight until my levels were back to where they needed to be.

"This isn't the first time it's happened, and it won't be the last." I looked down at my fingers and forced myself to untangle them. "It's because of getting sick when I was younger. Sometimes I don't notice when I've overdone it."

"I should have noticed though," Dorian growled. "You could have been hurt far worse."

I shifted onto the bed and patted beside me. "Will you sit here?"

"I'll crush you," he said softly.

"You won't. I just want to cuddle. Please?" I was pleading, and he narrowed his gaze at me, but he lowered the railing and settled in. I sank into his warmth, finally breathing for the first time.

"You passing out like that nearly took ten years off my life. Probably more." He kissed the top of my head, and I nestled into his side. Thankfully, it was on his non-burned side, but I had a feeling even if it wasn't, Dorian wouldn't have cared. I would have though. I would do anything not to hurt him.

"I always try to take care of myself, but I guess I hadn't really paid attention to exactly how many times I'd had to catch my breath."

"Wellesley," he growled out.

"I know. I know. I'll do better. I just sometimes forget."

"Does anyone else know that you deal with this sometimes?" he asked softly.

I shook my head. "No. I don't want people to think I'm weak." There, I said it out loud.

"I don't think anybody who knows you would ever think that, Harper Wellesley. But you should tell your friends. So they can be on the lookout. Because we both know that you don't take care of yourself the way you should."

I pinched his hip softly. "You don't do the same."

"I'm learning. Because you're making me."

I looked up at him then and kissed his chin. "Then I guess you'll have to make me."

"You don't have to keep what happened to you as a child a secret from your best friends. Or at least you don't have to keep the consequences of that a secret. Okay? I don't want you to ever feel like you have to hide things from me. And I want others to keep an eye out on you too."

There was so much to unpack from that, so I just leaned into him a little more and let out a breath. "Sometimes I feel like I tell you all my secrets, but I don't know any of yours."

It must have been the meds making me say that,

because I shouldn't have said that aloud. We were just finding our equilibrium, and I wasn't owed any of his.

But Dorian's arms tightened around me, and he let out a breath. "I can tell you one. One that nobody else knows."

I froze, my hold tightening once more. "You can trust me," I whispered.

"I trust you with everything, Wellesley."

And then he let out a breath and told me exactly why he was avoiding his family.

And everything changed.

Chapter 14

DORIAN

Mom: You can't continue to push me out of your life. I'm your mother.

Mom: If you continue to act like this, I will have to change your mind.

Mom: The more you act like that man, the more you do resemble a Cage.

Mom: If you don't call me back, I will tell them the truth about who you are.

Mom: How could you stay in that house? You know what that house means.

Mom: I'm going to tell them.

Me: Tell them all you want. You're the one who will end up hurt more than me.

I ran my hands over my face, then tossed my phone onto the bed.

Why had I even replied back to her? Just feeding into my mother's narcissistic personality would be the end of it.

"Are you okay?" Harper asked as she walked out of the bedroom, squeezing the water out of her hair with a towel. I swallowed hard and just stared at her.

I loved watching her move, watching her walk. And frankly, at this point, I loved watching her breathe because a week ago she had scared the shit out of me.

She'd stayed overnight for observation, and we came back to her apartment. Lucky lay on the small armchair in the corner, watching her every move as well. He had been just as scared as I had been after we'd come home, and he'd watched Harper like the guard dog he was.

Since I was close enough to him, I reached out and ran my fingers through his fur. He bumped my hand for deeper pets, and I just smiled.

"I'm fine. Just glaring at my phone."

Her gaze went to the middle of the bed where the phone lay, and she turned back to me. "Your siblings or your mother?" she asked, and I held back a snort.

"I suppose it could be anyone at this point," I said drily.

"While I know why you're avoiding all of them, there's really only one that I wish you would avoid for the rest of time."

I moved forward then and slid my hands through her wet hair. Lucky let out a whimper, and I knew he was jealous I was now petting my girlfriend, but he would get over it.

"I don't plan on texting my mother back again. But yes, that was her."

Harper grimaced. "What did she say this time?"

"The usual bullshit. How I owe her." I paused. "And how she's going to tell my siblings the truth."

I hadn't known if I wanted to even say that out loud. Because there were probably only three people in this world who knew the truth. Maybe more if I thought about lawyers and other people good at keeping secrets, but in reality, it was just the three. And two of them were in this room.

"She wouldn't. She can't be that stupid."

I threw my head back and laughed. "Oh. She would be. To get me to do what she wants? She'll act the idiot."

"How is her ruining her own reputation—albeit whatever it is—going to help? All it does is hurt the both of you. Not that I think your family is really going to react in a way that will harm you."

"I don't know how they're going to react."

My phone buzzed again, and Harper pushed past me to pick it up.

"If it's my mother, just throw the phone out the window. I'll get a new one."

"It's Aston. I didn't read the text though. I'm not that into your privacy."

"I don't have any more secrets from you, Wellesley." And wasn't that a strange thought. Somehow Harper Wellesley had become the center of my universe. The person I shared everything with. It should scare me. It should terrify me, and while a part of me agreed and went down that path, the other part not so much. It felt as if that was what was right. What was needed.

Maybe I was just losing my damn mind.

"What did Aston say?" I asked.

Harper gave me a look and then plugged in my passcode, because of course she knew it now, to see.

"He says to call him back and stop hiding. Because they're wondering why you keep acting so grumpy since you're finally with a woman that can make you happy."

Her cheeks pinked and she looked up at me.

"Maybe I should read all of your texts if they're going to be that helpful."

Scowling, I took the phone from her.

"I'm not being grumpy."

"Says Mr. Grumperson."

"Is that what we're going to put on my stocking?"

"Yes. Though getting all those letters onto one part might be an issue. I'm not that crafty but I bet if I asked Ms. Patty she'd do it."

I rolled my eyes. "Yes. Because asking Ms. Patty to make a unique stocking for me for next Christmas won't invite any speculation on her part at all."

Harper just grinned, which was exactly what I wanted her to do. "They sure want to know exactly what's happening in this apartment, don't they?"

"I can feel them lurking beneath the boards."

"That's my team working, but sure."

I moved forward, cupping her face. "You don't have a fireplace up here. Do you even have a stocking?"

"I do, though I didn't really celebrate Christmas this year."

I winced, vaguely remembering the holiday myself. I'd been at Aston's, and the rest of the Cages had taken their turns. Trying to blend so many new traditions with different families wasn't easy. And I had been more standoffish than usual for good reason.

But the fact that Harper had spent it alone gutted me.

"I'm sorry I didn't reach out. I should have."

"I had dinner with Scarlett and Luna. Ivy was out of town. I wasn't alone." Harper smiled softly. "You're never really alone in Cage Lake."

Her home. That wasn't mine.

We were both steadfastly ignoring the fact that I didn't live in Cage Lake. I might be staying there for a time, but I did have responsibilities back home. From the way that her eyes darkened for just a moment, I wondered if she was thinking the same.

My phone buzzed again, and I sighed, looking at the family group chat blowing up.

They were all worried about me. Wondering why I was still in Cage Lake. Finally asking why I was fixing up that house. But I didn't answer. I was just so tired.

"You can put your phone on silent for now, but you do realize he'll just show up."

"Yes, but I need more time."

She cupped my face and kissed me softly. "Okay. More time it is."

I let my phone fall to the blanket and pressed my lips to hers. "I think I know what we could do to pass that time."

She smiled against my lips. "Oh?"

"Oh."

I crushed my mouth to hers, moaning into her. She ran her hands up my back, as we both moved into one another. Harper's nails dug into my back, and I slowly explored her mouth, taking everything in.

She tasted of mint and hot cocoa.

Lucky made a noise and moved out of the bedroom.

"I think we have officially scarred that dog," I said dryly.

"Oh no, we did that last night when you had me bent over the chair, and he came walking in to see what was going on."

"What? It was doggy style. He must have seen it before," I said so innocently that she just rolled her eyes.

"You have your hand on my tit and I want your dick in me right now, and you're making doggy style jokes?"

Said dick pressed against the seam of my pants. "Yes."

"Well okay," she teased, before she pulled off her T-shirt.

She had just showered, and now I was going to dirty her all up. And, because there was a God, she hadn't worn a bra. Her breasts were heavy, her nipples tight pink points that begged for my mouth. I leaned forward, licked at one, as my fingers played with the other.

"Dorian," she panted.

"Do you want my mouth on your nipples? Or on your pussy?"

"Do I have to choose?" she asked, shifting against me.

I just smiled before paying delicate attention to each

breast. Her tits overfilled my hands, and I had big hands. I was one lucky man.

I shoved down her sweats and groaned. "You're not wearing panties either?"

"I didn't feel like it."

"Don't sound all innocent. There's nothing innocent about you," I growled.

"You're the one that deflowered me," she sing-songed.

In answer, I lifted her by her thighs and tossed her on the bed.

She gasped, laughing, as I threw myself on top of her. She spread her legs, cradling me, as I licked up and down her neck, her jaw, down her breasts.

"I really want to fuck these," I mumbled.

"Would that feel good?"

I groaned. "I love teaching you all the new things."

She just grinned, and I continued to lick down her body. When I pinned her thighs wide and lapped at her cunt, she tried to shoot off the bed but couldn't.

"Play with your tits, I want those nipples hard and waiting for my mouth. I need to explore this beautiful pussy."

I sucked at her labia, then speared her with two fingers. When she groaned, I ran my thumb in circles over her clit. She came in a burst, gushing over my hand as I sucked and licked every ounce of her. "Sweet and tart. Like my personal drug."

She blushed from head to toe, and I just continued to eat her out, loving the way that she was still so new at this, so sweet. And so eager to learn.

I stood up, tossed off my shirt, and pulled down my pants and boxer briefs.

"Sit at the edge of the bed."

"Wow, I didn't know you were in the mood to order me around."

"Wellesley," I growled, and she shivered before scooting to the edge of the bed.

"Like this?"

I nodded and tapped her thigh. "Spread yourself for me. I want you wet and dripping by the time you're done." Eyes wide she did as I said, and I slid two fingers between her folds. "So swollen. It's going to be aching for my cock soon."

"So what are you going to do with my cock," she asked as she reached forward and gripped the base of me.

I groaned, head falling back. "I have plans for you."

She leaned forward slightly, and I took control, wrapping her hair with one fist and stopping her. Then I tapped her bottom lip with the tip of my cock, and her eyes widened.

"Soon. Lean back."

She frowned. "I don't get to taste you?"

"Eager much?"

"Of course."

I just grinned but pulled at her hair slightly so she would lean back.

"Now I want you to lift your breasts up and press them together. Present yourself to me."

"Oh." Her eyes wide, she did as she was told.

"So fucking hot."

I put my hand to her chin. "Spit."

Without even a second thought, she spit into my palm, and I held myself back, gripping the base of my cock. I was going to come, and it was going to be an issue. I rubbed my palm up and down my length, then spit down on my dick for good measure. Before she could say anything, I slid my cock in between her breasts, settling it over her heart.

"So warm, protective. Your tits are something else."

"Why was that the hottest thing I've ever seen?" She panted.

"Just wait."

Then I slid back, before continuing to move, fucking her breasts.

Her teeth bit into her swollen lips, as she continued to press her breasts tightly against my cock. The friction was nearly too much, but I didn't care. Instead I kept moving, loving the feel, and the way that she bounced on the bed for me.

"I'm going to come," I growled and pulled back. In answer, she arched her back, pressed her breasts together, and I came, spurting all over those luscious tits.

"So fucking beautiful," I whispered. I slid my hand around the back of her neck, gripping her throat, before I crushed my mouth to hers. Then I used my hand to rub myself into her chest, leaving her a sticky mess.

"I just showered," she teased.

"It's okay, I'll clean you up."

I moved her back onto the middle of the bed, before twisting her so she was on her hands and knees.

"Dorian!"

"I need to take care of this pussy of mine while I get ready for round two," I groaned, as I spread her cheeks and lapped at her core. She pushed her ass to my face, and I continued to lick and suck until I was ready again.

"I'm going to fuck this pussy, and you're going to call my name. Are you ready?"

"Always."

I pressed the tip of my dick to her, and then leaned down, slowly, oh so slowly, sliding balls deep inside her.

She was so tight, so wet, that I had to count to ten before I moved out again.

"Dorian. I'm so full. You're just...to say the obvious...big."

"You say the hottest fucking things."

"I have your cum all over me, so you better make me come. It gets kind of gross after a while."

I threw my head back and laughed, gripped her hips, and then slammed home.

It was hard and fast and raw, and I didn't care. We rode each other, thrust for thrust as I slammed into her. And when she came again, I pulled out of her, ignoring her whimper.

"Don't worry, you're going to ride me."

I positioned myself so I was at the edge of the bed, feet planted. She straddled me, and as our eyes met, I lowered her down over my cock.

"Dorian."

"You're so tight at this angle, baby. Are you ready for me?"

Her gaze met mine. "I'm ready for anything."

Grinning, I tipped her hips as she rocked on me, and she set the pace. In this position she could fall if I didn't hold her, so I wasn't going to fucking let her go. Instead I played with her breasts, loving the way she had my mark all over that beautiful body of hers. And when I slid my thumb over her clit, she came again, her pussy fluttering over my cock. I pulled her forward, hand on the back of throat, as I kissed her, moving fast as I pounded into her from below. And when I came, filling her, we both groaned, shaking.

"That was, that was…" She didn't finish her sentence though. Instead she sat on my lap, hand on her chest, as she fought for breath.

Everything from the past few moments vanished from my mind as ice slid over me.

"Wellesley? Fuck. Did I hurt you?" I slid out of her and cradled her to me. "Baby. What's wrong?"

"I'm just catching my breath. I'm fine."

But then I saw them, the bruises on her hips, the slight red marks on her throat. The fact that it was taking her far too long to catch her breath. I had done all that.

"I hurt you. Fuck. I was too rough. You were a damn virgin, and I hurt you. I treated you so fucking rough I marked you." I set her down on the bed and scrambled up, looking for my jeans.

"Don't you dare leave. And don't you dare call what we were just doing anything as cheap or not what we wanted."

I whirled, jeans in hand as I stared at her. "I hurt you."

"And my scratch marks are on your back. What the fuck, Dorian? Yes, I was a virgin, but both of us were in this bed just now. We both came multiple times. Sure it took me a moment to catch my breath, but I'm healthy again. I'm cleared for sex, and we had sex yesterday. Stop freaking out." She walked towards me, her breasts bouncing and sticky, and I dropped the jeans. I just pulled her to my body, rubbing my cheek on the top of her head. She clung to me, shaking.

"I'm a fucking bastard."

"Maybe. But you need to stop freaking out every time that I need to catch my breath, or you realize that both of us like it rough."

My heartbeat finally began to slow but I couldn't let her go. She was my ending, my beginning, my sin, and my salvation. "Sometimes it just hits me that you're *Wellesley*, you know?"

"Somehow that made sense. But I'm going to need you to stop reacting that way. Because it's starting to hurt."

"Fuck. I'm sorry." I leaned down and captured her lips as I held her close.

I was in love with Harper Wellesley. And I was a bastard. And I had to stop finding ways to hurt her so she would push me away. Because I had a feeling as soon as I told the others the truth, she would be the only one left. And I had no idea what the hell I was supposed to do with that.

Chapter 15

DORIAN

Harper had been correct.

Only it had taken three days for my entire family to show up.

In those three days, I had barely seen her. She had multiple events at work, and I was later going to be forced to attend the St. Patrick's Day prep event. I didn't even know that Cage Lake did things like a St. Patrick's Day party.

I was pretty sure I had never been there in the month of March. But the whole town was treating me like I would always be there.

I ran my hand over my chest. I'd have to figure out exactly what I was going to do soon, because I wasn't letting Harper go.

In those three days, I had come back to the house

rather than stay at Harper's apartment and now Lucky and I were working on the staircase.

"A hammer no, that's a wrench. I need a hammer."

Lucky just tilted his head, expressive eyebrows saying far more than a bark could.

"Yes, I know I could reach it myself, but I thought we were learning something. We're creating a bond."

Again. A tilt of a head. This time I felt judgement.

"I'm sorry you saw me naked before, it was an accident. We'll make sure you're safe in the other room from now on."

"Can you make this promise to all of your siblings?" a familiar voice said from a distance.

I froze, wondering why I was surprised he was here. Ford came around the side of the house. The sleeves of his Henley pushed up even though it was getting damn cold with the storm rolling in later that evening.

Then again, knowing how Cage Lake weather worked, the storm could wait a couple of days. It's just what it did.

My youngest brother, or at least the youngest brother I had grown up with, moved closer and leaned against the side of the house.

"You don't call, you don't write, you don't answer the damn doorbell," Ford muttered.

"Shouldn't you be with your husband and pregnant wife?" I asked.

At that, Ford's smile grew wide and his entire expression brightened. "I have sonogram photos. Do you want to see?" Lucky moved past me to Ford and my brother leaned down, running his hands up and down Lucky's body. "I'll show you, not Mr. Grumpy Gus."

"Why do people call me grumpy? I thought that was Hudson."

"You are out grumping me. That's got to say something," Hudson snarled as he walked around the house.

I sighed as nearly all of my brothers came forward. The only one not here was Kyler, but from what I remembered of his schedule, since I was keeping up with him on social media, he was in New York right now.

I looked over at my six brothers and frowned. "You leave the girls at home?" I asked, wondering why it felt like we were missing so many siblings.

It wasn't as if we had all grown up together. It hadn't been that long since I'd even found out that Isabella, Sophia, Kyler, Emily, and Phoebe existed. And yet not having them here when there were so many of us felt off—like we were hiding something. At least one good thing had come from Loren Cage's infidelity and the other Cage mom's secrets. We'd made our own family. Even if sometimes I didn't feel like I could be part of it or even that I *should* be part of it.

"They'll be along soon." Aston said as he studied me. "Kyler would've been here as well, but he has a sold out show tonight." A small smile played over his face. "When he and his band come to Red Rocks, I've made sure to get us the space we need to attend."

My lips twitched. Of course he did. He was the big brother who always fixed things, but I didn't think he was going to be able to fix this.

"How is your leg doing?" Flynn asked softly, and it surprised me. He wasn't as bouncy as usual, but maybe again, none of us were acting the way we were supposed to these days.

I shrugged. "Better than before I did my physical therapy, and working on the house here has helped."

"And you're not doing a piss poor job of it," Hudson said.

I stared between the two and wondered when they had decided to be the exact opposite of twins. Flynn's hair was getting slightly longer, but Hudson's was down to his shoulders. Flynn also tended to shave, but he'd let his beard grow slightly.

My lips curled. "Thank you, I live to serve."

James cleared his throat. "I hear that you've been saying something like that to a certain Ms. Wellesley."

"If you're going to dig into my personal life, I'm going to need a beer." I stomped off, Lucky at my side.

"Even the dog loves him more, that's the Dorian I know," Theo teased.

I sighed and let the familiar sound of my brothers piling in after me fill my ears. When we had been kids, we'd been together always. Yes, I had Joshua, and each of my siblings had had their own best friends. Hell, Ford even married his best friend, but we were a tight crew as Cages. No matter that our parents tried to split us apart.

Hell, my mom loved me but hated Flynn and now Aston. My dad could barely stand me but also hated Hudson. It never made any sense to me, and it wasn't like we told each other those things. Maybe that was the problem. Maybe it was time to just tell them.

Theo leaned forward. "Oh, the good stuff. I love Ashford Brews."

It wasn't a local company, but still a small town around here. It was damn good, and we had a family connection through Phoebe and Ford in the careless way of family trees.

"So... do you want to tell us what the hell's going on with you?" Hudson asked, staring at me.

"Since when did you get so chatty?" My jaw clenched and it took all within me to force myself to relax.

"Since you stopped speaking to us," James whispered. "I know that you went through an unimaginable hell. I can't even begin to imagine."

"No, you can't. None of you can," I snapped.

"No, we really can't," Flynn said softly, "but we've giving you time to try to figure out what the hell you want. Or even just to heal. But maybe we gave you too much space."

"Like enough rope to hang myself?" I asked.

Theo's eyes widened. "Don't even joke like that."

I held my hands up, my beer dangling from my left. "I'm not going to hurt myself. It's not like that. I promise." I'd already lost my best friend, and I wasn't about to hurt anyone else in my life by going in a direction that would be the end. That, at least, I knew for sure.

"You know the reason we're here is because we're worried about you," Aston said in that deep fatherly voice he had learned over time.

Maybe it was because he had been more of a father even with such a small age gap between us than our own father. *Father.* What a word. It didn't mean much. Especially to me.

Aston continued. "I have been truly worried for a while now. How I could help you, how we were failing you."

I swallowed hard. I knew I'd been caught up in my own mess, my own healing, but I hadn't realized how hard I'd been on everyone else even if they'd been quiet about it. "You weren't failing me. You gave me a place to stay. My house had too many stairs and you let me growl and be mean at your place."

"And you still ran away here." Aston met my gaze, and it took all within me not to flinch.

"And why here?" Hudson asked suddenly. "Why this place? The piece of land that we didn't even know about until you said you were staying here. It's between two pieces of Cage family land, part of the main trust, but it's a different slice. So what the hell?"

"You don't need to tell us everything, but we're here for you," Ford said. "We've all kept our secrets, sometimes for good reason, but we're worried."

"I was far more worried before," Aston added. "Until I saw you with Harper."

"Yeah?" I asked, my voice biting.

Aston just raised his brows. "She might be too young for you, but what do I know? She makes you happy."

I snorted. "You're going to pull the age card?"

"Blakely and I don't have that much of an age gap," Aston said with a shrug. "And frankly, you don't have one either. Not in the way you're thinking. You two fit. I have no idea how you're going to make it work once you're ready to head back to the city, and I know you've been thinking about that."

"I'll figure it out," I put in quickly.

"I hope so. Because like I said, I'll kick your ass if I have to," Theo put in, his gaze on mine.

"I'm not going to hurt Harper. I love her." I pressed my lips together, annoyed with myself for even saying the words out loud. I hadn't even said them to her.

"Damn," Flynn said, sounding like his old self before he whistled through his teeth. "Each Cage is falling quickly. Surprising."

"Of course you love her," Hudson said. He rolled his eyes and took a sip of his beer. "Everyone in Cage Lake knows it."

"Is there a small town paper that tells everyone these things?" James asked, looking intrigued.

"Yes, but you just need to ask Ms. Patty and she'll let you know everything," I added dryly.

That made the others laugh since we all knew of Ms. Patty, even if we hadn't lived here full-time.

"Why this house, Dorian? Why did Dad leave it to you?" Hudson being Hudson pressed once the laughter died down. He was like a dog with a bone. That should have annoyed me since the man kept his secrets close to the vest...but I was too tired to anymore.

I swallowed hard before chugging the rest of my beer. "Dad left it to me because I kept his secrets while he kept mine."

Nobody said a thing and I knew they were letting

me breathe. Finally. "Dad had more than one mistress, not just Constance. He slept with dozens of women all over the world. I don't know how he found the time, but he did."

"He was always a bastard," Flynn growled.

"Completely. But this is one of the places that he would meet women. Usually from the resort. He'd pick them up, bring them here. Then one day Joshua and I came out to play in the small creek in the back. It was between two Cage houses, so we just walked over the land like we owned it." I snorted. "I just didn't realize that Dad *did* own it."

"He made you keep that a secret?" James asked and shook his head. "What exactly did you walk in on?"

"They were in the yard fucking against a tree. Because that's exactly the image I wanted to see." Bile coated my tongue, and I went for another beer. "Fucking against the tree out in the open and Joshua and I just walked past. I thought he would kill me. He looked so damn angry, that vein on the side of his neck bulging. He pulled up his pants and I was so startled, I was like a deer in headlights. And when he caught me by the neck and shoved me into another tree, I just laid there. Joshua had run off because he thought I was right behind him. He eventually came back, but thankfully Dad didn't hear him. I met his gaze and tried to tell him not to do anything because it was just Dad."

"If he wasn't dead, I'd kill him again," Aston snapped.

"You'd have to take a number," Hudson said so coolly that right in that moment, I knew Hudson would kill a man if he had to. Maybe he already had.

I swallowed hard, trying not to relive the fear that had slammed into me when I'd been younger. "He threatened me, said he'd beat me and take my money, that I wasn't allowed to tell anyone."

"But Mom already knew about the cheating. Was it because of a scandal?" Flint asked, sounding utterly confused.

"Later I learned that Mom knew about one mistress, not the rest, and that would've endangered the company. They didn't have a prenup," I said.

"Are you fucking kidding me?" Aston snapped. "There was paperwork for Mom."

I shook my head. "There was the postnup, which is apparently a thing, and that's what the lawyers confused us with. The postnup is what allowed Dad to keep a mistress and keep the secrets. And why Mom is so fucking annoyed with the way that the trust is set up now, about how we have to have dinners and shit once a month, because hers is all twisted up in that. I'm so glad I'm not a lawyer."

"Damn straight," Flint growled.

"I'm so sorry he threatened you," Aston said as he moved forward, but I stiffened. "What else?"

I met their gazes and swallowed hard. "I would've found a way to tell you guys, but you used to suck at keeping secrets. But then he told me something else." They didn't say a thing, and Lucky leaned against my leg. I ran my hand over his head, taking comfort from the love of Harper's life. "He told me that he wasn't the only cheater. That Mom cheated too." I looked up at each one of my brothers and met their similar gazes. "Mom cheated just like Dad did, and I was the result." For a moment it was so silent you could hear a pin drop and then everyone roared at once.

"What the fuck?"

"She has to be lying."

"You look like us."

Countless things were thrown at me, and I just set down my beer and rubbed my temple. "I have the DNA test. I'm not a fucking Cage. Yes, Loren Cage is on my birth certificate, but I have no idea who the hell my biological father is."

"So that's why Mom acts the way she does," Hudson snarled, letting out a breath "Because you're the one she feels isn't touched by Loren."

I nodded. "It's sick, twisted, but that's it. I'm not

even a Cage. The other Cages? The girls and Kyler? We don't share any blood. That's the bombshell. I'm a half of a half at that point. However the math works for it. I'm not a Cage. After all this, I'm not a fucking Cage."

I tried to move past Aston, but instead he gripped my shoulder and glared at me. "Stop it right there. We are not Loren Cages. He can go fuck himself. The only reason that we even started doing these dinners was to save the company and this town. Not to deal with whatever megalomaniacal issues that man dealt with. But we are all family, all of us. The girls and Kyler? They're not our halves. They are siblings just like you. Fuck whatever the others say."

"I'm just going to let Aston continue this, because yes," Flynn said, throwing up his hands.

"Why the fuck are you keeping up with this house then?" Ford asked, his voice low.

"Because I need to fix something. Everything's just breaking down around me. And I don't know, I thought maybe if I fix this, it would all just go away, and I wouldn't have to worry about the fact that I'm not even related to the girls and Kyler."

"You're our brother, that's who you are. Fuck genetics." Hudson shrugged as we all stared at him. "Fuck it. I'm twins with this asshole over here, but I act more like James and Ford than anyone," Hudson added after he pointed towards Flynn.

"We're all different and we all look very similar," James put in.

"But I'm not even Loren Cage's son."

"Maybe you're better off," Theo said dryly. That made me laugh and the others joined.

Finally, I let out a breath and continued. "I don't want the rest of the world to know. I mean, your significant others, and the other siblings. Wellesley knows."

"Of course she does," Aston said, his lips twitching.

I flipped him off. "The will has my name, and not anything about genetics or anything like that. So it's not going to affect the town or anything, right?" I asked my voice soft.

"If it does, we'll figure it out together," Aston said. "But please refrain from keeping big secrets from us and stop working on this damn house."

Hudson shook his head. "Fixing it up after so much neglect isn't going to make Dad a better person. He's still dead, gone and buried, and he will always have a legacy of being an asshole."

"Cheers to that," Flynn said as he held up his beer bottle to his twin. I did the same. I held up mine, and we each toasted to the fact that my father was the worst of the worst.

"I already cut Mother out, by the way." Aston shrugged. "I won't bring this up with her. Not unless you want us to, but I don't know what the hell's going on with her."

"She's losing it for sure," Hudson added.

James cleared his throat. "We'll have to deal with her at some point."

I shrugged. "But I'm done. I'm done pretending that I can deal with being her so-called favorite."

"Well, she's an asshole too," Flynn said as he held up his beer once more.

We all toasted to that. And I sat down on one of the couches in the far too big cabin that was once the Ackerson place and that I knew I would never be able to fix up and hung out with my brothers. And when each of the sisters showed, surprising me, I laid down, drank another beer, and told them all about another Cage family secret.

I had kept it to myself for so long that it felt weird to be open about it. But as I looked at the people surrounding me, Aston and the others were right. I might not carry the same blood as everyone in this room, but these were my family members.

This was my family.

Lucky perked up and moved his way to the door.

As Harper walked in, her gaze bright, I stood up

and moved towards her, ignoring the cheers and cat calls as I did so. And when I pressed my lips to hers, I knew I wasn't alone. That my family was right behind me, and in my arms. I just needed to figure out exactly what to do about that.

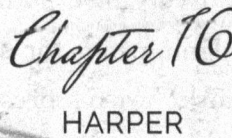

Chapter 16

HARPER

"The wind is sure picking up out there," Dorian said as he looked out the darkened window. We hadn't bothered to pull down the blinds, since the moonlight was the only thing that really showcased how glaring the snow was. He reached out at that moment and flipped on a switch, so the outdoor light illuminated everything we could have missed, and now we could see the snow coming down hard.

I wrapped my arms around him, pressing my cheek between his shoulder blades.

"I should take Lucky out before the storm gets any worse."

Dorian patted my hands and leaned back.

"I can do it. It's too cold out there for you."

I rolled my eyes. "I've lived in the mountains for longer than you. I can handle it."

He turned then, but I still kept my arms wrapped around his waist. Then he pushed my hair back from my face and smiled. Ever since he had told his family what had been burdening him for so long, he looked lighter. As if the world wasn't pressing down on his shoulders.

"Yes, you can do it. And I trust you to know your own lungs, but I don't mind. I could use some fresh air."

"Is everything okay?"

He leaned down and kissed the tip of my nose. "It is. I'm just wondering why I'm here."

I froze, everything in me shaking. But I tried to act as if I wasn't falling apart inside.

This was it. This is when he said he was having fun, but it was time. He was no longer needing to hide from his family anymore. He was finally figuring out what he needed in life. And living in Cage Lake with a bakery owner, and who only rented a tiny apartment with her giant dog, wouldn't be part of that.

I should have known it would be coming. Yes, he liked me. Yes, we were having a good time. But this wasn't forever. He would realize exactly what he wanted, and I would have to deal.

"I wish I knew what was going on in that mind of

yours. Because your eyes are so expressive right now. Like Lucky's."

I narrowed my gaze. "My eyebrows are nowhere near as expressive at Lucky's, thank you very much."

Lucky took that time to bark, and I nodded, as if my dog had just stood at my side.

"Fine, Lucky wins. But I'd love to know what you're thinking."

I put on a bright smile and shook my head. "Nothing. Why don't you take him out, I'll make some hot cocoa."

"Are you going to add the Bailey's this time?"

"Of course. We have that caramel Bailey's now."

"Why is that stuff so good?" he asked as he went to slide on his shoes.

"Because it's full of sugar?" I asked, laughing.

"That is true. But I'd love a hot cocoa. And I'll take care of Lucky. Don't worry."

"I won't," I whispered.

The house rattled, the wind coming harder. I frowned, hoping that the power would stay on. My apartment did well during storms, as the place was older and well insulated. And I knew Dorian's house on the lake would be the same.

The large broken-down Ackerson place that was slightly larger than a grand cabin probably wasn't the best place to ride out the storm. Not to mention the emotional toll that it had over him. But we'd wanted the space away from the rest of town for the night, but I had a feeling it was the wrong decision.

"I swear the temperature dropped like twenty degrees in the past hour," Dorian said as he shook off the snow and shivered. I had moved forward with my towel and rubbed down Lucky.

"I put another log on the fire, so we should be okay there. Are you okay, buddy?" I asked as I rubbed off any snow that Lucky had brought in. Even between his toes. I hated when the snow got clumpy, because it just stayed there and lowered his body temperature.

Lucky licked my face, and I grinned.

"Go curl in front of the fire. We've got you." I kissed his cheek, and Lucky padded off.

The lights flickered, and I froze. "Crap. We should have stayed in town. Even dealing with everybody stopping by."

I shook my head. "I was just thinking that. This place really gets weird during storms."

He reached out and pulled me to him. I let myself sink into his warmth, trying not to stress about anything I had felt before this. We would figure it out. We had to. I wasn't just going to let him go, but I would wallow a bit. A girl had rights.

"Whenever the storms hit Denver, my place shakes

a bit, just because of the wind slicing, but not like this. I swear I can hear every creak and groan."

Why did him talking about his place in Denver surprise me? I'd literally just been thinking of it. He didn't live here. I knew that, he knew that, and it was just a matter of time before we all had to form a plan.

Because I loved Dorian Cage, and I wasn't going to let him go easily.

But putting myself out there seemed like the hardest thing in the world to do. And I wasn't sure if I knew how to even take that step.

"I have hot cocoa in the kitchen. At least we can warm up that way."

He frowned at me but took my hand as we moved forward. In that moment, the lights blinked out.

"Fuck. The generator should go on, at least for a few lights, and things in the kitchen."

But nothing came back on.

"Shit. Hudson and I fixed it, but there must be something else wrong. I'll go down in the basement and work on it."

Though we were on a mountain incline, the basement was still a walkout. But with as much snow that was coming down, he'd have to go down the rickety stairs in order to make that happen.

"This sounds like a horror movie. Maybe we should just pile up under blankets?"

"As much as I'd love to get naked and pile under blankets with you, we should at least check the generator."

"I didn't mention being naked."

His brows rose. "Well, we'll have to be naked to conserve body heat."

I rolled my eyes. "If that's what you think. I'll get naked with you. Don't worry."

"You're such a giver." He pulled out his phone to use as a flashlight, and I did the same.

"How do we have no service? We always have the best service up here."

"Storms must be shittier than usual. Usually we only have service problems on the north side of the lake."

"I'm going with you," I said as Lucky pressed his entire body to my thigh.

Underneath the glow of a flashlight, Dorian glared.

"I can handle it. You and Lucky need to stay up here and stay safe."

"So you're saying the basement isn't safe?"

"I've got it. Don't worry."

Huffing out of breath, I went into the kitchen and pulled out the heavy duty flashlight. I didn't want to drain our phones.

"Take this please."

"Deal." He pressed a hard kiss to my lips, and we

headed towards the basement door. I got another flashlight out of the hall closet and saved my phone battery. Not that it would be helpful without any service.

The house shook once again, this time harder.

"Is there a way for us to get to one of the houses on the lake right now?" I asked, my voice slightly fearful.

"I'm not driving in this weather. And honestly, I don't think my right leg could handle that kind of pressure."

"Dorian."

"It's fine. It's just been a long day."

And with that, he headed down the stairs.

"Please talk to me, so I know where you are."

"You can still see me, baby. But of course I will. What are you planning on making for dinner tomorrow?" he asked as he turned down the corner.

"Oh, so I'm making dinner now?" I asked, my teeth worrying my lip.

"You offered, remember?"

I blinked. "Oh fine you win. Maybe my chicken Alfredo lasagna?"

"I have no idea what that is but it sounds amazing."

"I'll bake fresh bread of course."

"I would expect nothing less from my favorite baker." He paused, then said, "I still don't know why the hell this generator isn't working. Everything looks to be connected. Fuck."

"Maybe it just takes a minute?" I asked, the anxiety in my system increasing. The house shook once again, and a window in the corner of the living room shattered.

Wind and snow barreled in, and I couldn't help but scream.

"Oh my God."

"Stay away from the window, I'm coming up."

"Dorian. What the hell's going on?"

"This house is going to come down around us. Fuck this house."

He stood at the bottom of the stairs, ready to come up, when everything happened at once.

The edge of the house facing the east side of the mountain shook before parts of the siding just sheared off. Lucky barked, and I reached out for him, until a wind gust shoved its way into a large board. The board broke off, and I tried to move out of the way to protect Lucky, but it nudged at my side, slamming into me. The scream ripped from my throat as Dorian tried to run up the stairs, but the house shook impossibly harder. I fell back toward the stairs, snow and debris coming at me as Lucky continued to bark, and then I hit the third stair down. The breath knocked out of me, but I didn't stop moving. Instead I kept going, falling through the staircase.

"Harper! Wellesley!"

I covered my head with my arms as I slammed into the ground, everything feeling as if I'd been shattered at once.

I let out a shaky breath, my palms damp, as I realized I'd fallen into the spare blankets and pillows that had been stored down here.

"I'm okay," I rasped, my body ice cold. "I fell on blankets. I'm okay." I looked up at Dorian, who stared at me through the hole in the floor. How had he gotten up the stairs so quickly?

But then I realized I was deeper into the basement than he had been. And somehow he'd moved up the broken stairwell to look down to where I'd fallen.

"Don't move. Whatever you do, baby, don't move."

Lucky kept barking as Dorian pushed him back, and I frowned.

I was fine, I could feel my toes and fingers move. It wasn't that bad of a fall.

And then, everything came back.

Sharp pain radiated through me as if jagged claws ripped through my stomach.

And then I looked down at the steel rod protruding from my side right above my hip.

I'd been skewered.

And until that moment, I couldn't feel it.

And then there was nothing.

"I'M FINE. I KEEP TELLING YOU I'M FINE."

"You had a steel bar shoved through your abdomen. It's going to take a while until I know that you're fine."

"It didn't puncture any major organs somehow. And yes I lost blood, but you were able to get me to the doctor."

Somehow, through magic or perseverance, my body had come out only slightly broken.

The pillows and blankets had stopped my fall, but the steel rod had sliced through me. It narrowly missed my spleen. And I knew if it had even nicked my spleen, I probably would have bled out.

When I had mentioned that, Dorian had shuddered, his entire face paling. So I would never mention that again.

"I'm fine. The doctors say I'm fine. And you're fine. Lucky's safe with Ivy, and we never have to go back to that godforsaken house again."

Dorian leaned forward and cupped my face, kissing me softly.

"I owe Hudson everything."

"I know. I'll bake him a cake."

His lips twitched as he sat down and took my hand.

There had been a mini avalanche in Cage Lake. Or at least to the east of it. The old house that Dorian had been working on had been hit the worst. Part of the place had just been sliced off, and it would take a while to repair if Dorian didn't just bulldoze it.

Hudson had been at the tip of the avalanche, and had followed it down, white-knuckling it all the way in his four-wheel-drive truck to us.

He had a satellite phone and was able to get a hold of the emergency services and get us out.

I still was a little bit blank on how everything had happened, and how they'd gotten me off the steel rod. I didn't want to ask, but I would later.

But for now I knew the Cage men had saved my life.

Hudson would be getting many cakes.

"You scared the shit out of me."

"Well, it was very scary. I don't want to do that again."

I knew I was trying to make light of it to help him, but if I dwelled on it too much, I knew anxiety would slam into me. And I didn't want that right then.

I just wanted to know that we would both be safe.

"I'm never going back into that house. We'll just have to stay at my house at the lake, your apartment, or downtown in Denver. We'll make it work."

I froze, trying to figure out exactly what he was saying.

"So you're going to find a way to stay in Cage Lake?" I asked, my breath shaky.

"Of course I am. I love you, Harper Wellesley. I love you so fucking much. We'll figure out where we're going to live and how to make it work. Your bakery is here, and I can travel. We'll work it out. But no matter what, my home is you, Wellesley. I almost lost you tonight. I almost lost *you*. I'm not losing you again."

Tears slid down my cheeks as Dorian kissed me softly, his lips chapped from being outside for so long. I tried to move my hand to reach up and brush my fingers through his hair, but my free hand was the one attached to the IV. Instead I just nuzzled into him, tears flowing.

"You love me?" I asked, my voice soft.

He leaned back and frowned at me. "Of course I fucking love you. I'm just sorry it took me screaming at you while you were passed out and impaled for me to say it."

"Wait. You told me you loved me before?"

He blushed. "Yes, I thought you were awake. Hell, I'm not good at this. I've never loved anyone before."

If I could, I would jump out of bed and dance, throwing myself in Dorian's arms. It would just have to happen later.

"I love you too you know. I was trying to figure out how to tell you. And how I wanted you to stay."

His face softened as he brushed his knuckles along my cheek.

"We'll make it work. I have family money for a reason. I might as well use it for good. But we're never, ever going down in a basement again."

"Damn straight. Maybe just ranch style homes from now on."

He grinned and kissed me once more.

"Excuse me, I thought the patient was supposed to rest," Hudson growled as he limped his way in. He wouldn't tell me how he had hurt himself, and Dorian wasn't budging.

These Cage men and their secrets; I was just going to have to figure them out myself.

"I am resting. And I'm thinking about what cakes I'm going to bake you."

Hudson rolled his eyes. "I like carrot cake."

"Nobody likes carrot cake," Dorian snapped.

"Yes, they do. And I like the cream cheese frosting."

Hudson snapped his fingers. "There you go. You don't have to bake me anything, Harper. The sound of that avalanche scared the hell out of me, and I was just glad I was there."

"You both saved my life. So I'm sorry, I'm baking things for you forever."

"Hey, I was the one with a satellite phone, why does

he get cake too?" Hudson asked, laughter in his tone that made me warm.

"She's my girlfriend and the love of my life. Of course I get cake, and pie. And other baked goods. And euphemisms with using baked goods."

I slapped at his chest with my good arm, ignoring the IV, and rolled my eyes.

"Really?"

"Sadly, that's the Dorian we know and love," Hudson said dryly.

"Well then okay. I'll take it."

"Damn straight you will," Dorian grumbled before he pressed his lips to mine, and I sighed happily.

I hadn't meant to fall in love with my best friend's brother. Or catch this particular Cage. But maybe, just maybe, my dog's name was right. And I was lucky.

Being impaled with a steel rod and all.

I grimaced, knowing I wasn't going to be able to make too many jokes about that anytime soon. But it didn't matter. Dorian was mine. And I was his. And we were going to figure things out.

Just as long as I never stepped in a basement again.

DORIAN

EVERYTHING HURT AND I WAS DYING. OKAY, NOT quite that bad but sometimes it felt like it. After all, I had been through worse.

I rubbed my knee and winced at the slight twinge in my ribs since I had moved too hard.

Well, fuck.

You would think I would be used to this whole being injured and figuring out how to deal with it thing, but apparently, I had forgotten how. Or I was losing my damn mind.

"Everything okay?"

I looked up to see Sophia standing there, her hands in front of her body, that soft and worried expression on her face.

Emily stood behind her, also looking just as worried, and I hated myself just a little bit in that moment.

I wasn't used to being the big brother to little sisters. I was used to being the asshole middle child who could grin his way out of most things.

And now two of my sisters were worried about me, and all I could do sometimes was yell and growl.

I needed to get over myself. After all, I would be okay, I had pretty much gotten the best out of the deal when it came to Harper after all.

Though the accident had taken ten years off my life, at least when it came to thinking about how Harper had been hurt, we were okay. And I had gotten far luckier than I had ever dreamed.

"Well, with that smile on his face, I suppose he is doing fine." Emily walked into the room, leaned forward, and kissed the top of my head. I had been sitting at the edge of the bed, trying to get the energy in order to get up and get downstairs to meet the family for dinner. For the first time in far too long, every single Cage in my generation would be there. The mothers weren't planning on being there, and for that I was grateful. My mother wasn't invited, and the other Cage mom had begged off, saying that she was going to take the grandmother's prerogative to watch the babies.

Sophia and Cale would be happy to have a few

moments to themselves, even surrounded by so many of our siblings.

"What do you mean?" I asked Emily, feeling awkward all over again.

"You're thinking about Harper, and with that smile on your face, I suppose you're going to do just fine."

I narrowed my gaze at her, wondering why she reminded me so much of Flynn. Genetics were such a weird thing.

"Is this what happens when you have younger sisters? You have to deal with their teasing?"

"Pretty much. And I'm not even the youngest."

"That is very true," Sophia said as she leaned over to grip the cane I had rested on the other side of the bed. My leg was killing me, and I was stuck using the cane for a bit longer. The wounds, the burns on the side of my body were finally healing to the point that it didn't hurt as much as it had even two months ago. But the new wounds from the storm weren't being nice.

"I always forget that you're not the youngest," I teased Emily.

She rolled her eyes. "It's because Phoebe is married and happy and all of that lovely glittery stuff. She cut in line, and if we were in regency time, I would have to have a speech about having no prospects and being a burden."

I snorted. "I'm sure we can find you a nice man who likes potatoes."

"You know *Pride and Prejudice?*" she asked, eyes wide.

"Of course, I do. Wellesley loves it."

Both women made cooing sounds, and I rolled my eyes.

"You know, it shouldn't surprise me that the two of you found each other, especially because she is Joshua's little sister, but now that I see you two together, it just makes sense."

"Damn right it makes sense," I said as Sophia grinned.

"Well, if you know a nice small town guy who's looking for maybe forever and maybe not forever, send them my way," Emily said as she fluttered her eyelashes.

"I'm not going to send anyone your way. Because then I'd have to kick their ass."

Her eyes widened. "Excuse me?

"I'm sorry, but you're my little sister. I have to be the overprotective asshole. I didn't get a chance to be that way with Phoebe and her husband."

"Is that really how it works?" Sophia asked.

"And you're telling me that Isabella or Kyler didn't act all growly and possessive with anyone you dated when you were younger?" I asked.

Sophia cringed. "Isabella was always the one that tended to do research and interrogate our dates. But she likes Cale, so I guess I was okay there."

"She let you marry him."

"And you act as if I didn't do my own reconnaissance," a deep voice said from the doorway and I looked up to see Kyler Cage Dixon standing there, leaning slightly with his arms crossed over his chest. His hair was far longer than it had been the last time I saw him, and the dark circles under his eyes told me that while his world tour was kicking ass, it was also kicking *his* ass.

"Kyler! You made it!" Emily said as she threw herself into her brother's arms. He caught her in a blink, that smile on his face wide and true.

"Of course, I came. I had to make sure this asshole stops hurting himself."

I rolled my eyes as I tried to stand up. I couldn't help the groan that escaped my lips, and suddenly Sophia was there, helping me.

"I broke my leg once when I was younger, and it was still during the time when I was growing, and between that and the fact that I refused to stop dancing, I resented the hell out of having to use a cane. So I completely understand."

I leaned forward and kissed Sophia's cheek. "I hate

it. But I'll be okay. After all, we all know it could have been worse."

She reached forward and squeezed my hand, and I looked up into Kyler's narrowed eyes.

"Something you want to say, little brother?

"I don't know if I like the fact that so many of you are older than me," Kyler said with a snort. "And I'm just here to say that I'm glad you're okay. It must have been scary, not able to get to Harper the way you needed to."

I swallowed hard as Emily wiped away a tear. "Well, it all works out in the end," I said, trying to sound far more positive than I felt. But then again, with Wellesley at my side, maybe I could be that positive guy. The guy who just made things make sense.

"Are we having a party in here?" Flynn asked as he stole Emily from Kyler's arms and hugged her tight.

The two beamed up at each other, and that's when I knew there was a reason that the two got along so well. They were like two sides of a coin.

With so many years lost between all of us, not knowing that the others existed, it was nice to see the connections forming. I didn't know all of my siblings well, but I was damn well going to learn them.

After all, I had gotten my second chance, and my third.

"We were just making sure the old man could

hobble his way down the stairs," Kyler said dryly. Sophia smacked him in the chest, and he just smiled.

"Love you."

"Oh fuck off," she said, and I burst out laughing.

"I didn't know you cursed," I teased.

"Well, you're just going to have to get to know me. And now, I'm going to go find my husband, because all of you make me insane. And he's the only calm one."

"That's because he's not related to any of us," Emily said with a sly smile, and I just laughed and made my way to the door. Kyler reached out and gripped my elbow as I stumbled a bit, and I didn't even resent him for it.

After all, we were family.

Somewhat learning each other.

We made our way downstairs, and I was grateful that Aston once again had a large enough house for all of us. This one might be on the lake, but it was still enough space for the group.

Ford, along with his husband and wife, Noah and Greer, stood off to the side, laughing at something that Paige was saying. She leaned against her husband Cain, and that's when I remembered that Noah and Cain were cousins.

Our family was complicated as hell, but that family probably could match us in our craziness.

Sophia was already in Cale's arms, the two whispering to each other, and I held back a smile at that. They were so damn happy, and since I was just as happy with Wellesley, I couldn't really make fun of that anymore.

Aston, Blakely, Isabella, and Weston were all in the kitchen, working on wine and appetizers, and since nobody else was helping, I had a feeling that everyone had been kicked out of the room before I'd even come downstairs.

Weston's brother and twin sisters were also in the living room, speaking with James and Theo. What was funny was that I usually saw Theo more than anyone. He was a chef and owned one of the best restaurants in Denver, and now that I was up in Cage Lake so often, I didn't get to see him as much. I was going to have to change that though. After all, I missed my brother. I missed my family. I had been hiding from everybody a little too often these days.

"Hey, there you are."

I looked up as Hudson came forward, a scowl on his face. There was something going on with him, and I had no idea what it was. But maybe one day he'd actually let me figure it out. My family had given me enough time to deal with my own secrets, and then they had badgered me until I told them the truth.

In the end, it hadn't felt too big of a secret. Because

it was just genetics. It wasn't real. Not in a sense that it should matter to me.

Every single person in this room was my family in some connected way. And that's all that mattered.

After all, technically I wasn't blood related to half of the people in this house right now. But I didn't care about that. Not anymore. And I knew they sure as hell didn't care.

I was a Cage because of the people in this room, not my mother's indiscretions, and not the asshole man who tried to raise me and failed.

"What's up?" I asked Hudson as he came forward.

"I know you said you were going to plan on selling that old place, but I want it."

I blinked. "What?" There was no way I'd heard him right.

Hudson wouldn't look at me, his voice gruff. "The old cabin. The Ackerson place. I want it."

"Why do you want it? It's a piece of shit. And it nearly killed me and Wellesley." I'd rather burn it to the ground than step foot in that place again.

"I know it's a piece of shit, but I just have an idea. I'll buy it from you over market price. But I don't want it out of the family."

That was it. My brother had officially lost his damn mind. "I don't know if it was technically really part of something that we want our family legacy to be."

"No, not that. I just like the real estate."

I narrowed my gaze. "Are you fucking with me?"

"It's between two of our lots, I don't want a stranger there. Just let me have my way. For once. Just let me."

Considering Hudson never asked for things, yes he sometimes demanded things like privacy, but he was usually the guy who just did things on his own and didn't ask for help.

So if he wanted this, it was for a reason. Maybe it was privacy, maybe it was something I was never going to understand. "I'll sell it to you for five dollars. How's that?"

My brother blinked at me, jaw dropping. "Is this how you do business down in Denver with all of your companies?"

"No, he knows if he sells it for more than that, I'll get grumpy."

My entire body warmed as I looked over at Wellesley. I knew she had to deal with a few things at the bakery, and had been downright mean to me when I had said I would stay with her. I hadn't wanted her out of my sight, but I had finally given in.

Because I loved her, and frankly, she could kick my ass. And I would probably deserve it.

"Baby," I said, my spine softening.

She wrapped her arms around me, as I did the same

to her. We were both still healing, and while she was not allowed to lift anything heavy, she still liked to spend a couple of hours a day in the bakery.

I had almost lost the love of my life, and I was never going to let myself forget that.

"Hi. Sorry I'm late. Scarlett dropped me off, so I didn't walk anywhere. I promise. Now, sell the place to him like you said you were for five dollars. And if Hudson fights you on it, I'll sick Scarlett on him."

"That's mean," my brother growled, but I just threw my head back and laughed.

"I love you so fucking much," I said softly.

"I love you too. And I know I'm the luckiest girl in the world. Just saying."

I leaned forward and captured her lips with mine, ignoring the hoots and hollers in the room.

My entire family was watching at this point, and I could not care less. All that mattered was I had Harper Wellesley in my arms. Our life wasn't perfect. And we weren't going to be okay and happy every day. We had suffered losses that seemed insurmountable, but we would survive. There was truly no other option. She was my everything. The one person I would protect no matter what. The person I loved more than anyone.

Hudson sighed. "Fine, five dollars. But don't you dare sick Scarlett on me." Hudson growled a bit more and stomped off to the kitchen, ignoring everybody who told him to just sit down and relax. None of us seemed like relaxing tonight.

I wrapped my arms a little tighter around Harper, knowing that we were both still a little sore.

Sore enough that it had been far too long since I'd felt her around me, the heat of her, the need of her. And from the way that her eyes darkened, I knew she was feeling the same thing.

"Six more days," she whispered.

I groaned and captured her lips with mine. Somebody threw a folded up napkin at me, and I ignored it, holding Harper closer.

This was our new home. Maybe not underneath this roof, but my other house on the opposite end of the lake. I could work remotely, and we could go down to the city when needed. Hell, if Wellesley let me, we'd be opening another Rising Cage in Denver. We could always use another bakery in the family.

We would find a way to make our jobs work in both places, so that way we wouldn't have to choose.

I pressed my lips to her temple as we made our way to the large dining table that my brother had expanded to fit everybody. And even with extra chairs, it was a tight fit.

"I never would've guessed I would have to find another damn table to make all of us fit in this house," Aston said with a laugh.

"I know a guy, I'll figure it out," Hudson said with a shrug of his shoulders, but he didn't elaborate.

I didn't know what *I knew a guy* meant, but I had a feeling that by the time we did a dinner like this again with the whole lot of us, we'd have space to fit.

Because that was my brother, all of them. They got shit done, confused you, and made sure you remembered exactly what our family was about.

"Maybe we can stretch it to only five days," Wellesley whispered into my ear, and I groaned.

"Woman," I growled.

She threw her head back and laughed, looking like a dream I had never allowed myself to believe in.

I would do anything to have Joshua back, to have the man who was like a brother to me, my best friend. But that couldn't happen. And there were no second chances when it came to some of the most important things in life.

But he had given me a gift. Part of his heart.

My Wellesley.

And I would do everything in my power to make sure the world knew I was worthy of her. As I looked around this family of mine, some by blood, some by circumstance, I knew I was damn lucky. I had almost given in to the darkness, almost given up. But in the end I was here. My family was here.

And Wellesley was mine. No ifs. No goodbyes.

Just everything. This time, I didn't mind calling myself a Cage. Because this was the family we had made, not the ones our parents had tried to destroy. One day Wellesley would be one too. If that didn't bring a smile to my face, and a roll to Joshua's eyes, I didn't know what would. I had given in and fallen in love with my best friend's little sister.

And it was the best decision I would ever make.

Chapter 18

HUDSON

WHEN I HAD MOVED BACK TO CAGE LAKE, I HADN'T thought much of it. In fact, it wasn't technically moving back to the town as I had never lived there permanently. I'd only been there during the summers and some other vacation times with the family. I'd lived all over the country after high school, because I had enlisted rather than dealing with certain parts of my family. Not my brothers, those I could handle. No, it was the rest of them.

Being overseas hadn't been a picnic. I held back a shudder trying not to go too far down that path. And yet here I was, in a town that was not my own, but I had nowhere else to go. I didn't want to live in a big city, didn't want to live in a place that I had to truly start over again. I just wanted to live in the woods and not deal with people. And yet I was never allowed to do that because apparently when you lived in a small town, all you did was deal with people. That was not in the terms of service when I decided to move here.

Because of course my family owned the damn town. Maybe not the title of each property, but enough of them that they named the damn thing after us. There was really no going back to normalcy and anonymity after that.

In retrospect, moving to a town that held my last name probably wasn't the best place to hide, but I hadn't quite been thinking clearly when I had come here.

So now I had to deal with people. Daily.

Because once my dad had died, may he rest somewhat in peace, somebody had to take care of all the properties. And it wasn't like he had been doing a good job of it. So Aston, James, and Flynn had been doing a decent job of it—with Flynn being the one who dealt with things in the majority once Dad had walked away from the company. But Flynn rarely came to Cage Lake with his full time job at Cage Enterprises in Denver.

So when I had decided to move back permanently, they'd all been so happy. Not that I was back in the country, well, maybe. But no, because now somebody could do their dirty work. And that of course made it sound like we were part of the mob or something. And I wasn't sure we were. I mean, I'd been away for a while, and who knew what some of my brothers got up to, but I was pretty sure we were clean on that front. Dad, however? Dad I wasn't quite sure about.

We owned multiple businesses, residential properties, and land, which we knew we would never develop so we could keep the town looking how it needed to. Like it wasn't some overrun piece of land in the Colorado mountains. Which to these days, was hard to find. The number of developers who came after my family, including stomping up to my fucking house, was ridiculous. Once they got to know me though, nobody came by my house. They knew better than that. And I hadn't even shot at one of them. I was growing.

I held back a snort at that. Okay, maybe not particularly growing, but I was too tired to deal with that bullshit. And now they knew it.

So while the Cages owned many of the businesses in town, our biggest source of income was right on the edge of town.

And the source of my annoyance. And possibly my nemesis.

I hated the resort. Full of uppity rich people who did not care about anybody else. They paid for their overpriced hot toddies, cocoa, bourbon, and rental skis.

Because while most people brought their own, some people wanted to rent something from the Cages. Because apparently that meant something to them.

If they only knew all of our family secrets. Of course I didn't even know all of our family secrets, and the media had given most of it away.

But when Isabella had met Weston and decided to spend half of her time in Cage Lake, I was thrilled. Yes, because I liked my sister—not that I would ever tell her that. But also, because she, a brilliant forensic accountant, was also going to take on the responsibility of dealing with the business side of the resort.

While I didn't go through books or anything, not unless they needed me to, I was the guy that all of the business owners spoke to if they needed something.

It was my worst nightmare.

I just wanted to do my art in peace and pretend everyone else didn't exist.

It was kind of hard to do that when you had eleven siblings. Many of which were starting to find their significant others so therefore adding more people to my circle.

And since Isabella was out of town, doing something with Weston's siblings, I really hadn't paid attention, which meant I had to deal with the resort.

I was just not okay with that.

I rubbed my temples as I made my way inside the

back entrance. The place was closing down, although just the public areas. There was twenty-four-hour room service, a full-time concierge, and people would be milling about throughout their rooms, but the main lobby would be quiet.

The daytime staff would be gone, and the nighttime staff would come in.

I didn't need to speak to any of them. Instead I just needed to fix a couple things. I wasn't a damn handyman, and I wasn't in the mood to be alone at home.

And how was that for irony. Because I was the dumbass who pushed people away so I could stay at home alone, and now I didn't want to deal with it.

And it had nothing to do with that phone call. Or that nightmare.

I walked inside and nodded at a guest who happened to be going to their room. They were decked out in their finery, weaving a bit from their alcohol consumption, but she just smiled before leaning into her husband. Or at least who I thought was her husband. I wasn't going to judge.

The guy scowled at me, and I scowled right back. I didn't really fit in with this crowd with my worn jeans, flannel, and beard that I needed to trim. But they could just deal with it. My hair was too long at this point too, and I was starting to match my twin's look of roughness, but then again, he was usually a little cleaner cut than I was.

He just cursed more than me.

At least that's what I told myself.

I didn't know why we kept this resort open. Yes, it was great for the town, yes it was good income for the company. But why did we have to do something in which we had to make rich people happy?

And now I was just being an idiot.

I moved down the hall towards the back offices. After I slid my key card to get through security, I tried to think about all the things I needed to get done tonight. I wanted to work on my art piece, but it was turning out to be far more difficult than I thought. Maybe I would head down to Harper's later and work on another mural. That would clear my head. And I liked my brother's girlfriend. She might seem sweet and innocent, but she could kick anybody's ass if they ever decided to come and hurt her family. And the Cages were now her family.

I liked her.

I could be doing art. I could be working on my house. I could be doing anything else. But instead I was at this damn resort trying to fix a doorknob that kept getting stuck.

Again, not my job, but if I kept my hands busy, I

wouldn't have nightmares. And that sounded a lot better to me.

When I got to the manager's office though, I frowned. The door was open, not locked in place like it usually was. Scarlett was damn good with security. She was damn good at most things, which was why we always butted heads. Because I didn't like her knowing that I thought she did a damn good job. She got all uppity and looked down at me. And I wasn't in the mood to deal with that.

But she never left the door open.

I slid my hand in my pocket, gripping my knife, as I slowly opened the door. She stood there, alone, as I scanned the room, but it took me a moment to let go of the knife.

Because while she was alone, she wasn't sitting at her desk working.

Instead the image in front of me made my jaw tense, and anger surged to the surface.

Scarlett, in all her beauty, with her light blonde hair flowing down her back, and that icy way she could put down anybody who tried to hurt her, stood in front of her mirror, her main shirt off and over the chair, and only in her pants and tank top.

And there were bruises all over her. She pulled up part of her shirt since I knew she hadn't seen me yet, and the dark bruises turning blue and green there put a metallic taste in my mouth.

"Who. Hurt. You?"

She met my gaze in the mirror, her eyes widening. Her face went deathly pale, before her jaw tensed, and that familiar snarl covered her face. She whirled, sliding down her top.

"Get out!" she yelled, as she scrambled for her shirt.

I moved forward, hands at my sides. I was a good foot taller than her, and could scare the shit out of her, but it wasn't like I could look any smaller than I was. But I'd be damned if she didn't tell me what the hell happened.

"I repeat. Who hurt you?"

She quickly buttoned up her blouse, her hands shaking.

"I'm fine," she lied. Because it was a damn lie. "I went skiing and hurt myself. I was just checking the bruises."

I leaned forward and reached out to grip her chin. My breath caught as the bruise on the side of her jaw had only just now revealed itself to me when she turned.

And she flinched. *Fucking flinched.*

I let my hand drop, and I told myself to breathe. "Don't fucking lie to me."

"And maybe you should just get over yourself. I don't owe you any answers. Get out. You may own this place, but you don't own me. Get out, get out, get out, get out."

She repeated the words over and over again, before her knees went weak, and tears slid down her face.

I had never once seen Scarlett Blair crack. Not in all the times that we'd yelled at each other, fought, or poked at each other just because we knew we could handle it.

And that scared me more than anything.

I reached out and caught her before she hit the ground and held her to my chest.

Because I knew exactly who had done this.

And I tried not to let the memories slam into me. Because this was all too familiar, and I had failed the first time.

I would kill him. I didn't tell her that, I just let her break down in my arms. But I vowed to myself right then and there, I would kill him.

Just like before.

Next in the series? Hudson changes the game in One Quick Obsession.

AND IF YOU'D LIKE TO READ A BONUS SCENE YOU CAN FIND IT HERE! I LOVE THIS SCENE SO MUCH!

If you'd like to read the next Generation with the
Montgomery Ink Legacy Series:
Bittersweet Promises

In the mood for more small town romance? Check out the Ashford Creek series with LEGACY. Or as I like to call it "The Small Town of Single Dads".

Bonus Epilogue

DORIAN

"I'M NOT GOING INTO THE CREEPY BASEMENT."

I looked over at my wife and shook my head. "I'm not asking you to go into the creepy basement. I'm asking you to go into the walkout basement with me so you can see the lounge area that we're putting in. You and I both know that if I move the sectional to a certain place, and it's wrong, I'm going to get in trouble."

Wellesley narrowed her gaze at me. "Excuse me. Are you saying that I am going to nag you like some wife who doesn't care about her husband's needs?" She put her hands on her hips, and I tried not to laugh.

My wife had to be the most beautiful woman in the entire world.

It didn't matter that she was now a Wellesley Cage, I was always going to call her Wellesley. And even though she glared at me, that little line between her brows deepening ever so much, I just wanted to kiss that look right off her face.

Of course, if I did so, I would have to deal with the rounded belly separating us.

I wasn't going to mention that she was larger than she had been though, because that was asking for me to be pushed down the stairs into the not haunted, nearly finished walkout basement.

I had some survival skills.

"Why don't you take a seat, and we can talk about the sectional later."

"Why don't you just record it for me, and I will tell you where to put the sectional."

I narrowed my gaze at her, wondering why she didn't want to go down to the basement. Of course, the last time we'd been near a basement in the other house, things had gone to shit.

"Are you okay? Is something wrong?" Alarm slammed into me, and I was moving then, knowing I was going into dangerous territory. Instead I cupped her face, then looked down at her belly between us. "Is it the babies?"

Her whole face brightened as she leaned into my palm.

"The babies are fine. They're still cooking. However, my ankles are now twice the size that they were yesterday, and frankly, I don't want to go down the stairs. There. I'm cranky."

I leaned down and brushed my lips against hers. "I just looked at your ankles and they look the same as yesterday."

I checked those ankles and every inch of her often. Her mother had dealt with hypertension during Joshua's birth, and so I was going to make sure that the love of my life had a healthy, safe, and relatively boring pregnancy.

Of course, with my siblings butting in with every single part of this pregnancy, there really wasn't much normalcy or quietness to go around.

"Are you sure?"

"Well, let's double check."

Without a word, I lifted her up into my arms, ignoring her squeal of protest. She immediately wrapped her arms around my neck as I carried her to the living room.

We lived in our home on the lake, the one that I had owned for years, and Harper had really made it ours versus just a place where I put up my feet as part of a vacation.

We also had a house in Denver and still owned the apartment over Harper's bakery. I refused to let her pay rent to the Cages since she was one now, and that was a fun fight that ended up with her bent over the table and both of us enjoying our meals a little too much.

We didn't rent out the place, but it was a nice apartment for when visitors came and didn't want to stay in one of the big houses, or frankly, if we got snowed in in the middle of town and had nowhere else to go. At the moment though, it was for a short-term lease for one of Harper's new workers. A single mom who needed a place to stay, so Harper was letting them stay for a dollar a week. The only reason we even had to do that was so our accountants didn't yell at us. Again.

I swore our accountant and lawyer loved to yell at us. It was their fault we were in most of these messes.

I set Wellesley on the couch with her feet up, and before she could say a word, I set out sparkling water for her and got her favorite white cheddar popcorn.

"Now, I realize that I'm giving you salt and water when you're worried about your ankles, but you're allowed this much per day."

"I love the fact that you are trying to tell me what I'm allowed to eat, but I appreciate it," she said with a laugh. She moaned as she took a couple of bites of the popcorn, and I opened my mouth to see if she would even notice I wanted some too. When she threw it and I caught it with ease, we both cheered.

"We're getting better at that."

"I know, right? You're no longer hitting me in the eye."

She blushed and shook her head. "That was one time."

"Each eye."

I moved to sit next to her on the couch and shifted her so her feet were now on my lap so I could rub her arches.

She moaned as I dug my thumb in, and I just grinned at her.

"Have I ever told you how hot you are?"

"I didn't realize you had a breeding kink."

"You really need to stop reading those books where you learn these words, Wellesley."

"Like age gap?" She fluttered her eyelashes, and I couldn't help but tickle her feet. When she kicked me in the nuts though, I froze.

"Sorry," she sing-songed.

"You don't sound too sorry," I rasped, wondering if this pain would ever end. But if I mentioned something like that, she would probably glare at me, considering the lovely pain of being pregnant and then childbirth was going to win any argument for a good while now.

And considering what I knew some of my family members had gone through with their pregnancies, Wellesley and I were just fine with me doing everything she said and trying not to fuck it up.

"What's with that look?" she asked after a moment.

"Do you think I'll make a good dad?" I asked, the question not a new one between us.

She reached out to try to touch my face, but with her pregnant belly between us, it was a little difficult. So I leaned to the side and let her run her hands through my hair.

"I think you're going to be an amazing dad."

"I don't even know who my biological father is, and the dad who raised me didn't really raise me."

"No, they didn't. And they are not the dads that showed you how to be a father. I know Aston isn't that much older than you, but he and your other brothers raised you far better than any other Cage could. Not to mention you and Joshua ran wild and figured out how to be grown men I could be proud of."

I leaned again, this time nearly crawling over her without touching her belly so I could kiss her softly on the mouth.

"I love you, Wellesley."

"I love you too, Cage. And I truly believe you're going to be a great father. Mostly because the amount of siblings you have won't allow for any other answer."

That just made me snort. "That is very true. I have a lot to live up to with them."

"And they all have a lot to live up to you as well. I

mean, the playboy Dorian falling for the small town baker? You're a little ridiculous."

"And that's why I love you. You always make sure that we settle into our own normalcy."

"I do my best. Now, I suppose I'll let you lead me down to the basement of doom. Mostly because I want to see if you put the couch where it needed to be."

"See, I knew you had ulterior motives."

"Always."

"Come on, Wells, let's get you loaded."

"I feel like you're calling me big, but since I feel like I have eight babies in me, a full litter rather than two, I don't blame that thought. I still blame the Cages for the fact that your family has so many twins," she snapped.

"I am sorry about that. At least I'm not a twin. That would get confusing."

"The number of twins in your family and adjacent to it are confusing enough."

"How about we move the couch exactly where it needs to be, and then we'll break it in."

I winked as my hand went around her chest, cupping her breast.

She glared at me and then moaned as I rolled her nipple between my thumb and forefinger.

"Okay, I suppose I'll let you make me come."

"You're so nice."

"And giving. If I can reach your dick, I promise I'll make sure you get off too."

I barked out a laugh, as we made our way downstairs and did indeed break in the couch. Carefully, strategically, and to a point that Wellesley's toes curled, and my eyes rolled to the back of my head.

There was a reason that though we hadn't planned this pregnancy, it had come so quickly. We couldn't keep our hands off each other.

And though I was damn scared of being a father, I couldn't wait.

Because I had Wellesley. And together we could handle anything.

Harper

THERE WAS A MOMENT IN TIME WHEN I HAD WALKED into one of the Cages' homes and saw Dorian holding Sophia's daughter. In that moment, I had nearly fallen to my knees, my ovaries bursting. Because the man that I had loved, even though I didn't really know what that meant, was holding a baby. So watching Dorian, with his dark stormy eyes and broken heart, holding his niece had changed everything for me. Hell, that night had changed everything for me in more ways than one.

And now the damn man was holding one of our babies as I held the other, and my ovaries might not be bursting because everything felt as if I had been pulled through a pasta machine, however, everything felt different.

Because I was a mom. Dorian was a father.

And he was holding our baby.

When he looked up and met my gaze, I swallowed hard, tears sliding down my face.

"I have no idea how we're going to do this, but this is amazing," he whispered.

I nodded, looked down at my child, and knew that life was never easy, but in this moment, life was worth everything.

"You have so many aunts and uncles watching out for you," I whispered, and Dorian let out a rough chuckle. "So many that you're going to need a spread-sheet to know them all. And then when you add in your cousins? It's a little scary. But don't worry. Because no matter what, you're all going to stand against the world together. And you have the best of both worlds because you have a twin. Someone that will love you with their whole soul because you shared so much space for so long. And you have a mommy and daddy who love you and will fight and burn down the world for you."

"Damn straight," Dorian growled.

"Language."

"They can't understand. I'm just a blob to them."

"Okay, Mr. Blob," I mumbled, my lips tilting into a smile. I looked down at my baby again and sighed. "You have so much love pouring towards you, and you'll never be alone. I promise. Even when we annoy you." Again, Dorian chuckled. "And remember, you have an uncle who's watching you from afar. An uncle who would have loved meeting you."

Dorian cleared his throat. "Your uncle was my best friend. And I trusted him with everything. So I'm damn happy that he trusted me with your mom."

"Again, language," I said with a laugh.

Dorian moved to sit next to me on the large bed, and we cuddled the babies close to us. This was our first quiet moment as a little family, and my heart ached.

Because this was the beginning of everything, and I wasn't quite sure how we were going to do this.

But before I could say anything, to voice my worries, the door opened, and the Cages piled in one after another. They each washed their hands and came over to check on our new little family. And I realized just then, it wouldn't matter if I felt like I couldn't do this. Because we would never be alone.

I had once been afraid that I was the only member

left of my family. Standing alone in the abyss as darkness settled in.

But that was no longer the case.

Because I had a family who loved me, who needed me, and who stood by me day in and day out.

And our babies would feel the same.

I was a Cage. A Wellesley Cage.

And our family was ready to face whatever came at us next.

Next in the series? Hudson changes the game in One Quick Obsession.

If you'd like to read the next Generation with the Montgomery Ink Legacy Series: Bittersweet Promises

In the mood for more small town romance? Check out the Ashford Creek series with LEGACY. Or as I like to call it "The Small Town of Single Dads".

A Note from Carrie Ann Ryan

Thank you so much for reading **IF YOU WERE MINE.**

This story broke my heart but in the best ways possible. I had no idea the journey Dorian and Harper would take me on and I'm so grateful for the time I had with them.

As a widow, writing and reading about loss honestly helps me figure out my place in the world. I know that's not the same for everyone, but being the one left behind makes me focus on what I need to do in order to feel like I earned it.

Which honestly, isn't the thought process a person truly needs. So writing about Dorian's guilt and Harper's solitude truly was an incredible experience. And I hope you loved their book!

Up next is One Quick Obsession with Hudson and Scarlett. I will say this book is EVERYTHING and I cannot wait to show you more!

In case you'd like to read Phoebe's romance, you can read about her and Kane in His Second Chance!

And Ford finds his match with Greer and Noah in Best Friend Temptation!

The Cage Family

Book 1: The Forever Rule (Aston & Blakely)

Book 2: An Unexpected Everything (Isabella & Weston)

Book 3: If You Were Mine (Dorian & Harper)

Book 4: One Quick Obsession (Hudson & Scarlett)

Next in the series? Hudson changes the game in One Quick Obsession.

AND IF YOU'D LIKE TO READ A BONUS SCENE YOU CAN FIND IT HERE! I LOVE THIS SCENE SO MUCH!

If you'd like to read the next Generation with the Montgomery Ink Legacy Series: Bittersweet Promises

In the mood for more small town romance? Check

out the Ashford Creek series with LEGACY. Or as I like to call it "The Small Town of Single Dads".

If you want to make sure you know what's coming next from me, you can sign up for my newsletter at www. CarrieAnnRyan.com; follow me on twitter at @CarrieAnnRyan, or like my Facebook page. I also have a Facebook Fan Club where we have trivia, chats, and other goodies. You guys are the reason I get to do what I do and I thank you.

Make sure you're signed up for my MAILING LIST so you can know when the next releases are available as well as find giveaways and FREE READS.

Happy Reading!

From One Way Back to Me

ELI

WHEN MY MORNING BEGINS WITH ME STANDING ankle-deep in a basement full of water, I know I probably should have stayed in bed. Only, I was the boss, and I didn't get that choice.

"Hold on. I'm looking for it." East cursed underneath his breath as my younger brother bent down around the pipe, trying his best to turn off the valve. I sighed, waded through the muck in my work boots, and moved to help him. "I said I've got it," East snapped, but I ignored him.

I narrowed my eyes at the evil pipe. "It's old and rusted, and even though it passed an inspection over a year ago, we knew this was going to be a problem."

"And I'm the fucking handyman of this company. I've got this."

"And as a handyman, you need a hand."

"You're hilarious. Seriously. I don't know how I could ever manage without your wit and humor." The dryness in his tone made my lips twitch even as I did my best to ignore the smell of whatever water we stood in.

"Fuck you," I growled.

"No thanks. I'm a little too busy for that."

With a grunt, East shut off the water, and we both stood back, hands on our hips as we stared at the mess of this basement.

East let out a sigh. "I'm not going to have to turn the water off for the whole property, but I'm glad that we don't have tenants in this particular cabin."

I nodded tightly and held back a sigh. "This is probably why there aren't basements in Texas. Because everything seems to go wrong in these things."

"I'm pretty sure this is a storm shelter, or at least a tornado one. Not quite sure as it's one of the only basements in the area."

"It was probably the only one that they had the energy to make back in the day. Considering this whole place is built over clay and limestone."

East nodded, looked around. "I'll start the cleanup with this water, and we'll look to see what we can do with the pipes."

I pinched the bridge of my nose. "I don't want to have to replace the plumbing for this whole place."

"At least it's not the villa itself, or the farmhouse, or the winery. Just a single cabin."

I glared at my younger brother, then reached out and knocked on a wooden pillar. "Shut your mouth. Don't say things like that to me. We are just now getting our feet under us."

East shrugged. "It's the truth, though. However much you weigh it, it could have been worse."

I pinched the bridge of my nose. "Jesus Christ. You were in the military for how long? A Wilder your entire life, and you say things like that? When the hell did you lose that superstition bone?"

"About the time that my Humvee was blown up, and when Evan's was, Everett's too. Hell, about the time that you almost fell out of the sky in your plane. Or when Elliot was nearly shot to death trying to help one of his men. So, yes, I pretty much lost all superstition when trying to toe the line ended up in near death and maiming."

I met my brother's gaze, that familiar pang thinking about all that we had lost and almost lost over the past few years.

East muttered under his breath, shaking his head. "And I sound more and more like Evan these days rather than myself."

I squeezed his shoulder and let out a breath, thinking of our brother who grunted more than spoke these days. "It's okay. We've been through a lot. But we're here."

Somehow, we were here. I wasn't quite sure if we had made the right decision about two years ago when we had formed this plan, or rather *I* had formed this plan, but there was no going back. We were in it, and we were going to have to find a way to make it work, flooded former tornado shelters and all.

East sighed. "I'll work on this now. Then I'll head on over to the main house. I have a few things to work on there."

"You know, we can hire you help. I know we had all the contractors and everything to work with us for some of the rebuilds and rehabs, but we can hire someone else for you on a day-to-day basis."

My brother shook his head. "We may be able to afford it, but I'd rather save that for a rainy day. Because when it rains, it pours here, and flash flooding is a major threat in this part of Texas." He winked as he said it, mixing his metaphors, and I just shook my head.

"You just let me know if you need it."

"You're the CEO, brother of mine, not the CFO. That's Everett."

"True, but we did talk about it so we can work on

it." I paused, thinking about what other expenses might show up. "And what do you need to do with the villa?"

The villa was the main house where most things happened on the property. It contained the lobby, library, and atrium. My apartment was also on the top floor, so I could be there for emergencies. Our innkeeper lived on the other side of the house, but I was in the main loft because this was my project, my baby.

My other brothers, all five of them, lived in cabins on the property. We lived together, worked together, ate together, and fought together. We were the Wilder brothers. It was what we did.

I had left to join the Air Force at seventeen, having graduated early, leaving behind my kid brothers and sister. After nearly twenty years of doing what we needed to in order to survive, we hadn't spent as much time with one another as I would have liked. We hadn't been stationed together, so we hadn't seen one another for longer than holidays or in passing.

But now we were together. At least most of us. So I was going to make this work, even if it killed me.

East finally answered my question. "I just have to fix a door that's a little too squeaky in one of the guestrooms. Not a big deal."

I raised a brow. "That's it?"

"It's one of the many things on my list. Thankfully,

this place is big enough that I always have something to do. It's an unending list. And that the winery has its own team to work on all of that shit, because I'm not in the mood to learn to deal with any of the complicated machinery that comes with that world."

I snorted. "Honestly, same. I'm glad there are people that know what the fuck they're doing when it comes to wine making so that didn't have to be the two of us."

I left my brother to this job, knowing he liked time on his own, just like the rest of us did, and went to dry my boots. I was working by myself for most of the day, in interviews and other "boss business," as Elliot called it, so I had to focus and get clean.

I wasn't in the mood to deal with interviews, but it was part of my job. We had to fill positions that hadn't been working out over the past year, some more than others.

Wilder Retreat was a place that hadn't been even a spark in my mind my entire life. No, I had been too busy being a career military man—getting in my twenty, moving up the ranks, and ending up as a Lieutenant Colonel before I got out. I had been a commander of a squadron, and yet, it felt like I didn't know how to command where I was now.

When my sister Eliza had lost her husband when he was on deployment, it had been the last domino to fall in the Wilder brothers' military career. I had been ready to get out with twenty years in, knowing I needed a career outside of being a Lieutenant Colonel. I wasn't even forty yet, and the term retirement was a misnomer, but that's what happened when it came to my former job.

East had been getting out around that time for reasons of his own, and then Evan had been forced to. I rubbed my hand over my chest, that familiar pain, remembering the phone call from one of Evan's commanders when Evan had been hurt.

I thought I'd lost my baby brother then, and we nearly had. Everett had gotten hurt too, and Elijah and Elliot had needed out for their own reasons. Losing our baby sister's husband had just pushed us forward.

Finding out that Eliza's husband had been a cheating asshole had just cemented the fact that we needed to spend more time together as a family so we could be there for one another.

In retrospect, it would have been nice if Eliza would have been able to come down to Texas with us, to our suburb outside of San Antonio. Only, she had fallen in love again, with a man with a big family and a good heart up in Fort Collins, Colorado. She was still up there and traveled down enough that we actually got to get to know our sister again.

It was weird to think that, after so many years of

always seeing each other in passing or through video calls, most of us were here, opening up a business. And all because I had been losing my mind.

Wilder Retreat and Winery was a villa and wedding venue outside of San Antonio. We were in hill country, at least what passed for hill country in South Texas, and the place had been owned by a former Air Force General who had wanted to retire and sell the place, since his kid didn't want it.

It was a large spread that used to be a ranch back in the day, nearly one hundred acres that the original owners had taken from a working ranch, and instead of making it a dude ranch or something similar, like others did around here, they'd added a winery using local help. We were close enough to Fredericksburg that it made sense in terms of the soil and weather. They had been able to add on additions, so it wasn't just the winery. Someone could come for the day for a winery tour or even a retreat tour, but most people came for the weekend or for a whole week. There were cabins and a farmhouse where we held weddings, dances, or other events. We had some chickens and ducks that gave us eggs, and goats that seemed to have a mind of their own and provided milk for cheese. Then there was the main annex, which housed all the equipment for the retreat villa.

The winery had its own section of buildings, and it

was far bigger than anything I would have ever thought that we could handle. But, between the six of us, we did.

And the only reason we could even afford it, because one didn't afford something like this on a military salary, even with a decent retirement plan, was because of our uncles.

Our uncles, Edward and Edmond Wilder, had owned Wilder Wines down in Napa, California, for years. They had done well for themselves, and when we had been kids, we had gone out to visit. Evan had been the one that had clung to it and had been interested in wine making before he had changed his mind and gone into the military like the rest of us.

That was why Evan was in charge of the winery itself now. Because he knew what he was doing, even if he'd growled and said he didn't. Either way though, the place was huge, had multiple working parts at all times, and we had a staff that needed us. But when the uncles had died, they had left the money from the sale of the winery to us in equal parts. Eliza had taken hers to invest for her future children, and the rest of us had pooled our money together to buy this place and make it ours. A lot of the staff from the old owner had stayed, but some had left as well. Because they didn't want new owners who had no idea what they were doing, or they just retired. Either way, we were over a year in and doing okay.

Except for two positions that made me want to groan.

I had an interview with who would be our third wedding planner since we started this. The main component of the retreat was to have an actual wedding venue. To be able to host parties, and not just wine tours. Elliot was our major event planner that helped with our yearly and seasonal minute details, but he didn't want anything to do with the actual weddings. That was a whole other skill set, and so we wanted a wedding planner. We had gone through two wedding planners now, and we needed to hire a third. The first one had lied on her résumé, had given references that were her friends who had lied and had even created websites that were all fabrication, all so she could get into the business. Which, I understood, getting into the business is one thing. However, lying was another. Plus, we needed someone with actual experience because we didn't have any ourselves. We were going out on a limb here with this whole retreat business, and it was all because I had the harebrained idea of getting our family to work together, get along, and get to know one another. I wanted us to have a future, to be our own bosses.

And it was so far over my head that I knew that if I didn't get reliable help, we were going to fail.

Later, I had a meeting with that potential wedding planner. But first, I had to see what the fuck that smell was coming from the main kitchen in the villa.

The second wedding planner we hired was a guy with great and *true* references, one who was good at his job but hated everything to do with my brothers and me. He had hated the idea of the retreat and how rustic it was, even though we were in fucking South Texas. Yes, the buildings look slightly European because that was the theme that the original owners had gone for. Still, the guy had hated us, hadn't listened to us, and had called us white trash before he had walked away, jumped into his convertible, and sped off down the road, leaving us without help. He had been rude to our guests, and now Elliot was the one having to plan weddings for the past three weeks. My brother was going to strangle me soon if we didn't hire someone. And this person was going to be our last hope. As soon as she showed up, that was.

I looked down on my watch and tried to plan the rest of my day. I had thirty minutes to figure out what the hell was going on in the kitchen, and then I had to go to the meeting.

I nodded at a few guests who were sipping wine and eating a cheese plate and then at our innkeeper,

Naomi. Naomi's honey-brown hair was cut in an angled bob that lit her face, and she grinned at me.

"Hello there, Boss Man," she whispered. "You might need to go to the kitchen."

"Do I want to know?" I asked with a grumble.

"I'm not sure. But I am going to go check in our next guest, and then Elliott needs to meet with the Henderson couple."

"He'll be there." I didn't say that Elliot would rather chew off his own arm rather than deal with this, considering we had a family event coming in, one that Elliot was on target with planning. The wedding for next year was an important one, so we needed to work on it.

Naomi was a fantastic innkeeper, far more organized than any of us—and that was saying something since my brothers and I knew our way around schedules, to-do lists, and spreadsheets. Naomi was personable, smiled, and kept us on our toes.

Without her, I knew we wouldn't be able to do this. Hell, without Amos, our vineyard manager, I knew that Evan and Elijah wouldn't be able to handle the winery as they did. Naomi and Amos had come with the place when we had bought it, and I would be forever grateful that they had decided to stay on.

I gave Naomi another nod, then headed back to the kitchen and nearly walked right back out.

Tony stood there, a scowl on his face and his hands on his hips. "I don't understand what the fuck is wrong with this oven."

"What's going on?" I asked as Everett stood by Tony. Everett was my quiet brother with usually a small smile on his face, only right then it looked like he was ready to scream.

I didn't know why Everett was even there since he was part responsible for the financials side of the company and usually worked with Elliot these days. Maybe he had come to the kitchen after the smell of burning as I had after Naomi's prodding.

Tony threw his hands in the air. "What's going on? This stove is a piece of shit. All of it is a piece of shit. I'm tired of this rustic place. I thought I would be coming to a Michelin star restaurant. To be my own chef. Instead, I have to make English breakfasts and pancakes with bananas. I might as well be at a bed and breakfast."

I pinched the bridge of my nose. "We're an inn, not a bed and breakfast."

"But I serve breakfast. That's all I do these days. That and cheese platters. Nobody comes for dinner. Nobody comes for lunch."

That was a lie. Tony worked for the winery and the retreat itself and served all the meals. But Tony wanted to go crazy with the menu, to try new and fantastical items that just weren't going to work here.

And I had a feeling I was going to throw up if I wasn't careful.

"I quit," Tony snapped, and I knew right then, it was done for. I was done.

"You can't quit," I growled while Everett held back a sigh.

"Yes, I can. I'm done. I'm done with you and this ranch. You're not cowboys. You're not even Texans. You're just people moving in on our territory." And with that, Tony stomped away, throwing his chef's apron on the ground.

I was thankful that the kitchen was on the other side of the library and front area, where most of the guests were if they weren't out on one of the tours of the area and city that Elliott had arranged for them. That was the whole point of this retreat. They could come visit, and could relax, or we could set them up on a tour of downtown San Antonio, or Canyon Lake, or any of the other places that were nearby.

And yet, Tony had just thrown a wrench into all of that. I didn't know what was worse, the smell of burning, Tony leaving, the water in the basement that wasn't truly a basement, or the fact that I was going to smell like charred food and wet jeans when I went to go meet this wedding planner.

"You're going to need to hire a new cook," Everett whispered.

I looked at my brother, at the man who did his best to make sure we didn't go bankrupt, and I wanted to just grumble. "I figured."

"I can help for now, but you know I'm only part-time. I can't stay away from my twins for too long," Sandy said as she came forward to take the pan off the stove. "I wish I could do full time, but this is all I can do for now."

Sandy had come back from maternity leave after we had already opened the retreat. She had been on with the former owners and was brilliant. But she had a right to be a mom and not want to work full time. I understood that, and I knew that Sandy didn't want to handle a whole kitchen by herself. She liked her position as a sous chef.

I was going to have to figure out what to do. Again.

"I'll get it done," I said while rubbing my temples.

"You know what we need to do," Everett whispered, and I shook my head.

"He'll kill us."

"Maybe, but it'll be worth it in the end. And speaking of, don't you have that interview soon? Or do you want me to take it?" His gaze tracked to my jeans.

I shook my head. "No, help Sandy."

Everett winced. "Just because I know how to slice an onion, it doesn't mean I'm good at cooking."

"I'm sorry, did you just say you could slice an onion? Get to it," Sandy put in with a smile, pointing at the sink. "Wash those hands."

"I cannot believe I just said that out loud. I just stepped right into it," Everett said with a sigh. "Go to the interview. You know what to ask."

"I do. And I hope we don't get screwed this time."

"You know, if we're lucky, we'll get someone as good as Roy's wedding planner, or at least that woman that we met. You know who she is." Everett grinned like a cat with the canary.

I narrowed my eyes. "Don't bring her up."

"Oh, I can't help it. A single dance, and you were drawn to her."

"What dance? You know what? No, I don't have time. We have to work on lunch and dinner. Tell me while you work," Sandy added with a wink.

Everett leaned toward her as he washed his hands. "Well, you see, there was this dance, and he met the perfect woman, and then she got engaged."

Sandy's eyes widened. "Engaged? How did that happen? She was dating someone else?" she asked as she looked at me.

I pinched the bridge of my nose. "It was at Roy's place when we were looking at the venue to see if we wanted to buy the retreat here." I sighed, I knew if I just let it all out, she would move on from this conversation, and I would never have to deal with it again. "Somehow, I ended up at a wedding there, caught the garter. This woman caught the bouquet, and she happened to be the wedding planner. We danced, we laughed, and as she walked away, her boyfriend got down on one knee and proposed."

"No way!" She leaned forward with a fierce look on her face, her eyes bright. "What did she say?"

"I have no clue. I left." I ignored whatever feeling might want to show up at that thought. Everett gave me a glance, and I shook my head. "Enough of that. Yes, the wedding that she did was great, but I honestly have no idea who she is, and she has a job. She doesn't need to work here." And I didn't know what I would do if I saw her again or had to work with her. There had been such an intense connection that I knew it would be awkward as hell. But thankfully, she had her own business and wasn't going to come to the Wilder Retreat for a job.

I left Sandy and Everett on their own, knowing that they were capable, at least for now. And I knew who we would have to hire if she said yes, and if my other brother didn't kill me first.

I washed my hands in the sink on the way out, grateful that at least I looked somewhat decent, if not a little disheveled, and made my way out front, hoping that the wedding planner who came in through the doors would be the one that would stick. Because we needed some good luck. After the day we've had, we needed some good luck.

I turned the corner and nearly tripped over my feet.

Because, of course, fate was this way.

It was her.

Of all the wedding planners from all the wedding venues, it was her.

In the mood to read another family saga? Meet the Wilder Brothers in One Way Back to Me!

From Bittersweet Promises

LEIF

"NOT ONLY DID YOU CONVINCE ME TO SOMEHOW GO on a blind date, it became a double date. How on earth did you work this magic on me, cousin?" I asked Lake as she leaned against the pillar just inside the restaurant.

Lake grinned at me, her dark hair pulled away from her face. She had on this swingy black dress and looked as if she were excited, anxious, nervous, and happy all at the same time. Considering she was bouncing on her toes when usually Lake was calm, cool, and collected, was saying something. "I asked, and you said yes. Because you love me."

"I might love you because we're family, but I still think we're making a mistake." I shook my head and pulled at my shirt sleeves. Lake had somehow convinced me to wear a button-up shirt tucked into gray pants, I even had on shiny shoes. I looked like a damn banker. But if that's what Lake wanted, that's what I would do.

Lake might technically be my cousin, even though we weren't blood-related, but we were more like brother and sister than any of my other cousins.

I had siblings, as did Lake, but with the generational gap, we were at least a decade older than all of our other cousins. That meant, despite the fact that we had lived over an hour apart for most of our lives, we'd grown up more like siblings.

I loved my three younger siblings and talked to them daily. Unlike some blended families, they *were* my brothers and sister and not like strangers or distant family members. I didn't feel a disconnect from the three of them, but Lake was still closer to me.

Probably because we were either heading into our thirties or already there, where most of our other cousins were either just now in their early twenties or still teenagers in high school. With how big we Montgomerys were as a family, it made sense that there would be such a widespread age group. That meant that Lake and I were best friends, cousins, practically siblings, and sometimes the banes of each other's existences.

We were also business owners and partners and

saw each other too often these days. That was probably why she convinced me to go on a blind double date. But she had been out with Zach before. I, however, had never met May. Lake had some connection with her that I wasn't sure about, and for some reason Lake's date had said yes to this double date.

And, in the complicated way of family, I had agreed to it. I must have been tired. Or perhaps I'd had too many beers. Because I didn't do blind dates, and recently, I didn't do dates at all.

Lake scanned her phone, then looked up at me, all innocence in her smart gaze. "You shouldn't have told me you wanted to settle down in your old age."

I narrowed my eyes. "I'm still in my early thirties, jerk. Stop calling me old."

"I shouldn't call you old since you're only a few years older than me." She fluttered her eyelashes and I flipped her off, ignoring the stare from the older woman next to me. Though I was a tattoo artist, I didn't have many visible tattoos. Most of mine were on my back and legs, hidden from the world unless I wanted to show them. I hadn't figured out what I wanted on my arms beyond a few small pieces on my wrists and upper shoulders. And since tattoos were permanent, I was taking my time. If a client needed to see my skin with ink to feel comfortable, I'd show them my back. My body was a canvas, so I did what I could to set people at ease.

But I still had the eyebrow piercing and had recently taken out my nose ring. I didn't look too scary for most people. But apparently, flipping off a woman, growling, and cursing a time or two in front of strangers probably made me appear too close to the dark side.

"Yes, I want to settle down, but this will be awkward, won't it? Where the two of us are strangers, and the two of you aren't?" I wanted a life, a future, and yeah, one day to settle down with someone. I just didn't know why I'd mentioned it to Lake in the first place.

"If it helps, May doesn't know Zach, either. So it's a group of strangers, except I know everybody." She clapped her hands together and did her version of an evil laugh, and I just shook my head.

"Considering what you do for a living and how you like to manipulate things in your way, this makes sense. Are you going to be adding a matchmaking company to your conglomerate?"

Lake just fluttered her eyelashes again and laughed. Lake owned a small tech company that made a shit ton of money over the past couple of years. And because she was brilliant at what she did, innovative, and liked pushing money towards women-owned businesses, she owned more than one company at this point and was an investor in mine. I wouldn't be surprised if she found a way to open up a women-owned matchmaking company right here in town.

"It might be fun. I can call it Montgomery Links." Her eyes went wide. "Oh, my God. I have to write that down." She pulled out her phone, began to take notes, and I pinched the bridge of my nose.

"You know I trust you with my actual life, but I don't know if I trust you with my dating life."

Lake tossed her hair behind her shoulder as she continued to type. "Shut up. You love me. And once I finish setting you up, the rest of the family's next."

"Oh, really? You're going to get Daisy and Noah next?" I asked, speaking of two more of our cousins.

"Maybe. Of course, Sebastian's the only one of the younger group that seems to have a serious girlfriend."

I nodded, speaking of our other familial business partner. Sebastian was still a teenager, though in college. He had wanted to open up Montgomery Ink Legacy with me, the full title of our company. There was a legacy to it, and Sebastian had wanted in. So, though he didn't work there full-time, he was putting his future towards us. And in the ways of young love, he and his girlfriend had been together since middle school. The fact that my younger cousin was better at relationships than I was didn't make me feel great. But I was going to ignore that.

"You're not going to start up a matchmaking service, are you? Or maybe an app?"

"Dating apps are ridiculous these days, they practically want you to invest in coins to bid on dates, and that's not something I'm in the mood for. But maybe there's something I can try. I'll add it to my list."

Lake's list of inventions and tech was notorious, and knowing the brilliance of my cousin, she would one day rule the world and might eventually cross everything off that list.

"Oh, here's Zach." Lake's face brightened immediately, and she smiled up at a man with dark hair, piercing gray eyes, and an actual dimple on his cheek.

Tonight was not only about my blind date, but me getting the lay of the land when it came to Zach. I was the first step into meeting the family. Oh, if Zach passed my gauntlet, he would meet the rest of the Montgomerys, and we were mighty. All one hundred of us.

"Zach, you're here." Lake's voice went soft, and she went on her tiptoes even in her high heels as Zach pressed a soft kiss to her lips.

"Of course, I'm here. And you're early, as usual."

Lake blushed and ducked her head. "Well, you know me. I like to be early because being on time is late," she said at the same time I did, mumbling under my breath. It was a familiar refrain when it came to us.

"Zach, good to meet you," I said, holding out my hand.

The other man gripped it firmly and shook. "Nice to meet you too, Leif. I know you might be the one on a blind date soon, but I'm nervous."

I chuckled, shaking my head. "Yeah, I'm pretty nervous too. Though I'm grateful that Lake's trying to look out for me."

My cousin laughed softly. "You totally were not saying that a few minutes ago, but be suave and sophisticated now. Or just be yourself, May's on her way."

I met Zach's gaze and we both rolled our eyes. When I turned toward the door, I saw a woman of average height, with black straight hair, green eyes, and a sweet smile. I didn't know much about May, other than Lake knew her and liked her. If I was going to start dating again after taking time off to get the rest of my life together, I might as well start with someone that one of my best friends liked.

"May, I'm so glad that you're here," Lake said as she hugged the other woman tightly.

As Lake began to bounce on her heels, I realized that my cousin's cool, calm, and collected exterior was only for work. She was bouncing and happy when it came to her friends or when she was nervous. I knew that, of course, but I had forgotten how she had turned into the mogul that she was. It was good to see her relaxed and happy.

Now I just needed to figure out how to do that for myself.

May stood in front of me, and I felt like I was starting middle school all over again. A new school, a new life, and a past that didn't make much sense to anyone else.

I swallowed hard and nodded, not putting out my hand to shake, thinking that would be weird, but I also didn't want to hug her. I didn't even know this woman. Why was everything so awkward? Instead, I lifted my chin. "Hello, May. It's nice to meet you. Lake says only good things."

There, smooth. Not really. Zach began to move out of frame, with Lake at his side as the two went to speak to the hostess, leaving May and me alone.

This wasn't going to be awkward at all.

The woman just smiled at me, her eyes wide. "It's nice to meet you, too. And Lake does speak highly of you. Also, this is very awkward, so I'm so sorry if I say something stupid. I know that your cousin said that I should be set up with you which is great but I'm not great at blind dates and apparently this is a double date and now I'm going to stop talking." She said the words so quickly they all ran into one breath.

I shook my head and laughed. "We're on the same page there."

"Okay, good. It's nice to meet you, Leif Montgomery."

"And it's nice to meet you too, May."

We made our way to Lake and Zach, who had gotten our table, and we all sat down, talking about work and other things. May was in child life development, taught online classes, and was also a nanny.

"I'm actually about to start with a new family soon. I'm excited. I know that being a nanny isn't something that most people strive for, or at least that's what they tell you, but I love being able to work with children and be the person that is there when a single parent or even both parents are out in the workforce, trying to do everything."

I nodded, taking a sip of my beer. "I get you completely. With how my parents worked, I was lucky that they were able to get childcare within the buildings. Since they each owned their own businesses, they made it work. But my family worked long hours, and that's why I ended up being the babysitter a lot of the times when childcare wasn't an option." I cleared my throat. "I'm a lot older than a lot of my cousins," I added.

"Both of us are, but I'm glad that you only said yourself," Lake said, grinning. She leaned into Zach as she spoke, the four of us in a horseshoe-shaped booth. That gave May and me space since this was a first date and still awkward as hell, and so Lake and Zach could cuddle. Not that that was something I needed to be a part of.

"Oh, I'm glad that you didn't judge. The last few dates that I've been on they always gave me weird looks because I think they expected a nanny to be this old crone or someone that's looking for a different job." She shrugged and continued. "When I eventually get married and maybe even start a family, I want to continue my job. I like being there to help another family achieve their goals. And I can't believe I just said start a family on my first date. And that I mentioned that I've been on a few other dates." She let out a breath. "I'm notoriously bad at dating. Like, the worst. Just warning you."

I laughed, shaking my head. "I'm rusty at it, so don't worry." And even though I said that, I had a feeling that May felt no spark towards me, and I didn't feel anything towards her. She was nice and pleasant, and I could probably consider her a friend one day. But there wasn't any spark. May's eyes weren't dancing. She wasn't leaning forward, trying to touch my hand across the table. We were just sitting there casually, enjoying a really good steak, as Lake and Zach enjoyed their date.

By the end of dinner, I didn't want dessert, and neither did May, so we said goodbye to the other couple, who decided to stay. I walked May to her car, ignoring Lake's warning look, but I didn't know what exactly she was warning me about.

"Thanks for dinner," May said. "I could have paid. I know this is a blind date and all that, but you didn't have to pay."

I shook my head. "I paid for the four of us because I wanted to be nice. I'll make Lake pay next time."

May beamed. "Yes, I like that. You guys are a good family."

"Anyway," I said, clearing my throat as I stuck my hands in my pockets. "I guess I'll see you around."

May just looked at me, threw her head back, and laughed. "You're right. You are rusty at this."

"Sorry." Heat flushed my skin, and I resisted the urge to tug on my eyebrow ring.

"It's okay. No spark. I'm used to it. I don't spark well."

"May, I'm sorry." I cringed. "It's not you."

"Oh, God, please don't say that. 'It's not you. It's me. You're working on yourself. You're just so busy with work.' I've heard it all."

"Seriously?" I asked. May was hot. Nice, but there just wasn't a spark.

She shrugged. "It's okay. I'll probably see you

around sometime because I am friends with Lake. However, I am perfectly fine having this be our one and only. You'll find your person. It's okay that it's not me." And with that, she got in the car and left, leaving me standing there.

Well then. Tonight wasn't horrible, but it wasn't great. I got in my car, and instead of heading home where I'd be alone, watching something on some streaming service while I drank a beer and pretended that I knew what I was doing with my life, I headed into Montgomery Ink Legacy.

We were the third branch of the company and the first owned by our generation. Montgomery Ink was the tattoo shop in downtown Denver. While there were open spots for some walk-ins and special circumstances, my father, aunt, and their team had years' worth of waiting lists. They worked their asses off and made sure to get in everybody that they could, but people wanted Austin Montgomery's art. Same with my aunt, Maya.

There was another tattoo shop down in Colorado Springs, owned by my parents' cousins, who I just called aunt and uncle because we were close enough that using real titles for everybody got confusing. Montgomery Ink Too was thriving down there, and they had waiting lists as well. My family could have opened more shops and gone nationwide, even global if

CARRIE ANN RYAN

they wanted to, but they liked keeping it how it was, in the family and those connected.

We were a branch, but our own in the making. I had gone into business with Lake, of course, and Sebastian, when he was ready, as well as Nick. Nick was my best friend. I had known him for ages, and he had wanted to be part of something as well. He might not be a Montgomery by name, but he had eaten over at my family's house enough times throughout the years that he was practically a Montgomery. And he had invested in the company as well, and so now we were nearly a year into owning the shop and trying not to fail.

I pulled into the parking lot, grateful it was still open since we didn't close until nine most nights, and greeted Nick, who was still working.

Sebastian was in the back, going over sketches with a client, and I nodded at him. He might be eighteen, but he was still in training, an apprentice, and was working his ass off to learn.

"Date sucked then?" Sebastian asked, and Nick just rolled his eyes and went back to work on a client's wrist.

"I don't want to talk about it," I groaned.

The rest of the staff was off since Nick would close up on his own. Sebastian was just there since he didn't have homework or a date with Marley.

"Was she hot at least?" Sebastian asked, and the client, a woman in her sixties, bopped him on the head with her bag gently.

"Sebastian Montgomery. Be nice."

Sebastian blushed. "Sorry, Mrs. Anderson."

I looked over at the woman and grinned. "Hi, Mrs. Anderson. It's nice to see you out of the classroom."

She narrowed her eyes at me, even though they filled with laughter. "I needed my next Jane Austen tattoo, thank you very much," the older woman said as she went back to working with Sebastian. She had been my and then Sebastian's English teacher. The fact that she was on her fifth tattoo with some literary quote told me that I had been damn lucky in most of my teachers growing up.

She was kick-ass, and I had a feeling that she would let Sebastian do the tattoo for her rather than just have him work on the design with me as we did for most of the people who came in. He had learned under my father and was working under me now. It was strange to think that he wasn't a little kid anymore. But he was in a long-term relationship, kicking ass in college, and knew what he wanted to do with his life.

I might know what I want to do with my work life, but everything else seemed a little off.

"So it didn't work out?" Nick asked as he walked

up to the front desk with the clients after going over aftercare.

"Not really," I said, looking down at my phone.

The client, a woman in her mid-twenties with bright pink hair, a lip ring, and kind eyes, leaned over the desk to look at me.

"You'll find someone, Leif. Don't worry."

I looked at our regular and shook my head. "Thanks, Kim. Too bad that you don't swing this way."

I winked as I said it, a familiar refrain from both of us.

Kim was married to a woman named Sonya, and the two of them were happy and working on in vitro with donated sperm for their first kid.

"Hey, I'm sorry too that I'm a lesbian. I'll never know what it means to have Leif Montgomery. Or any Montgomery, since I found my love far too quickly. I mean, what am I ever going to do not knowing the love of a Montgomery?"

Mrs. Anderson chuckled from her chair, Sebastian held back a snort, and I just looked at Nick, who rolled his eyes and helped Kim out of the place.

I was tired, but it was okay. The date wasn't all bad. May was nice. But it felt like I didn't have much right then.

And then Nick sat in front of me, scowled, and I

realized that I did have something. I had my friends and my family. I didn't need much more.

"So, you and May didn't work out?"

I raised a brow. "You knew her name? Did I tell you that?"

Nick shook his head. "Lake did."

That made sense, considering the two of them spoke as much as we did. "So, was it your idea to set me up on a blind date?"

"Fuck no. That was all Lake. I just do what she says. Like we all do."

I sighed and went through my appointments for the next day. "We're busy for the next month. That's good, right?" I asked.

"You're the business genius here. I just play with ink. But yes, that's good. Now, don't let your cousin set you up any more dates. Find them for yourself. You know what you're doing."

"So says the man who dates less than me."

"That's what you think. I'm more private about it. As it should be." I flipped him off as he stood up, then he gestured towards a stack of bills in the corner. "You have a few personal things that made their way here. Don't want you to miss out on them before you head home."

"Thanks, bro."

"No problem. I'm going to help Sebastian with his consult, and then I'll clean up. You should head home. Though you're doing it alone, so I feel sorry for you."

"Fuck you," I called out.

"Fuck you, too."

"Boys," Mrs. Anderson said, in that familiar English teacher refrain, and both Nick and I cringed before saying, "Sorry," simultaneously.

Sebastian snickered, then went back to work, and I headed towards the edge of the counter, picking up the stack of papers. Most were bills, some were random papers that needed to be filed or looked over. Some were just junk mail. But there was one letter, written in block print that didn't look familiar. Chills went up my spine and I opened it, wondering what the fuck this was. Maybe it was someone asking to buy my house. I got a lot of handwritten letters for that, but I didn't think this was going to be that. I swallowed hard, slid open the paper, and froze.

"I'll find you, boy. Oops. Looks like I already did. Be waiting. I know you miss me."

I let the paper hit the top of the counter and swallowed hard, trying to remain cool so I didn't worry anyone else.

I didn't know exactly who that was from, but I had a horrible feeling that they wouldn't wait long to tell me.

. . .

Read the rest in Bittersweet Promises! OUT NOW!

Acknowledgments

After so many books, you'd think I'd run out of people to thank but honestly it feels like the opposite. There are so many people who got me here and I'm so grateful.

To Brigid & the Discord - y'all. The patience and deception of this group is strangers is unmatched and I'm so grateful of all of you. Finding a group of people who come from all walks of life as well as so many different processes is fantastic. Thank you for keeping me on target and bringing me back from the abyss.

Brandi - Thank you again for all of your help with this book and everything you do behind the scenes. The Shrimp also thanks you.

Britt, Fedora, and Lillie - Thank you so much for all of your dedication with this book! I couldn't do this without you.

Lesheera - Your hard work behind the scenes is so appreciated!

LB - You are a touchstone. I know that's a surprise to you. But you are. THANK YOU for all you do.

Brianna, Ann, Classy, Lauren Brooke, and Ashley - I love this team and I'm so happy that I can trust my worlds to you. Thank you!

To the Ryan Family...I love you guys. Each passing year brings us closer together and the fact that I can talk my books out with you just brings me so much joy.

K - I love that you found romance and so many books I love. But you still cannot read my books. Sorry. Big Sister Rule #40. LOL

And last but certainly not least, thank you to my readers. I've been on this journey for over a decade and still earn so much. But the one thing that never changes is your dedication and love for my books. So THANK YOU. And I will keep doing what I can to be worthy of your love of my books.

Love you!

~Carrie Ann

Also from Carrie Ann Ryan

The Montgomery Ink Legacy Series:

Book 1: Bittersweet Promises (Leif & Brooke)

Book 2: At First Meet (Nick & Lake)

Book 2.5: Happily Ever Never (May & Leo)

Book 3: Longtime Crush (Sebastian & Raven)

Book 4: Best Friend Temptation (Noah, Ford, and Greer)

Book 4.5: Happily Ever Maybe (Jennifer & Gus)

Book 5: Last First Kiss (Daisy & Hugh)

Book 6: His Second Chance (Kane & Phoebe)

Book 7: One Night with You (Kingston & Claire)

Book 8: Accidentally Forever (Crew & Aria)

Book 9: Last Chance Seduction (Lexington & Mercy)

Book 10: Kiss Me Forever (Brooklyn & Reece)

Book 11: His Guilty Pleasure (Dash & Aly)

The Cage Family
Book 1: The Forever Rule (Aston & Blakely)
Book 2: An Unexpected Everything (Isabella & Weston)
Book 3: If You Were Mine (Dorian & Harper)
Book 4: One Quick Obsession (Hudson & Scarlett)
Book 5: Pretend it's Forever (???? & ????)

Ashford Creek
Book 1: Legacy (Callum & Felicity)
Book 2: Crossroads (Bohdi & Keira)
Book 3: Westward (Atlas & Elizabeth)

Clover Lake
Book 1: Always a Fake Bridesmaid (Livvy & Ewan)
Book 2: Accidental Runaway Groom (Jamie & Sharp)

The Wilder Brothers Series:
Book 1: One Way Back to Me (Eli & Alexis)
Book 2: Always the One for Me (Evan & Kendall)
Book 3: The Path to You (Everett & Bethany)
Book 4: Coming Home for Us (Elijah & Maddie)
Book 5: Stay Here With Me (East & Lark)

Book 6: Finding the Road to Us (Elliot, Trace, and Sidney)

Book 7: Moments for You (Ridge & Aurora)

Book 7.5: A Wilder Wedding (Amos & Naomi)

Book 8: Forever For Us (Wyatt & Ava)

Book 9: Pieces of Me (Gabriel & Briar)

Book 10: Endlessly Yours (Brooks & Rory)

The Falling for the Cassidy Brothers Series:

Book 1: Good Time Boyfriend (Heath & Devney)

Book 2: Last Minute Fiancé (Luca & Addison)

Book 3: Second Chance Husband (August & Paisley)

Montgomery Ink Denver:

Book 0.5: Ink Inspired (Shep & Shea)

Book 0.6: Ink Reunited (Sassy, Rare, and Ian)

Book 1: Delicate Ink (Austin & Sierra)

Book 1.5: Forever Ink (Callie & Morgan)

Book 2: Tempting Boundaries (Decker and Miranda)

Book 3: Harder than Words (Meghan & Luc)

Book 3.5: Finally Found You (Mason & Presley)

Book 4: Written in Ink (Griffin & Autumn)

Book 4.5: Hidden Ink (Hailey & Sloane)

Book 5: Ink Enduring (Maya, Jake, and Border)

Book 6: Ink Exposed (Alex & Tabby)

Book 6.5: Adoring Ink (Holly & Brody)

Book 6.6: Love, Honor, & Ink (Arianna & Harper)

Book 7: Inked Expressions (Storm & Everly)

Book 7.3: Dropout (Grayson & Kate)

Book 7.5: Executive Ink (Jax & Ashlynn)

Book 8: Inked Memories (Wes & Jillian)

Book 8.5: Inked Nights (Derek & Olivia)

Book 8.7: Second Chance Ink (Brandon & Lauren)

Book 8.5: Montgomery Midnight Kisses (Alex & Tabby Bonus(

Bonus: Inked Kingdom (Stone & Sarina)

Montgomery Ink: Colorado Springs

Book 1: Fallen Ink (Adrienne & Mace)

Book 2: Restless Ink (Thea & Dimitri)

Book 2.5: Ashes to Ink (Abby & Ryan)

Book 3: Jagged Ink (Roxie & Carter)

Book 3.5: Ink by Numbers (Landon & Kaylee)

The Montgomery Ink: Boulder Series:

Book 1: Wrapped in Ink (Liam & Arden)

Book 2: Sated in Ink (Ethan, Lincoln, and Holland)

Book 3: Embraced in Ink (Bristol & Marcus)

Book 3: Moments in Ink (Zia & Meredith)

Book 4: Seduced in Ink (Aaron & Madison)

Book 4.5: Captured in Ink (Julia, Ronin, & Kincaid)

Book 4.7: Inked Fantasy (Secret ??)

Book 4.8: A Very Montgomery Christmas (The Entire Boulder Family)

The Montgomery Ink: Fort Collins Series:

Book 1: Inked Persuasion (Jacob & Annabelle)

Book 2: Inked Obsession (Beckett & Eliza)

Book 3: Inked Devotion (Benjamin & Brenna)

Book 3.5: Nothing But Ink (Clay & Riggs)

Book 4: Inked Craving (Lee & Paige)

Book 5: Inked Temptation (Archer & Killian)

The Promise Me Series:

Book 1: Forever Only Once (Cross & Hazel)

Book 2: From That Moment (Prior & Paris)

Book 3: Far From Destined (Macon & Dakota)

Book 4: From Our First (Nate & Myra)

The Whiskey and Lies Series:

Book 1: Whiskey Secrets (Dare & Kenzie)

Book 2: Whiskey Reveals (Fox & Melody)

Book 3: Whiskey Undone (Loch & Ainsley)

The Gallagher Brothers Series:

Book 1: Love Restored (Graham & Blake)

Book 2: Passion Restored (Owen & Liz)

Book 3: Hope Restored (Murphy & Tessa)

The Less Than Series:
Book 1: Breathless With Her (Devin & Erin)
Book 2: Reckless With You (Tucker & Amelia)
Book 3: Shameless With Him (Caleb & Zoey)

The Fractured Connections Series:
Book 1: Breaking Without You (Cameron & Violet)
Book 2: Shouldn't Have You (Brendon & Harmony)
Book 3: Falling With You (Aiden & Sienna)
Book 4: Taken With You (Beckham & Meadow)

The On My Own Series:
Book 0.5: My First Glance
Book 1: My One Night (Dillon & Elise)
Book 2: My Rebound (Pacey & Mackenzie)
Book 3: My Next Play (Miles & Nessa)
Book 4: My Bad Decisions (Tanner & Natalie)

The Ravenwood Coven Series:
Book 1: Dawn Unearthed
Book 2: Dusk Unveiled
Book 3: Evernight Unleashed

The Aspen Pack Series:
Book 1: Etched in Honor
Book 2: Hunted in Darkness

Book 3: Mated in Chaos

Book 4: Harbored in Silence

Book 5: Marked in Flames

The Talon Pack:

Book 1: Tattered Loyalties

Book 2: An Alpha's Choice

Book 3: Mated in Mist

Book 4: Wolf Betrayed

Book 5: Fractured Silence

Book 6: Destiny Disgraced

Book 7: Eternal Mourning

Book 8: Strength Enduring

Book 9: Forever Broken

Book 10: Mated in Darkness

Book 11: Fated in Winter

Redwood Pack Series:

Book 0.5: An Alpha's Path

Book 1: A Taste for a Mate

Book 2: Trinity Bound

Book 2.5: A Night Away

Book 3: Enforcer's Redemption

Book 3.5: Blurred Expectations

Book 3.7: Forgiveness

Book 4: Shattered Emotions

Book 5: Hidden Destiny

Book 5.5: <u>A Beta's Haven</u>
Book 6: <u>Fighting Fate</u>
Book 6.5: <u>Loving the Omega</u>
Book 6.7: <u>The Hunted Heart</u>
Book 7: <u>Wicked Wolf</u>

The Elements of Five Series:
Book 1: From Breath and Ruin
Book 2: From Flame and Ash
Book 3: From Spirit and Binding
Book 4: From Shadow and Silence

Dante's Circle Series:
Book 1: <u>Dust of My Wings</u>
Book 2: <u>Her Warriors' Three Wishes</u>
Book 3: <u>An Unlucky Moon</u>
Book 3.5: <u>His Choice</u>
Book 4: <u>Tangled Innocence</u>
Book 5: <u>Fierce Enchantment</u>
Book 6: <u>An Immortal's Song</u>
Book 7: <u>Prowled Darkness</u>
Book 8: Dante's Circle Reborn

Holiday, Montana Series:
Book 1: <u>Charmed Spirits</u>
Book 2: <u>Santa's Executive</u>
Book 3: <u>Finding Abigail</u>

Book 4: <u>Her Lucky Love</u>
Book 5: Dreams of Ivory

The Branded Pack Series:
(Written with Alexandra Ivy)
Book 1: <u>Stolen and Forgiven</u>
Book 2: <u>Abandoned and Unseen</u>
Book 3: <u>Buried and Shadowed</u>

About the Author

Carrie Ann Ryan is the New York Times and USA Today bestselling author of contemporary, paranormal, and young adult romance. Her works include the Montgomery Ink, Redwood Pack, Fractured Connections, and Elements of Five series, which have sold over 3.0 million books worldwide. She started writing while in graduate school for her advanced degree in chemistry and hasn't stopped since. Carrie Ann has written over seventy-five novels and novellas with more in the works. When she's not losing herself in her emotional and action-packed worlds, she's reading as much as she can while wrangling her clowder of cats who have more followers than she does.

www.CarrieAnnRyan.com

www.ingramcontent.com/pod-product-compliance
Lightning Source LLC
Chambersburg PA
CBHW011143100726
47899CB00010B/3153